"About u... tonight..."

Caitlin felt color moving up her neck. She wasn't up for some clumsy apology, and she didn't want to hear why their kiss had been a mistake. "Don't worry, Michael. I've read about these things. When people are thrown together in dangerous circumstances, their emotions go haywire, that's all," she said with forced lightness.

"Caitlin, that's not—"

"Look, you don't have to apologize. I know someone like you would never be interested in a person like me. I'm nobody, just ordinary, just an ex-housewife from the suburbs. I understand."

Michael stood there dumbfounded. Was she blind? Couldn't she see she was driving him crazy with wanting her? "What on earth do you see when you look at yourself?" he asked. "*I* see a beauty. A beautiful woman I've waited too long to have." And then he reached for her.

Dear Reader,

The year is coming to a close, so here at Silhouette Intimate Moments we decided to go out with a bang. Once again, we've got a banner lineup of books for you.

Take this month's American Hero, Micah Parish, in *Cherokee Thunder*. You met him in the first book of author Rachel Lee's Conard County series, *Exile's End,* and now he's back with a story of his own. Without meaning to, he finds himself protecting woman-on-the-run Faith Williams and her unborn child, and suddenly this man who shunned emotion is head over heels in love. He's an American Hero you won't want to miss.

Reader favorite Ann Williams puts her own spin on an innovative plot in *Shades of Wyoming*. I don't want to give anything away, so all I'll say is beware of believing that things are what they seem. In *Castle of Dreams,* author Maura Seger takes a predicament right out of the headlines—the difficulties a returning hostage faces in readjusting to the world—and makes it the catalyst for a compelling romance. Award-winner Dee Holmes checks in with another of her deeply moving tales in *Without Price,* while March Madness find Rebecca Daniels writes a suspenseful tale of a couple thrown together and definitely in danger in *Fog City*. Finally, welcome new author Alicia Scott—a college student—whose *Walking After Midnight* takes gritty reality and turns it into irresistible romance.

And 1993 won't bring any letup in the excitement. Look for more of your favorite authors, as well as a Tenth Anniversary lineup in May that you definitely won't want to miss. As always, I hope you enjoy each and every one of our Silhouette Intimate Moments novels.

Yours,

Leslie Wainger
Senior Editor and Editorial Coordinator

FOG
CITY

Rebecca Daniels

Silhouette® ™
INTIMATE MOMENTS®
Published by Silhouette Books New York
America's Publisher of Contemporary Romance

SILHOUETTE BOOKS
300 East 42nd St., New York, N.Y. 10017

FOG CITY

ISBN: 0-373-07467-0

First Silhouette Books printing December 1992

REBECCA DANIELS

will never forget the first time she read a Silhouette novel. "I was at my sister's house, sitting by the pool and trying without much success to get interested in the book I'd brought from home. Everything seemed to distract me—the kids splashing around, the sea gulls squawking, the dog barking. Finally, my sister plucked the book from my hands, told me she was going to give me something I wouldn't be able to put down and handed me my first Silhouette novel. Guess what? She was right! For that lazy afternoon by her pool, I will forever be grateful." That was four years ago, and Rebecca has been writing romance novels ever since.

Born in the Midwest but raised in Southern California, she now resides in Northern California's San Joaquin Valley with her husband and two sons. She is a lifelong poet and song lyricist who enjoys early morning walks, an occasional round of golf, scouring California's Mother Lode region for antiques and traveling.

TYVMFE—Maureen Porras,
whose friendship has meant so much.

Chapter 1

Caitlin MacKenzie stepped into the shower and let the warm, comforting spray relax her tired body. She'd had a wonderful day. This first session of the West Coast Booksellers convention had been a frantic one, but she hadn't minded. She'd met many new people and had enjoyed the various seminars. As reluctant as she'd been about coming to San Francisco's Park Regency Hotel and attending the conference alone, she was almost glad now that Chloe had talked her into it.

Two years ago the idea of going anywhere or doing anything without Brian would have been out of the question. But all that had changed when he announced he wanted a divorce because he'd fallen in love with a twenty-year-old secretary in his law office. Caitlin had taken the news very hard. She'd spent twelve years trying to be the perfect wife to Brian. What would she do without him? How would she survive on her own?

Well, she had survived, and in the past twenty-four months she'd discovered she could do plenty without her ex-husband. Especially be happy. Still, losing her husband to a younger woman had taken its toll on her confidence and self-esteem. Facing life as a thirty-five-year-old divorcée wasn't always easy. The plain, unvarnished truth of the matter was that men weren't interested in women her age; they were interested in women *half* her age. It wasn't right, and it was hardly fair, but it was just another benefit of society's unyielding double standard that all women faced at one time or another.

Turning off the spray, Caitlin stepped from the tub and reached for her towel. Thank God for Chloe, she thought with a smile as she patted herself dry. If it hadn't been for Chloe and her support over the past couple of years, she never would have made it. Brian had never approved of her friendship with Chloe Mitchell, whose free-spirited, bohemian-type life-style had never quite fitted in with his picture of what was "acceptable." But that hadn't stopped the two women from being friends.

It was Chloe who had pushed and prodded Caitlin, who had gotten her out of the house and into the real world again in those dark days after the divorce. She'd insisted Caitlin come to work for her and help run the small up-scale bookstore she owned and operated. It was also Chloe who had insisted she attend this conference.

Reaching for the bulky terry-cloth robe and wrapping it around her, Caitlin couldn't help but feel a little proud of herself. Maybe as far as accomplishments went this wasn't very significant, but making it through this day on her own had been a giant step in a two-year struggle toward self-sufficiency.

He stood in the blackness, feeling the beads of perspiration trickle down his forehead. The steady drone of the shower from the bathroom beyond the thin wall behind him sounded like thunder.

Sweat poured down his bearded face, falling into his eyes and stinging them. He swiped an impatient hand across his forehead. Despite the cool night outside he was burning up with heat.

Listening to the incessant hum of the water, he swore viciously beneath his breath. Was the person going to stay in that damn shower forever? He wanted whoever it was in there to come out. He wanted this over with.

The abrupt silence brought him up short, bringing all his senses to full alert. The shower had stopped.

No screaming. He couldn't have any screaming. All he needed was for her to shut up and cooperate. But God help her if she screamed.

The first thing Caitlin noticed when she opened the bathroom door was the darkness. She stopped, peering warily into the room. That was odd, she thought to herself. She was certain the lamp on the bureau stand had been on just before she'd stepped into the shower.

She glanced down at the two small drinking glasses, neatly wrapped and lined up on the counter by the sink. Of course, she thought, breathing a little sigh of relief. The maid. Caitlin had knocked a glass off the table with her suitcase when she unpacked earlier, and she'd called for the hotel maid to help clean up the scattered pieces. The young woman had been vacuuming the shards of glass when Caitlin went into the bathroom for her shower. No doubt the maid had switched off the lights when she left the room—automatic reflex.

Stop being so jumpy, she reminded herself, reaching up to pull the towel from the turbanlike hold on her hair. Shaking out her long, damp strands, she carelessly tossed the towel over the rack beside the sink and stepped gingerly out of the bathroom, feeling her way toward the light switch.

When it happened, it happened so fast that her reflexes were slow in coming. The rough hand clamped down hard on her mouth, and a strong arm grabbed her from behind, pulling her against a hard wall of muscle and bone. She'd been too confused to panic at first, too baffled to realize what was happening, but that didn't last long. Confusion soon gave way to realization, and realization to horror.

Her hands came up, pawing helplessly at the hand over her mouth. She couldn't breathe, couldn't think. She struggled frantically, but the arms that held her were like steel bands.

"Quiet!" he said in a gruff whisper at her ear.

But she couldn't be quiet. Fear was churning inside her; she was desperate for a means of escape. Her arms felt powerless, her legs thrashed helplessly around. She tried desperately to free herself, but the arms that held her remained firm and unyielding. It was so dark, and she was so frightened.

"Damn it, *shut up!*" he demanded.

But Caitlin heard nothing. She recognized only fear, and fear demanded that she fight.

He knew she was scared, but damn it, why couldn't she just be quiet? He didn't want to hurt her. He just wanted her to cooperate with him, do as he said.

She was tall and, even though he was easily able to lift her bare feet off the carpet, she fought him wildly. In their struggle her hair splayed across his face, feeling cool and damp. In some part of his mind he registered the gentle fragrance of shampoo, bath oils and beauty bars, but he didn't have time to think beyond that. It was all he could do to keep her flailing arms and legs from throwing him off balance.

Gradually, however, he began to feel her strength begin to slip. At last, he sighed in relief. Her struggle was valiant, but finally it ended in an exhausted slump. Her tired arms and legs hung limp and lifeless, but his hold remained firm.

"You have to be quiet," he whispered finally.

For the first time he felt as though she might have heard him, for her body tensed at the sound of his voice. They stood together in the darkness, listening to the labored sounds of their breathing blend and combine.

"Just shut up and I won't hurt you," he told her. He eased the pressure of his hand against her mouth by a fraction.

Caitlin felt the brush of his lips against her ear when he spoke, and a chill ran down her spin. It was so dark, and her terror fed on the blackness. Fear had her senses reacting to him with an almost superhuman clarity. She had become aware of details, of nuances, of subtleties that would have gone unnoticed under normal conditions. She was cognizant of each slight shift of his weight, of each shallow catch in his breath, of each scant lessening of pressure on his hold. She felt the roughened texture of the skin along his hands, felt the scratchy stiffness of his beard along her cheek, smelled the pungent, musty odor of fish and the ocean that clung to his clothes. His body felt huge behind her, and his hold on her like iron. His ragged breathing sounded like a tempest in her ear, and his heartbeat like thunder.

He held her for what seemed like hours, long enough for her fear to turn to dread. She was too frightened for tears, too numb to cry. She squeezed her eyes tight, and willed herself not to think, yet she couldn't stop her thoughts from spinning. Let him take what he wanted—money, jewels, anything. But when her mind threatened to move beyond those obvious things, terror consumed her again. She squeezed her eyes even tighter in an effort to block out those nightmare images.

He was restless. Now what did he do? Tie her up? Toss her into a closet? All he really wanted was for her to shut up long enough to give him some time to think.

His grip remained firm around her despite the fact that she was calm at the moment. He knew he couldn't trust that she would remain that way. Once her strength returned she'd more than likely turn into a wildcat again. He had to decide fast how he wanted this thing played out while she was still fairly easy to control. He wasn't sure how much time he had.

Shifting his hold, he silently cursed again the people and the circumstances that had brought him to this point. He was no James Bond, no Indiana Jones, yet standing in the darkness of a stranger's hotel room he felt as though he'd stepped into the world of both those fictional characters.

Only seven days earlier Jorge had lain dying in his arms on a hot, dusty street in Lima. Yet there had been no time to mourn. Those bastards who'd murdered Jorge were after him now, too. The tramp steamer he'd escaped Peru on had been dark and filthy, but he'd made a promise to his dying friend and he was determined to honor it. The trick would be to stay alive long enough to keep his word.

He was on the run and he was desperate, desperate enough to break into the hotel room, desperate enough to take its occupant hostage. But it couldn't be helped. He'd never been accused of running away from a fight, but now he was fighting for his life, and God help anyone who got in his way.

Without warning Caitlin felt his hold on her tighten again. Terrified, she tried to resist, but her arms and legs were too weak. Half dragging her, he crossed the room toward the door.

For an instant Caitlin was filled with hope. Was he planning to leave? Could it be that this nightmare would end as suddenly as it had begun? Would he push her aside and escape down the hall?

He peered through the peephole. The corridor outside her room looked deserted, but looks could be deceiving. He had to be sure, and until he was he wasn't going anywhere.

Caitlin would hardly allow herself to breathe. She prayed he would open the door and leave. But when he turned with her and moved away from the door, hope died a terrifying death.

He dragged her to the bed. It had been in his mind to sit her down and try to make some explanation, to convince her if she were to cooperate that no harm would come to her. In his mind it seemed reasonable. He would let her know up front what he expected of her and then they both could get on with it. He'd talk to her calmly, rationally, logically. She'd understand what it was he needed, and she wouldn't be afraid of getting hurt. Only…when he walked to the bed and forced her down upon it, there was nothing calm, nothing rational, nothing logical about her reaction.

In her worst nightmare Caitlin couldn't have imagined anything more frightening. As he pushed her onto the mattress, she knew without a doubt that her terror had only just begun. If all he'd wanted was her money or her jewelry, he could have had them by now and been long gone. There was only one other reason he'd stuck around this long, and imbued with new strength she wasn't going to let him take her without a fight.

He was caught off guard when she sprung for him like a tigress. She lunged off the bed, hands clawed.

"Damn it, woman!" he growled, grabbing her by the wrists. "Sit down."

"No!" Caitlin gasped, struggling. "I won't. Help! Someone help me!"

The force of her attack had surprised him, causing him to lose his balance. What the hell was the matter with her? He had to shut her up—fast—before someone heard her. Swearing under his breath, he clamped a hand hard on her mouth and wrestled her down. As arms and legs grappled, they went sprawling across the bed together.

Finding herself horizontal on the bed beneath this looming hulk of a man made her struggle all the more furiously. The weight of his body was suffocating and made it difficult for her to breathe. And the darkness—so black and threatening—played havoc with her equilibrium. The room spun. She felt dizzy and light-headed.

He waited, watching as she struggled against him as he pinned her beneath him on the bed. Then, like the mainspring of a clock as it gradually unwound, he watched as her strength slipped away and she fell back exhausted.

"Are you finished?" he asked after a moment.

Caitlin bristled at his sarcasm. Too exhausted, she didn't answer.

"All right," he said reasonably. With his free hand he held her wrists together above her head, giving them a rough jostle for emphasis. "Keep your mouth shut and you won't get hurt." His other hand was still pressed tightly over her mouth. "Now, if you promise not to scream, I'll take my hand away. Got it? Keep quiet, understood?"

Caitlin nodded. All she could think about was getting his hand from her face and getting him off her. Cautiously he eased the pressure on her mouth slightly.

So far so good.

When he released her mouth, Caitlin gasped noisily for air. In an instant his hand trapped her again.

"Remember," he warned, pressing hard against her lips. "Not one sound." He let his hand fall away from her face, and when he was satisfied she wouldn't cry out, he pushed himself to a sitting position, straddling her. "Good." He nodded, looking down at her.

Despite the floor-length windows that opened to the city, it was so damn dark in the room that he could only make out a vague outline of her face. But he didn't need to see her face to know she was tired. Her exhausted body trembled beneath him.

"That's better," he said, rubbing at a spot on his shoulder where she'd managed to land a blow. "If you promise to shut up and stay put, I'll get up. Deal?" He couldn't see her nod, but he felt the bed move. Smiling, he leaned down. "Since I don't hear any objections, I take it we agree."

"D-deal," Caitlin answered in a raw whisper.

Slowly moving his leg, he lifted himself off the bed. Without turning away from her he backed toward the windows and glanced out at the gloomy night. A heavy fog dulled the magnificent skyline, contributing to the darkness and throwing an eerie glow around the city.

Okay, so now what should he do? He just needed some time, damn it. It hadn't really been his intent to frighten her, but at the moment keeping her afraid suited his purposes.

Caitlin gasped for breath. She didn't dare move, but she kept her eyes glued to her attacker. Against the drab glow from the lights outside she could make out the tall, jagged outline of him silhouetted by the window. His long hair was shaggy, his shoulders broad, and when he turned his head to glance outside, she could see the outline of a straight, angular nose and scruffy beard.

She felt enormously better with him off her, and her tired, worn-out body began to relax. But when he turned toward her again, every muscle came to full alert.

"W-what are you doing?" she stammered, scrambling back against the headboard.

"Calm down," he ordered impatiently. "Look, I realize you're scared, but believe me, I'm not interested in your virtue." Slowly he moved toward the door. "You might say I'm a little pressed for time."

He used that same arrogant sarcasm he'd used earlier, and Caitlin seethed inside. At the door he spied through the peephole again, then quickly moved back across the room to the bed.

"All you have to do is just sit there. Got it? You won't get hurt as long as you just sit there and keep your mouth shut, understand?" In the dimness he could see her nod.

The restlessness was almost unbearable. He felt like a caged animal, trapped and exposed. He paced back to the door, checked the peephole again, then crossed back to the windows. Cold sweat made his skin feel clammy and uncomfortable. If he only knew whether those bastards were still out there or not.

Caitlin watched him prowl the room, moving back and forth from the door to the window and back again. He didn't speak to her, didn't acknowledge her in any way. She began to wonder after a while if he'd forgotten she was even there. His relentless pacing and constant restlessness was infectious, and she began to feel jumpy and agitated, too.

The sudden knock on the door could have been a gun-shot in the darkness; it had sounded that loud to Caitlin. He leaped across the room to the bed, hurling her to her feet. His hand clamped down hard on her mouth, and he dragged her with him to the door. Squinting through the peephole, he swore violently under his breath.

"Ask who it is," he ordered, his lips pressed against her ear. Slowly he eased his hand away from her mouth.

"Who is—" Caitlin's voice failed. She cleared her throat and tried again. "Who is it?"

"Room service." The voice from the corridor was heavily accented.

"Tell him it's a mistake," he growled into her ear. When she hesitated, his grip tightened and he gave her an impa-tient shake. *Tell him.*

Caitlin cleared her throat again. "I-I'm sorry. You've made a mistake." Pressed so closely to the door, she could see out the peephole. The greasy-haired, thick-necked man dressed in a hotel uniform looked blurry and distorted through the small round opening, but even with his fea-tures contorted he looked thoroughly frightening.

"No one inside ordered room service?" the loathsome-looking waiter called back.

"You've made a mistake," Caitlin called again. From the peephole she watched him turn to leave. She was al-most relieved when she saw him walk off down the corri-dor, even though it meant she was again left alone with the dark stranger who held her.

Shoving her to one side, he checked the peephole and swore violently again. That had been one of them. Those dirty bastards hadn't given up. They were still lurking around the hotel, looking for him. Grabbing Caitlin by the arm, he pulled her back to the bed.

He shoved her onto the mattress. "Sit there and be quiet," he ordered gruffly. Distracted, he ran an impatient hand through his hair. His mind scrambled; he had to come up with something fast.

Caitlin scooted into the middle of the bed and sat upright against the headboard. She trembled as a new fear began to consume her. What was going on? Who was that awful man at the door just now? What did he want? What did this stranger want? She'd been worrying about robbery or rape until now, but something else was going on here. What could it be, and what did it have to do with her?

With wide eyes she watched the dark figure of the man roam around the room. Panic made her mind race. What was going to happen to her? Was she going to die? Was he going to kill her?

Fear caused thoughts to come into her mind in a jumbled array of images—flashing back and forth from life and death to trivial and insignificant. She thought of Brian, of Chloe, and about her Wednesday night ceramics class. She couldn't die. There was so much she hadn't done yet. She regretted never having had a child, never having finished reading Hermann Hesse, never having gone to Europe. She remembered she'd forgotten to tell Chloe where she'd stored that new shipment of books that had come into the shop just before she'd left, and she thought of all the unfinished ceramic pottery she'd left. If she died tonight, what would happen to that hidden carton of books, and who would finish firing her pots?

Thinking about all those things made her furious—with herself rather than her assailant. If she were going to die in this hotel room tonight, it made her angry to think of all the mistakes she'd made in her life, all the time she'd wasted. She should never have allowed Brian to bully her into marrying him as soon as she'd graduated from small La Verne College. He'd just finished La Verne's law school that same June and had wanted her to move with him to his hometown of Stockton, California.

Why hadn't she waited? Why hadn't she given herself a chance to experience a little of life, to test her own wings? But instead she'd gone from the cloistered confines of campus life directly to the safe, sheltered world of marriage.

What a fool she'd been. While Brian had concentrated on his growing law practice she had devoted all her time to being the perfect loving wife. She'd met all the right people, joined all the right clubs, worked tirelessly for all the right organizations. She'd become Brian's best asset—the one he used most often to show off to his friends and to impress his clients.

How could she have been so stupid? She'd even let Brian convince her they should wait to start a family. She'd wanted a child desperately, but Brian had kept putting her off. No wonder she'd been devastated when she heard Brian and his "friend" were expecting. He'd given his young girlfriend the child he'd denied her for twelve long years.

She'd been a fool, and thinking about it now—now that it was too late—made her seethe. If, by some miracle, she made it out of this room alive and in one piece, she was determined never to allow herself to be denied again.

The anger felt good, primarily because it took the edge off her fear. The darkness still bothered her, though, still posed a threat. She watched the dark stranger who prowled restlessly around the room. She began to think that maybe he meant it when he said he wouldn't hurt her. After all, if that was what he wanted, what was he waiting for? He'd had plenty of time to hurt her—or worse—if that had been his plan. Yet all he'd asked from her was her silence.

If she could just see him, if she only knew what he looked like, maybe then she'd be better able to trust his word. Even though the draperies on the windows were open, the lights of the city weren't strong enough to cast more than a dim glow into the room. She had a few impressions, had caught a few glimpses here and there, but she'd been unable to put those random pieces together to form any kind of face.

She knew he was strong. Unconsciously she rubbed her wrists. The bruises on her skin and that powerful build of his certainly attested to his strength. And she'd felt and seen the outline of a beard. But still it wasn't enough. If only it weren't so dark. The darkness kept him a mystery, and the mystery still frightened her very much.

When the phone rang, Caitlin felt her heart leap into her throat—only it wasn't her heart at all. It was the hand of the stranger wrapped tightly around her neck. He was across the room and onto the bed before she'd even had a chance to think.

"Don't answer it," he growled, pressing her back against the headboard.

Caitlin felt paralyzed, held prisoner by his hold, afraid to breathe, afraid to move. Even after the phone stopped ringing, they both remained frozen, staring at it as though anticipating another burst of sound. Finally his stranglehold on her eased and he lifted himself off the bed.

Caitlin's hands moved up to her neck and massaged the sensitive skin. She glared at the dark form pacing the room once again. He had no right, no right at all to manhandle her in such a way. Who did he think he was, anyway? She hadn't asked for any of this. Why couldn't he just do what it was he was going to do and get out and leave her alone?

She settled back against the headboard again and closed her eyes. This couldn't be happening, she told herself. Things like this just didn't happen to people like her. She was too careful, too cautious, too ordinary.

She tried to relax a little, calm herself down again, but within a half hour the telephone rang again. This time, however, Caitlin was ready for him. When he leaped onto the bed and grabbed for her, she swatted his hand away with her fist. Clearly surprised, he merely grabbed at her wrist.

"Who's calling?" he demanded.

"I don't know," she snapped. "You won't let me answer it."

The phone continued to ring and he swore under his breath. He felt like yanking the thing out of the wall.

"Maybe you better answer it," he said after a moment. His hand slid up from her wrist to grab her roughly by the upper arm. "But I'm right here," he reminded her through gritted teeth. "Get rid of whoever it is, and don't do anything stupid."

Slowly he reached down and picked up the receiver. Carefully he lifted it between them so they both would be able to hear.

"H-hel—" Her voice failed and she had to clear her throat. "Hello?"

"Hey, you're back, great." Chloe's voice sounded so familiar and endearing that Caitlin felt her eyes fill up with tears. "I tried a little earlier, but you must have been out. A wild party, I hope."

"Uh, no, no party," Caitlin mumbled, barely above a whisper.

"So how's it going?" Chloe asked excitedly. "What was the first day like?"

"It was ... uh ... great."

There was a slight pause, and Caitlin could imagine Chloe's eyebrows crinkling. "Everything okay?"

Caitlin felt the hold on her arm tighten. "Everything's fine. Why?"

"I don't know. You just sound kind of funny, that's all."

"No, I'm fine," Caitlin lied. "Just a little tired."

There was another pause, longer this time. "Is there someone there with you?"

He squeezed Caitlin's arms so tightly that she nearly cried out. "No, there's no one here."

Chloe giggled. "Caitlin MacKenzie, you have a man in your room, don't you?"

"No, nothing like that."

"You lie," Chloe gasped. "I know you and I know when you're lying. The first day! God, this is great. Better than I expected." She laughed. "Okay, look, I won't keep you, but remember, I want to know everything when you get home. Got it?"

"I've got it."

"Well, be careful, and remember, don't do anything I wouldn't do." She paused and laughed again. "But then you know I'd do just about anything. Take care. Bye."

The line clicked dead before Caitlin even had a chance to say goodbye.

He took the receiver from her hand and cradled it. "Okay," he said in his gruff, sarcastic tone, "you did good. Now sit back down and be quiet."

Chapter 2

The hours slowly crept by. Caitlin kept a silent count of their passing by watching the glowing red numbers change on the digital clock beside the bed. Sometime after midnight she watched as the stranger finally wound down and selected a spot on the floor beside the window.

Sitting Indian-style, he lowered himself onto the carpet and rested his head against the grass-cloth-papered wall. Turning his head, he gazed out the window, his features enigmatic and obscured by the darkness. Sitting there so casually, he seemed much less threatening.

She'd had several hours to cool down. *Sit down and be quiet,* he had said to her. Boy, that had made her mad. She didn't know who this guy was, but she was really beginning to dislike that damn sarcasm of his. And it wouldn't hurt him to learn a few manners, either.

She studied him carefully. In an odd sort of balancing way her courage had strengthened as her fear and anger had subsided. That, and the fact that for the past two

hours he hadn't so much as looked at her. She was beginning to think he really was going to leave her alone. Feeling braver than she had in hours, she cleared her throat
hesitantly. "A-are you hiding from the police?"

He turned his head and looked up at her. "Did that
creep out there look like a cop to you?"

"No, but he didn't look like a waiter, either," she remarked, matching his cynical tone.

He studied her shadowy face and couldn't help smiling.
Smart lady. "You're right about that."

"Look, it really doesn't matter to me what's going on,
but I've done what you've asked. Can't you just leave
now?"

Didn't he wish it was that easy. "Tired of me already?"

Caitlin cringed at the sarcasm, her anger flaring. "I'm
tired of being scared, if that's what you mean. I'm tired of
not knowing what the hell's going on. If someone's after
you, why don't you just call the police?"

Her little outburst surprised him. She'd been such a
quiet little mouse for the past few hours that he wouldn't
have expected it of her. But it looked as though the mouse
just might be a kitten, and the kitten had claws. "It's a little more complicated than that," he told her evasively.

"I don't give a damn what it is. I just want you to
leave."

He sat up, bringing his head away from the wall. He
didn't think he was capable of another struggle. For the
past twenty-four hours he'd been operating on pure
adrenaline and he was getting a little punchy.

"Okay, okay, look," he said, raising his hands in sur-
render. "I'll be honest with you. All I need is a
place . . . somewhere to lie low for a few hours. Just a few
hours, then I'll be out of here."

He sounded so reasonable, posing it almost as a request, as though she had a choice in the matter. "You'll leave by morning?"

Leaning back again, he raised his hand solemnly and gave a mocking laugh. "Scout's honor."

She snorted inelegantly. "You're no Boy Scout."

"You wound me," he retorted, feeling a little giddy from fatigue. "What makes you say that?"

"Scouts don't break into people's hotel rooms and terrorize them."

"I didn't terrorize you."

"You did, too," she argued. "Just what would you call it?"

He thought about it for a moment. "I might have . . ." He paused, searching for a word. "I . . . subdued you."

"Subdued?" she choked. "You don't leave bruises when you subdue a person."

"I didn't bruise you."

"Oh, no?" she insisted, raising her aching arms, even though she knew it was too dark for him to see. "My wrists? My arm?"

He sat up, wide awake now. "I really bruised you?" He felt the first flickering of guilt, the first inkling of regret. Up until that moment he hadn't thought of her as a person—not a real person, anyway. She'd just been someone who had gotten in the way, someone in the wrong place at the wrong time. He hadn't let himself think about what all this would do to her. He'd been desperate—like a wild and dangerous animal that was cornered and fighting for its life.

But he'd *bruised* her. He'd hurt her—this innocent woman, and she hadn't deserved any of it. Cursing under his breath, he balled his hands into fists. That didn't make him any better than those bastards who were after him.

God, when would this nightmare end? He wanted to keep his promise to Jorge and put everything to rest. He wanted to go back to being a civilized person again, someone who didn't inflict bruises on innocent bystanders.

"I'm really sorry," he murmured awkwardly into the darkness.

Caitlin shrugged. She really hadn't expected him to apologize. What was she supposed to say? That she forgave him? To think nothing of it? That accidents happen?

She absently massaged her sore wrist and leaned back heavily against the headboard. If only it wasn't so dark. Maybe then she wouldn't feel uncomfortable, and maybe she'd feel more inclined to believe him.

"So why are they after you?" she asked suddenly, her voice reverberating loudly in the silence, even though she spoke barely above a whisper.

"It's a long story," he said tiredly.

"I've got time."

He glanced up at her again. Yeah, he thought, and thanks to her, so did he for the time being. "I have something they want."

"Drugs? Money?"

He laughed. "You watch too much television."

"Well, if it's not drugs or money, then what do they want?"

He rolled his head to the side and gazed out at the lights and the fog of the city. Sitting there on the floor, talking to this stranger in the dark, he felt more relaxed than he had in days. The fatigue that engulfed his body actually felt good. He hadn't allowed himself to feel much since this whole thing started, and feeling himself succumb to the quiet of the night and the warmth of the room actually made him feel human again.

What *was* all this about? He wasn't even sure he knew himself. But one thing was certain. Jorge was dead. A good, honest man had been gunned down in broad daylight in front of a dozen witnesses, and yet no one had seen a thing. His friend had died trying to protect the country and a heritage he loved. And if it was the last thing he ever did, he would see to it that the miserable bastards who were responsible for Jorge's death were behind bars and their money-hungry scheme exposed once and for all.

"You wouldn't believe me if I told you," he mumbled wearily, turning his head back to the shadowy figure on the bed.

"Try me."

Try her? Try sorting it all out for a stranger? How do you try to explain greed, and violence, and insanity? How could he expect her to understand what he didn't understand himself? But maybe she was right. Maybe laying it all out in the darkness would help him to understand. He'd been carrying this thing around inside of him for so long now that he almost felt a need to unburden himself.

He leaned his head back and let his mind drift. When he spoke, his voice was a low, steady monotone. It seemed as if a million years had passed since that night in the cantina when Jorge slipped him that damn videotape for safekeeping.

Even then he'd had the uneasy feeling he was being watched. At first he thought he was just being paranoid. After all, Jorge's story about stolen antiquities, an underground black market, crooked Peruvian government officials and smuggled artifacts making their way into the Unites States via legitimate museum exhibitions in San Francisco sounded pretty menacing. But he knew all too well how tight security around their digs had become.

Michael Sinclair Seger had received grants and assignments from some of the most prestigious universities and museums in the country for his research and expertise as an archaeologist. He'd seen a lot in twenty years of field research and wandering the globe, but nothing close to what Jorge had stumbled onto. What was happening with the priceless artifacts of Peru had nothing to do with archaeology. It was corruption—plain and simple. Corruption, money, life and death.

Even though his work had taken him all over the world and to many fascinating areas of study, nothing intrigued him more than the pre-Columbian civilizations of South America. Over the past eight years he'd made many trips to various digs in the Peruvian Andes as he compiled information for his work on early Incan civilization. With each trip the vandalism and plundering had gotten worse. It had reached such alarming proportions that security patrols were now required to accompany all research teams at the digs. Jorge, a captain in the Peruvian security police, was hardly an alarmist, but he'd come to trust no one except Michael.

Jorge Chupaca was a proud Peruvian, and his friendship with Michael dated back more than a decade. The thought of his own countrymen selling the treasures of their heritage outraged Jorge, and after years of careful observation, he had finally put the pieces together. He had found a clear web of conspiracy and deceit and succeeded in capturing evidence—incriminating evidence stored on a videocassette—against Ernesto Balcolar, prominent curator of the Peruvian National Museum.

Working with a Peruvian national living in San Francisco, Balcolar was part of a group that was smuggling authentic works of antiquity from Peru's rich and mysterious past into the United States hidden in the packing crates of legitimate artwork and artifacts headed for North American museum tours. These smuggled treasures brought huge sums when sold on the black market to private collectors. And because of the enormous amounts of cash that were made readily available for these items, a clear way for corruption was paved. Jorge soon suspected that some of his superiors in the security police were involved in the smuggling as well as other high-ranking Peruvian government officials.

Not knowing how far the stain of corruption spread, Jorge made contact directly with U.S. Customs officials, not trusting his own State Department. Via a complicated network of telephone codes and faxed messages, Jorge supplied information to the customs agent in San Francisco who began a coordinated investigation, along with local law-enforcement and the FBI, to stop the illegal flow of antiquities through the Golden Gate. But then Jorge began to fear he had been compromised by someone in his own department. The videocassette had to reach the agent in San Francisco, and he could trust it to no one but Michael.

Jorge passed the tape to Michael that night in the cantina. He told Michael about his investigation and about the evidence on the videocassette. Michael knew Jorge wasn't the kind of man who panicked easily, but Jorge was frightened that night. Michael believed his friend when he said things had gotten dangerous, but just didn't realize how dangerous.

However, all that changed three days later when Jorge was gunned down in the street as they walked together in the square outside the government building in Lima. Michael promised, as he held his dying friend in his arms, that one way or another he would get Jorge's tape to his contact in the States. Trust the tape to no one else, his friend warned him just before he died.

That night Michael returned to the dig and found his tent ransacked. He suspected those responsible for Jorge's death had figured out that Jorge had passed the cassette to him and would stop at nothing to get their hands on the tape. Getting out of the country wouldn't be easy.

But he did make it out—barely—with the help of a few trustworthy workers at the dig. The smelly tramp steamer leaving Lima for San Francisco was a godsend. After greasing the right palms, Michael managed to secure passage for himself. Still, as he left the dig on the night of his departure, he had a nasty encounter with a couple of unsavory types who tried their best to stop him.

Michael wasn't a violent man, at least not until this whole thing had started. But in twenty years of traveling around the world he'd learned how to protect himself. Taking care of those two thugs only proved to him how imperative it was not to let Jorge's tape fall into the wrong hands.

After seven long days on the steamer, there was no sight better than the Golden Gate Bridge as they sailed beneath it at the mouth of San Francisco Bay. He actually let himself begin to relax. After all, things should be pretty smooth from then on. It would be impossible to do much with the tape that night, but first thing the next morning all he needed to do was to call Jorge's contact with U.S. Customs, deliver the tape and get all this over with. He wanted the people responsible for Jorge's death behind bars and then he wanted to get back to the things he knew, the things he understood and trusted, like his dig and his research.

Only... as he left the steamer with the cassette packed in his small canvas duffel bag and made his way along the docks, he got the uneasy feeling he was being watched again. Telling himself he was just being paranoid, he tried to ignore it.

He didn't even notice the black Mercedes at the end of the pier until he was practically right on it. Only then did its blacked-out windows, obscured license plates and unlikely location begin to look very ominous. Suspicious, he quickly changed directions and crossed a busy street at the end of the pier. He turned back in time to recognize the ugly thugs who leaped from the back of the car and began to follow him. They were the same men who'd tried to prevent him from leaving Peru.

Michael had never been to San Francisco and knew nothing about the city. But he needed a place to hide, and he needed it fast. He quickly scaled the barriers blocking access to the half-destroyed Embarcadero Freeway and made a run for the crowded traffic and chaos of Market Street just beyond. With his followers in pursuit he broke through the crowds of pedestrians and down a packed escalator into a busy BART station.

The Bay Area Rapid Transit station was filled with evening commuters. Underground rail trains sped in and out of the station at a frantic pace, filling up and depositing passengers. But the crowd wasn't enough to lose those bastards. They dogged his every step.

Feeling particularly vulnerable with Jorge's tape in his bag, he ducked into a public rest room and quickly hid the cassette behind the commode in one of the stalls. Once he felt it was safe to return he would retrieve the tape.

He made his way out of the BART station and back up to the street but was spotted once again. Running up Market Street, he darted in and out of the maze of city buses and commuter traffic in hopes of losing his pursuers. Block after block he ran, but his followers were tenacious in their pursuit.

Taking a sudden turn right, he changed direction, finding himself caught up in a noisy crowd that was embarking from an airport shuttle bus at the entrance of a huge hotel. He allowed himself to be herded along with them into the hotel's lobby.

Once inside he just stood there in the crowded lobby for a few moments, hoping he might have lost his pursuers. But when he caught a glimpse of greasy black hair, he realized all hope was lost. He made it into the elevator just as the large doors began to close, noticing his pursuers scramble for the next elevator.

He did his best to ignore the curious stares of the elevator's other occupants, trying to be as inconspicuous as possible. But it was a little difficult given the circumstances. His breathing was labored and heavy from the long run and sweat streamed down his face. And after seven days in the bowels of a tramp steamer his khaki trousers and safari jacket were permeated with the smell of fish and the sea.

When the elevator finally stopped at the tenth floor, he'd raced out, running down the plush corridor, frantic for a means of escape. Just as he heard the landing bell of the other elevator carrying those three ugly creeps, he had seen a maid coming out of one of the rooms—her room.

"So," he said thoughtfully now, inhaling deeply and gazing up at her blurred silhouette on the bed, "now you know."

Caitlin had sat listening to Michael in stunned silence. She'd imagined him a jewel thief, a rapist, even a drug smuggler, but a globe-trotting archaeologist? Never in a million years.

And the tale he'd told her—stolen antiquities, corrupt officials, secret tapes—sounded more like the plot of a movie than something that could happen to real people. Yet, sitting in the darkness, listening to him talk, she had sensed instinctively that he had told her the truth.

"Wow," she mumbled unconsciously.

Michael had to smile at the honesty of her reaction. She hadn't tried to hide her response with some phony indifference or bogus nonchalance. She'd been amazed by what she'd heard, and she hadn't been afraid to show it.

"So now that you know I'm not going to murder you in your sleep, why don't you try to get a little rest," he suggested. "It'll be daylight in a couple of hours."

Caitlin slid down a fraction, resting her head against the hard surface of the headboard. Gazing at the ceiling, she thought about the story she'd just heard. "Your friend Jorge," she said suddenly.

"Yes?"

"I'm sorry."

The lump of emotion that had formed in his throat stayed there long after he heard the steady, even sound of her breathing. His own exhaustion gnawed at him, but his thoughts kept him awake.

She'd offered him her sympathy at the death of his friend. After all he'd put her through, after all he'd done, she'd still found it in her heart to feel an empathy for his loss. Amazing.

He had no idea who this woman was—what she looked like, where she was from, what she did—but he knew she was a decent person. Again he was badgered by guilt. The darkness had made it easier to talk, and as hard as it was for him to believe, he was almost glad he'd told her everything. She wasn't so afraid now, and he had to admit he felt better having unburdened himself. Normally he didn't trust many people with his secrets—especially women, and especially in the dark. Michael had learned the hard way to be very wary of darkness.

He remembered all too well the secrets he'd trusted to Alaura, the confidences he'd shared with her in the dark. He'd been so young back then, just finishing his undergraduate work, and the chance of studying with the famed Alaura Anderson had been pretty heady stuff.

Twenty years ago Alaura had been well on her way to becoming one of the foremost archaeologists in the country. For a green kid in his last year of college the chance to do fieldwork with someone of her caliber was like a dream come true. Despite the eight-year difference in their ages he found her an incredibly exciting woman, and when she singled him out for a special project, his fascination for the woman had soon turned to love.

They'd shared many long nights in the darkness of her tent. Little did he know that all the secrets he'd shared with her, all the ideas and intricate details of his new research breakthrough, would soon be shared with the world. When she published and took credit for the ground-breaking research he'd worked so hard and so long on, Michael had known he'd never trust another woman again. She'd not only stolen his project, but had broken his heart, as well.

But in her own way Alaura had been responsible for the drive and determination that had helped Michael establish his own career. He'd been intent on becoming successful at any cost, and he had. Of course, living the life of a virtual gypsy had left no time for long-term relationships or ties that bound him for too long in any one place. But after Alaura that was the way he'd wanted it. Women had their place in his life, but they were where and when he wanted them. The fact that relationships had turned empty and loneliness had become a way of life was irrelevant. He was convinced he was still better off.

Closing his eyes, he thought about the woman lying on the bed just a few feet away. She'd been pretty good about this whole thing all right. And in a few hours he'd do her a favor by getting the hell out of her life. Maybe he'd get her name and send her some flowers or something. Just to say thanks. Maybe a postcard from the dig.

God, he thought dizzily as the warmth and darkness of sleep consumed him, he must really be punchy to come up with something as corny as that.

Caitlin turned her head and glanced at the clock. It was early, just before six, but the first faint streaks of daylight had begun to make their way in through the windows. She'd little more than dozed on and off for the past few hours, but she felt wide-awake now.

Across the room the man sat, not having moved from the same spot on the floor. His body was poised perfectly still with feet on the floor, elbows resting on bent knees and head tilted back against the wall. But the room was still too dim to make out much else. Caitlin didn't know if he was sleeping, or staring, or...or anything. But as she sat propped against the headboard, looking down at him, she felt her level of anticipation rise with the sun outside.

As light slowly began to drift into the room, she was gradually able to make out more and more of him. Already she could discern pale, faded streaks in his hair, and was amazed.

He was fair. In the night she'd imagined him dark and brooding—black hair, black beard. But even in the first dim grayness of morning she could tell his hair was definitely light in color—blond or sandy brown.

The anger and the fear that had begun to vanish as he'd told her his story in the darkness seemed completely gone. He didn't look so menacing sitting there now. Not like the dark, scary criminal she'd first believed him to be.

Only... as morning slowly progressed and gray faded eventually to white, Caitlin found herself becoming uneasy for entirely different reasons.

Michael kept his head tilted back and watched her through slitted lids. With each careful degree of sunlight that found its way into the room he felt his stomach tighten a degree more.

Last night he hadn't needed any visual aids or lights to tell him that his frightened captive was slender and tall. Some part of his male brain had made note of the fact that beneath the bulky robe he had felt soft curves and shapely bends despite the circumstances and danger of the moment. But putting those soft curves together with long honey-colored hair, deep brown eyes and smooth ivory skin added dramatically to that awareness. This woman was beautiful, and he'd told her his secrets. That was a combination he'd become very uncomfortable with over the years.

He felt restless again, desperate to leave. He had to retrieve that tape before someone stumbled across it, if they hadn't already, but the streets below and the station would be practically deserted at this hour. He needed the safe cover of confusion and chaos of commuter hour madness, and that wouldn't be for a couple of hours yet.

A dozen times in the night he'd considered just telephoning the customs agent Jorge had named and giving him the location of the tape. That way the authorities could pick it up and he'd be out of this thing and headed back to Peru by the end of the day. Only that wasn't the promise he'd made his friend.

He'd come this far; it would be foolish to trust the tape to a voice on the telephone. He'd promised Jorge he'd personally deliver the cassette to his contact, and that was what he'd do.

But, damn, he wanted all this over with. He wanted to be back in the monotonous routine of his dig with its tedious work and predictable pattern. He wanted his tent and his research and to come and go as he pleased. He'd had enough intrigue and cloak-and-dagger crap to last him a lifetime. Enough running and hiding and looking over his shoulder.

And he'd had enough of darkness, and secrets, and honey-colored blondes with haunting brown eyes.

The minutes ticked by and the room became brighter. The fog outside misted the window with a fine sheen of moisture, making the city look cold and uninviting. They could clearly see each other now, but neither had made any attempt to move or speak.

When the phone rang, they both jumped violently. Michael leaped to his feet and Caitlin raised herself to her knees. They both just stared at the functional-looking, beige-colored device as though it were some sort of alien life-form. When it rang again, Caitlin looked up at Michael, confused.

Michael was confused, too. What was he supposed to do? Rush over and grab her again? Threaten her? It seemed a little inappropriate now. She wasn't exactly his captive any longer. The relationship between them had been blurred in the night. It was no longer a clear-cut case of captor and his captive.

"Answer it," he suggested simply.

Clearing her throat, Caitlin reached for the telephone. "Hello?"

Listening for a moment, she nodded and replaced the receiver. Turning to Michael, she shrugged sheepishly. "I left a wake-up call. I'm sorry."

In unison they both glanced at the clock. It was 7:00 a.m.

"You need to be somewhere?"

"The, uh, conference downstairs."

"What time?"

"No particular time," she answered honestly. It never occurred to her to lie. "I just didn't want to sleep in too late."

Michael checked the clock again, thinking aloud. "I've got about another hour."

"Another hour?" Caitlin asked. "Then you'll leave?"

He looked at her. For some ridiculous reason it irritated him to think she was so anxious to get rid of him. "I thought I'd call Customs from here," he explained caustically. "If that's okay with you."

Caitlin frowned at the sarcasm. "You're asking me?"

It had been a little strange. After bursting in last night and doing pretty much what he wanted, asking her permission suddenly seemed ridiculous. He wanted to tell her he was sorry about all that, about breaking in and pushing her around, but it wasn't dark any longer. Somehow, in the harsh light of day, some things just didn't get said.

Without waiting for an answer Caitlin reached for the telephone again. "I'll call down for some coffee. I don't know about you, but I could use some."

Michael nodded, thinking coffee sounded great about now. "Wait," he said suddenly, stopping her. "Don't forget. Just *one* cup. Got it?"

She understood. She was supposed to be alone in this room. He couldn't afford alerting attention to the fact that someone else was in here with her.

"One pot," she said, picking up the receiver. "One cup."

Chapter 3

It was 8:10, and Michael slammed the phone down hard, feeling anger and frustration welling up inside him. Downing the last dregs of cold coffee from the clear glass he had in his hand, he swore fiercely under his breath. What the hell was he going to do now?

The efficient-sounding female agent he'd spoken to at the U.S. Customs office had informed him that Special Agent Len Mason, Jorge's contact, was on a field assignment and wasn't expected back in the office until Monday morning. That was great, just great. It was only Friday. What was he supposed to do for the next three days?

And if he didn't get that damn tape from the BART station soon, he might as well forget about doing anything. The thing would be gone, and Jorge's evidence along with it.

But once Michael retrieved the tape, what then? Play cat and mouse with those South American malefactors for the next few days? Call a time-out? Become invisible?

Of course, the woman on the phone had tried to refer him to another agent, or at least get him to leave a name and a number where he could be reached in case Mason checked in. Again Michael had been tempted—go in, drop off the tape, make a formal statement, then split. It would have solved a lot of problems, this thing would be over and, God, he'd be on a rocket out of this town.

But he'd promised Jorge. He'd vowed to hand the tape to Mason and no one else. He couldn't go back on his word now. Somehow he'd make it until Monday—he'd figure out something. He'd figure a way out of here, get the tape and lie low for the next few days. But at the moment he didn't have a clue as to how he was going to do that.

He walked to the windows and stared out at the city's skyline. The fog was still heavy between the towering maze of buildings. He could hear the water from the shower in the bathroom, and he thought about how he'd stood in very nearly the same spot just a little over twelve hours ago and listened to those same sounds. But as he'd stood in the darkness last night he'd had no idea who had occupied that shower. Last night he hadn't fathomed hair like that, or eyes, or skin.

But now he knew. He knew, and the thought of her standing beneath that spray of water, her skin bare and wet and silky, her long, slick hair falling down her back...

Whoa, pal, what's going on here? he asked himself, reining in his wayward thoughts. This wasn't exactly the time for him to get all hot and bothered by a woman. Especially not this woman. She'd been too easy to talk to, too comfortable to be around. That in itself was enough to make him uneasy, but finding out she wasn't bad on the eyes made her downright dangerous.

No, what he needed to do was start concentrating on a way out of here, not about the woman in the shower. He had the tape and those creeps who were after him to think about, not to mention his own well-being. At least the woman had finally started to think of him as one of the good guys.

The good guys, he thought to himself. What a laugh. If nothing else, this whole thing had succeeded in showing him just how blurred the line between good and evil, criminal and saint really was.

He heard the water shut off, and soon she stepped out of the bathroom wrapped in the same thick robe she'd worn the night before. Last night in the darkness he'd grabbed her when she stepped into the room. But now, seeing her in broad daylight, he found he wanted to do that very same thing—only for very different reasons this time.

Great—as if he didn't have enough reason to get out of here. As if the tape and those creeps out there weren't enough. Now he had this woman bugging his thoughts and doing crazy things to his head.

"You know, I was wondering," Caitlin said a little hesitantly. She still held the towel from her shower and absently dried the long ends of her hair. "That man from last night, do you think there's a chance he might have just given up and left?"

Michael shrugged, remembering how many times in the night he'd wondered the same thing. "A chance maybe, but I doubt it. He and his buddies have come a long way for what they're after. I don't think they're going to give up very easily. Why?"

Caitlin didn't answer right away. She was a little reluctant to tell him what she'd been thinking about during her shower. Dropping her towel, she crossed her arms awkwardly over her chest. "I was just thinking," she said, coming across the room toward him. "You know, if we just worked on it a bit, we could probably make you look different enough that they wouldn't even recognize you. I mean, if you shaved the beard and maybe had some different clothes to put on."

Now that she'd started her excitement got the better of her and ideas began to flow. "This place is crawling with people attending the conference. You could just slip right in. We could leave the room together. Your friends out there aren't looking for a couple. You could just slide right by under their noses." She looked up at him with wide, excited eyes and blinked. "What do you think?"

Michael wasn't sure what to think. The whole thing had taken him by surprise—both the idea, and the fact that she'd come up with it. "I-I'm not sure how—"

"We could do it," Caitlin insisted enthusiastically, cutting him off. "I think there's a small department store right here in the hotel— Oh, better yet!" She climbed over the bed and rushed to the windows, pointing down. "That's Union Square, for heaven's sake. Macy's, Cable Car Clothier's, Brooks Brothers—the clothing world is at our feet."

Michael felt as though he'd missed something somewhere, as though the train had just left the station without him. He watched her throw open the closet and begin sorting through her clothes.

"I-I really appreciate you offering," he said as she rushed around in front of him. How had he lost control? "But I really don't have time for shopping and—"

"Well, of course you don't, silly." She laughed, imagining him browsing through department stores. "You're going to be too busy getting rid of that thing." She tilted her chin forward, gesturing to his beard. She pulled out a comfortable but stylish black cotton jersey jumpsuit with a wide brown suede belt. "While I'm out picking something up, you'd better hit the shower." Wrinkling her nose, she added, "I'm afraid that fish odor is a dead giveaway. There's a complimentary hotel shaving kit in the bathroom."

"Wait, stop," Michael demanded, grabbing her arm just as she headed back into the bathroom. Looking down into her soft brown eyes, he shook his head. "I can't ask you to do this."

"You haven't," she pointed out. "I'm offering."

There was a long pause. Michael still held her lightly on the arm. "Why are you doing this?"

"You're in trouble," she said simply. "And you need help."

His hand on her arm was making her uncomfortable. He'd never touched her before except to grab her. There was something very different in their contact now. She wasn't sure why she was willing to help him. While in the shower she'd told herself her motives were entirely selfish. After all, she wanted him to leave and she was just helping to make that possible. But now, looking up into his crystal blue eyes, she wasn't so sure.

Michael looked at her. There was such honesty in her eyes, such decency. His gaze traveled down to the ugly black and blue marks on her wrists, and he cringed again with guilt. "Thank you," he said, dropping his hands suddenly and turning away.

Caitlin stared after him for a moment, then picked up her things and slipped back into the bathroom to dress. This was probably not the smartest thing she'd ever done in her life, she decided as she closed the bathroom door behind her. It was foolish, dangerous and totally out of character for her. But he needed help, and she just felt she had to give it.

She dressed quickly, slipping her black-stocking feet into the stirrup pants of the jumpsuit and then into her low-heeled black shoes. By the time she finished her makeup, her hair had dried into a jumble of curls. Securing the belt around her waist, she gave herself a quick once-over in the mirror before leaving.

Acceptable, she told herself as she hurriedly surveyed her reflection, but no sweet young thing, either. She wondered as she reached for the doorknob if the stranger out there liked young women. Would he find a woman her age too old to be of any interest?

Stupid to even think about, she told herself as she pulled open the door. Just concentrate on helping him out, have your little adventure, then get your life back to normal.

Michael couldn't take his eyes off her. She looked incredible, and his stomach tightened into an uneasy knot. The black jumpsuit emphasized her tall, slender figure, but the crossed neckline plunged low, revealing a beguiling glimpse of full, round breasts. He swallowed so hard that he had to stop himself from gulping.

"Well, the bathroom's yours," Caitlin said quickly, careful not to look up at him. She'd rather not know if there had been admiration or indifference in those clear blue eyes. Besides, in the daylight those eyes of his had a way of making her feel very uncomfortable—sort of breathless and light-headed. "I shouldn't be too long. What sizes?"

"What? Oh, uh...thirty-four waist. Shirts about fifteen and a half, thirty-four, I guess," Michael answered a little sheepishly. Reaching into his pocket, he brought out his wallet, pulled out several large bills and handed them to her. "Some money."

Caitlin stared at the bills, trying to get her mind to compute. It seemed so odd, his giving her money, especially since he'd pretty much helped himself to anything he'd wanted since he'd gotten here. Of course, that was when she thought him a crook and a thief.

She took the money and shoved it into her wallet, then zipped her purse shut. She crossed the room toward the door. "I'll be back in a little while."

"Oh . . . uh . . ." Michael stammered.

Stopping, Caitlin turned around. "Yes?"

"Your name," Michael said quietly. "I don't even know your name."

"Oh," she said, breaking into a grin. She'd never even wondered about his name before. He'd just simply been "the stranger" to her. "It's . . . Caitlin. Caitlin Mac-Kenzie."

"Caitlin," he repeated, then extended his hand. "I'm Michael Seger."

With some apprehension Caitlin took Michael's outstretched hand. What was she supposed to say? Nice to meet you? How do you do? But when she looked up into his lucid blue eyes, she forgot about saying anything at all.

Michael took her soft, cool hand in his, wrapping his large palm around it. "Thank you, Caitlin. Thank you for helping me."

Caitlin stood in the elevator and cringed. That stranger—that Michael—must think she was a complete nincompoop. After all, she'd stood there like some starry-eyed teenager, ogling him, struck dumb by a pair of sky-blue eyes.

She squeezed her eyes tight and flinched as humiliation flooded through her veins. He must be having a good laugh right now. God, she hated women who couldn't control themselves around men—especially men they found attractive. And she had to admit she found the stranger—Michael—attractive.

But it was something more than his good looks that she found appealing. There was something about him— something more than those brilliant eyes, more than that tall physique, more than that impressive build.

It was excitement.

He was exciting—exciting and a little dangerous. He made her heart pound and her imagination spark. He both attracted and frightened her, and it was this combination that she was drawn to. She seemed to find everything about him exciting—the way he looked, the way he moved, the things he said. Yet always there was a shroud of mystery and a lot of questions.

Maybe it was the blend of excitement and intrigue that had her so willing to take chances and run risks. Exciting things happened around him, and Caitlin hadn't done many exciting things in her life. School had been school, and her life with Brian hadn't been what she would have called exhilarating. She'd always walked the straight and narrow, always playing it safe, betting only on the sure thing. She'd steered clear of long shots, of taking chances. In her thirty-five years she'd known safety, security, routine and certainty, but no real excitement.

But Michael Seger was excitement, Michael Seger was a long shot, Michael Seger was the chance of a lifetime, and she found herself drawn to him like a magnet.

Just then the elevator eased to a stop, and Caitlin was roused from her thoughts. As the doors swooped open, more people stepped aboard, heading for the lobby, and in one horrifying moment Caitlin recognized one of them. It was the greasy-haired stranger who'd posed as a room service waiter the night before.

Consciously she had to fight the urge to gasp in surprise and recognition, but managed to curb herself in time. But seeing him was like seeing something out of a nightmare. She took a deep breath to clear her lungs, hoping it would help to slow down the thunder of her heart. Then she grabbed the elevator handrail securely and steadied her shaking knees.

Don't stare, she warned herself, *and just try to act natural.* She kept her eyes focused on a point somewhere beyond his huge, hulking frame. Carefully schooling her face to display no reaction, she kept him in her peripheral vision.

His black beady gaze swept over the elevator's occupants, but as far as she could tell he hadn't looked at her with any more interest than any of the others. Easing the air slowly out of her lungs, she loosened her hold on the railing. For once she hadn't minded being overlooked.

After they traveled a few more floors, the elevator stopped again. The hulking, greasy-haired man was met by a companion—a man much smaller and far less threatening-looking than the first. The two spoke in low tones to each other in what sounded like Spanish to Caitlin, and yet it was different in some way. All the way to the lobby she listened intently to their conversation, even though she could understand nothing of what they said.

Obviously Michael's worst fears had been realized. They were still looking for him, still convinced he was hiding somewhere in the hotel. Of course, this only made Caitlin more determined in her mission to help him. Otherwise the chances of his getting out of this hotel without being spotted looked pretty grim.

Until this moment Caitlin wasn't sure she fully appreciated the danger this Michael person was really in. She'd been caught up in the excitement, had been so intrigued by the adventure that she hadn't thought about the danger in any real terms.

Watching these two thugs on the elevator, seeing their ominous expressions and ugly black eyes, she began to realize the seriousness of all of this. This was deadly and dangerous.

At the lobby she watched as the two men stepped off the elevator and disappeared in opposite directions. If Michael Seger hoped to get out of the hotel unnoticed by those two, this plan of theirs could very well be his only hope.

Carefully she made her way across the lobby, not wanting to run into any of the people she'd met and talked to from the conference the day before. She didn't want to have to answer any questions as to why she'd missed the breakfast activities, but her precaution proved unnecessary. She slipped across the lobby and out of the hotel unnoticed.

The street outside was its usual chaotic blend of people and machinery—pedestrians crowding the sidewalks and cars jamming the streets. Spotting Macy's down the block, she made a beeline for it.

"Damn!" Michael cursed, examining the damage in the mirror. Bright red blood oozed from the small cut on his chin, mixing with the shaving cream and stinging like hell. He scowled down at the small complimentary razor he held in his soapy hand and cursed again. Did they purposely make these things dull, or was it just their little sadistic joke?

Tearing a small piece of tissue from the box on the shelf, he dabbed his chin. Now he remembered why he'd grown the beard in the first place. Dull razors and no running water were a fact of life at the digs.

He finished shaving, trying as well as he could not to mutilate himself any further, then washed the rest of the suds from his face. Patting his skin dry, he carefully surveyed himself in the mirror. He'd had his beard for a long time, and he had to admit that its absence changed his appearance quite a bit. He just hoped it was enough to fool those creeps tailing him—at least long enough to enable him to give them the slip.

As he looked at himself, he had to smile. He hadn't even thought of shaving. She—Caitlin—had come up with it. What had made her think of it? What had made her think of him?

He'd been surprised by her willingness to help him, surprised she was willing to do anything for him given their inauspicious introduction. He'd found it amazing to think that she'd actually listened to and thought about his predicament and then taken it upon herself to help with a solution. He'd watched as her enthusiasm had caught hold and grown, how her eyes had widened with excitement and anticipation. He'd wanted to reach out and touch the honey silk of her hair, soothe those areas at her wrists where he'd marred that beautiful skin. He'd wanted to pull her into his arms and whisper her name over and over again, feel the sound of it on his lips and in his brain. Caitlin . . . Caitlin . . .

The smile on his face disappeared. He had to get out of here. Now. Today. As soon as possible.

This woman made him very uncomfortable. He wanted out, wanted to get away, to put some time and distance between himself and the image of those haunting brown eyes. Especially after seeing her in that black pant thing she'd worn this morning. She'd literally taken away his breath. The eyes, the hair, the figure, the voice, the heart, the soul—the whole package only made her all the more dangerous. Every bit as dangerous as those creeps out there looking for him.

Tossing the towel carelessly across the rack, Michael stepped into the shower. He closed his eyes and let the water beat against him, soaking his hair and body. This was another of civilization's little luxuries that he missed at the digs.

Reaching for the bar of soap from the dish, he brought it to his nose and smiled. She had smelled of the same clean, delicate fragrance last night when he grabbed her. She'd rubbed this same bar in her hands last night and again this morning, spreading its rich frothy lather all over that long, luscious body of hers. Her wet, slick skin would feel like satin, and his hands could slide smooth and effortlessly along—

Michael opened his eyes suddenly and swore violently. The curses echoed loudly, sounding hollow against the tiled walls. He had to get out of here.

It felt a little strange, she thought as she stepped off the elevator and headed down the hallway toward her room. She used to shop for Brian all the time, but picking out clothes and deciding on styles and colors for Michael was something entirely different. But it didn't matter if he liked the choices she'd made or not; he was simply in need of something different. She'd tried to pick out clothes that were comfortable and practical, and the fact that the colors she'd chosen would set off those brilliant blue eyes of his just happened to be a coincidence.

Caitlin glanced up and down the corridor one more time before slipping the card key into the slot. The hallway was deserted, just as it had been since she'd stepped off the elevator, but still she kept a watchful eye open. Since returning to the hotel, she'd seen no sign of the two men she'd spotted earlier, but caution had her taking a second look. She opened the door slowly, peering into the room a little apprehensively.

"Hello," she called quietly after the door swung shut. "I'm back."

Michael stepped from the bathroom, clad only in pants. "That didn't take long."

Caitlin could only stand and stare. The transformation from bearded to clean-shaven was extraordinary and took her completely by surprise. She'd found him attractive with a full beard and sweat-streaked hair, but not even that had prepared her for the sight of him now. His soft blond hair fell in tousled layers down his neck, and the high cheekbones and square jaw made the blue in his eyes seem that much more brilliant. Caitlin felt her heart skitter to a stop.

"Wow," she breathed out, blinking her eyes in disbelief. With a small shake of her head she pulled herself together. "That's quite a difference."

"Enough to fool our buddies out there?"

"I think so," she said, then remembered. "Oh! My God, that reminds me. I saw him—the one at the door last night."

Michael's brow creased deeply. "Where?"

"When I left earlier. He got on the elevator a couple of floors down. He met another man and they talked."

She described the other man to Michael, and he recognized him as one of the men from the Mercedes. He came forward quickly, unconsciously placing a protective hand on her arm. "He didn't . . . hurt you or anything?"

"No," Caitlin said, shaking her head. "He never even noticed me."

"I doubt that," Michael mumbled almost beneath his breath. He looked at his hand and wondered how the hell it had gotten on her arm. Where had that fierce need to protect come from? Angry, he let his hand drop to his side.

"What did you say?" Caitlin asked. He'd had such a fierce expression that it made her curious.

"Oh, uh..." he stammered, flustered. "I mean..." But Michael's words faded in an uncharacteristic loss of words. A man would have to be dead not to notice her, but she seemed to have no idea at all. Frustrated, he shook his head. "Forget it."

Caitlin looked up at him for a moment. He appeared angry, and she tried to think of what she might have said. Only she found she was having some difficulty concentrating. A rather pressing matter required her attention.

It had suddenly become imperative to her that she put some distance between them. The fact that he was standing just inches from her and that his broad, muscular chest was completely bare had finally penetrated her consciousness.

"Come see what I got," she said with forced enthusiasm, pushing past him and tossing her packages onto the bed. She felt better with him a little farther away, and he didn't seem to be quite so *naked*. "I hope these are all right."

"I'm sure it will be fine," he commented, following her to the bed.

"I looked at jeans, but I thought they might be too casual," she was saying as she pulled out a pair of deep charcoal-gray corduroy slacks. She looked up at him expectantly. "You know, in a place like this, if you're too casual, it might draw too much attention."

He looked down at her with a curious smile. "You sure you haven't done this before?"

"Of course." She laughed wryly, reaching for another bag. "I sneak men out of my hotel room all the time."

Michael laughed, but the wrinkles on his forehead remained. Did she? he wondered.

But he didn't wonder long. He was too caught up in the sight of her. Carefully he stepped back and watched in amazement as she pulled out shirt, shoes, socks, sweater. She chitchatted nervously about why she picked this one over that, why she thought one more suitable than another. She was unbelievable.

And her taste was impeccable. Michael had known men whose wives did all their shopping for them, and he'd always thought they looked like men who'd been dressed by women—bright colors, flashy styles, trendy designs. But that wasn't the case with Caitlin MacKenzie. She seemed to know instinctively what clothes a man would be comfortable with and look good in. The white oxford shirt she'd picked out was practical, the penny loafers classic, and the burgundy cable stitch cotton sweater on sale.

Caitlin finished arranging the new items on the bed and turned to reach for her purse. She realized then that Michael stood quietly watching her. Amusement blended with a less definable emotion on his face, and immediately she felt herself go hot all over.

Well, she'd done it again—managed to make an idiot of herself. She'd let herself go running off at the mouth— nervous and flustered, acting more like a ditzy teenager than a mature thirty-five-year-old woman.

He must think her a real dimwit, chattering on about color and sizes when all he was interested in was getting dressed and getting out of there.

"I'm sorry," she said, cringing. "I didn't mean to just rattle on."

"Don't be sorry," Michael scoffed with the wave of a hand. "And you weren't rattling."

"I get a little carried away sometimes," Caitlin said in her defense. "I used to drive Brian crazy—"

"Brian?"

Caitlin stopped cringing again. "Brian. My, uh, my husband."

A deep crevice opened up beneath Michael's feet and swallowed him whole.

"Or... rather... well, my ex-husband," Caitlin corrected.

Michael was instantly transported back to terra firma again—or as close as one could get in San Francisco.

"Ex-husband," he repeated.

"Yeah. He hated it when I talked about shopping." She shrugged and smiled apologetically. "I guess it is pretty frivolous. It's just that after you've been a housewife as long as I was you get pretty good at it." She smiled sheepishly and handed him some money. "I've even got change."

Michael stared down at the money in his hand and then back into her dancing hazel eyes. Did she have any idea how truly amazing she was? He didn't know about her ex-husband, but he was impressed, intrigued, beguiled and thoroughly fascinated.

Grabbing the clothes off the bed, he headed for the bathroom. He had to get out of here.

"What do you think?"

Caitlin wondered for a moment if San Francisco was experiencing one of those infamous tremors, or was it just the floor beneath her that shifted and swayed? Michael Seger, whomever or whatever he was, was an incredibly attractive man. And she realized right then, with her heart in her throat and her pulse racing like a sprinter, just how important it was that she get this man out of her life.

Desire had made itself known to her in one blinding flash. Maybe it was because she'd suppressed the feeling for such a long time. There had been no one in her life since Brian, just a lot of long, lonely nights, a lot of self-doubts and recriminations. But this stranger—this Michael—had cracked the wall that she'd dammed desire behind, and all kinds of emotions were now spewing out.

Every moment she spent with him her position would become more precarious, and far more dangerous. She wasn't a sophisticated woman of the world; she was just an ordinary person. She wasn't rich, or young, or famous, or special. She wasn't even the kind of woman a man like him would find interesting, but that didn't stop the flow of desire. Right or wrong, suitable or unacceptable, wise or simply foolish, she realized how much she wanted him—this man, this stranger, this Michael.

"Well?" he prompted.

"Hum? Oh!" Caitlin stammered, flustered now. "I, uh, I don't think they'll recognize you." Brushing past him, she quickly walked to the window and stared out at the steel-and-concrete skyline.

She felt foolish. Her feelings embarrassed her. She didn't even know the man, knew nothing about him. She had no business feeling the way she did. Proper women her age simply didn't go around getting all hot and bothered over virile, handsome strangers. Yet here she was, panting and flushed, with her hormones in an uproar, and thinking of any way she could to make him stay.

Michael turned and stared after her. She'd hardly looked at him, and for some ridiculous reason he was disappointed.

He checked his watch. Ten-thirty. He had to go. He *wanted* to go. There was the tape, the promise and the men who were after him. He was restless and uncomfortable, but despite all of that he found himself reluctant to leave.

But he'd had his shave, he had his change of clothes, and there was nothing to keep him any longer. Caitlin had been very helpful, but they were strangers, like ships that passed in the night. And those guys prowling around downstairs weren't playing games. Every moment he stayed would only put them that much closer to finding him and increase the chance of putting *her* in danger. Still, he found himself hesitating.

"I, ah, I suppose I should leave now," he said finally, despite the warring of his emotions.

"Right," Caitlin said tightly. It was stupid to feel bad, she told herself. She should be happy to see this end. She had a conference to go to, and she'd already missed enough of it. "I'll get my purse."

Caitlin hooked her purse over her shoulder, picked up her conference folder packet and handed it to Michael. He waited for her to pass, then followed her to the door. She dared not look up at him. Her feelings were right there, right on the surface, so clear and recognizable that surely he'd be able to identify them from even the most fleeting of glances.

At the door she paused. Carefully Michael turned the knob and quickly scanned the corridor. It looked deserted. They walked in silence toward the elevators. Pushing the down button, they stood staring at the illuminated indicator.

As they waited, several other hotel guests appeared, most carrying conference folders similar to the one Michael held, but there was no sign of the men from last night. Idle conversation moved around them, but they said nothing.

Caitlin was too bothered by her feelings to think much about danger or the fear of running into the men who were after Michael. It seemed far more important to keep him from discovering what she was feeling than to worry about being discovered.

But all that soon changed.

When the elevator finally arrived, the doors slid open quietly and Michael and Caitlin found themselves staring into the face of the thick-necked, greasy-haired South American who'd appeared at their door the night before.

Before Caitlin could even catch her breath, before she could even think of turning, or running, or even being afraid, she felt Michael's arm around her waist. "So what's next on the agenda?" he asked smoothly, pulling her close and gazing down at the conference folder.

"Uh…l-let me see," Caitlin stammered, staring up into his clear blue eyes. It took her a moment to realize that the hulking stranger had stepped to one side and, after having given them only the briefest of glances, looked right past them to scan the hallway beyond carefully. With knees trembling very badly Caitlin let Michael purposefully lead her onto the elevator right under the nose of his pursuer.

The elevator was quite full by the time the doors swished closed, and Michael and Caitlin were able to work their way to the back of the car. People chatted noisily around them, but the bulky South American stood aloof, slowly surveying the passengers.

Michael and Caitlin were making a point of studying the conference folder, pointing to one thing or another, but they were both aware when the hulking giant's eyes drifted to them. Caitlin felt Michael's hand at her waist tighten and pull her closer.

Caitlin was too afraid to move, even too frightened to breathe. The beady dark eyes of the stranger seemed to stay on them for an eternity, even though she knew it couldn't have been more than a few seconds. She took comfort in the warm security of Michael's hold on her, of the warmth of his body beside hers. Still, when that dark, menacing gaze shifted away, she went weak with relief.

The elevator stopped and started at several more floors as people got on and off. At each stop the stranger carefully eyed each newcomer and scanned the corridor of each new floor. Finally, at the lobby, the doors opened quietly and passengers in the crowded elevator began surging forward. The man had remained at the front of the car and was one of the first ones out.

Caitlin and Michael stepped off the elevator and stared after the stranger, watching until he disappeared into the crowd.

"Do you think he recognized you?" Caitlin asked, shifting her gaze to Michael.

"We're still here, aren't we?" he said, his arm still tightly holding Caitlin to him. Slowly he brought his blue gaze down to her and smiled. "But I wasn't sure there in the elevator."

"I was so scared," Caitlin sighed, sagging against him. "My knees trembled so badly I was sure he'd hear them knocking."

"You did great," Michael praised, unconsciously giving her a little squeeze. His smile faded slowly, and he lifted his gaze back to where the stranger had disappeared.

"You think he's gone?" Caitlin asked.

Michael shook his head. "I don't know." Looking back at her, he gave her another squeeze. "And I better not stick around to find out." Somehow their positions had shifted just enough to make them very close to a full-fledged embrace now. "Thank you, Caitlin MacKenzie."

Caitlin could only stare up into his eyes. What was there to say? Warily Michael lifted his fingers to her chin, gently tilting it up. Caitlin's heart leaped violently, thundering in her ears and her breath stalled in her lungs. She watched his lips move closer, closer...

"Caitlin! My dear, where have you been?"

Caitlin felt as though she'd been yanked out of a dream, forced to face reality unprepared. The voice had come from the elevators behind them. Stepping back, she turned and smiled weakly at the short, stocky woman who lunged off the elevator toward her. "Vivian, hello," she said, recognizing the Stockton bookstore owner she'd had dinner with the night before.

"We missed you at breakfast, dear," Vivian said, eyeing Michael with curiosity. "I guess you had other plans. Who's your friend, dear?"

"Ah, Vivian, this is...this is Michael," Caitlin stammered.

"Michael Seger," he finished for her, nodding politely. "Hello, Vivian."

"Hello, Michael," the older woman gushed, offering him her hand. She quickly turned and called to the others just stepping off the elevator. "Come over here, everybody. Meet Caitlin's friend."

Caitlin cringed as many of the people she'd met yesterday at the conference gathered around.

"Well, we better hurry," Vivian said once the introductions were made. "The eleven o'clock seminar is about to begin. Michael, will you be joining us?"

"Uh, no, Vivian," Michael told her graciously. "I just came by to see Caitlin."

"Well, I hope we'll see you again," Vivian said as she and the others started off. "Come along, Caitlin."

Caitlin turned and looked helplessly up at Michael. "I...I..."

"Go," Michael said, telling himself it was better this way. Give her back her life, let her get on with it, he told himself as he started to move away. "And thank you."

"Goodbye," Caitlin whispered.

They turned and went their separate ways.

Chapter 4

Michael told himself again that it was better this way. He was getting away just in time. He'd actually been ready to kiss her back there—actually been ready to throw caution to the wind and press those full, luscious lips of hers to his. But it was better this way, even though as he weaved his way through the crowded hotel lobby, it didn't exactly feel better.

Close call. That was how he'd remember Caitlin MacKenzie. Too close for comfort. He'd gotten out just in the nick of time, and he knew he should be thankful for that.

Yeah, he was on his own again, just the way he liked it. No one to bug him, no one to make demands on him, no one tying him down. Still, as he headed for the hotel's exit, he couldn't stop thinking about just how full and how wet those lips had been. How if he could have just held her, tasted those lips just once...

The soles of the new loafers were slick, and Michael literally skidded to a stop. Outside he could see the lumbering profile of his South American pursuer, meandering up and down the sidewalk among the valets and bellhops.

"Damn!" Michael muttered. Immediately he turned and headed for the exit on the opposite side of the lobby. However, standing just inside the door, smoking a short black cigar, was another of the men who'd been after him last night.

He'd been fairly certain that the character on the elevator hadn't recognized him earlier, but he couldn't be sure. There had been something in the way the ugly bastard had looked at them that had made him think their elaborate charade hadn't worked, but maybe that had just been his paranoia again. But regardless whether he'd been spotted or not, it was obvious his pursuers still believed he was hiding somewhere in the hotel.

He couldn't chance picking up the tape with those thugs following him. How could he hope to keep it out of their hands until Monday with them in hot pursuit? No, he had to figure a way out of the hotel without them seeing him— but how?

As he started back across the lobby, Michael's mind moved furiously—creating one plan and rejecting others. Glancing up, he spotted the concierge's desk, and an idea began to unfold in his brain.

The young woman behind the counter looked up expectantly and smiled as he walked up. "May I help you with something, sir?"

"Perhaps," he replied, acting on the notion as it formed in his mind. "I'm considering purchasing a large antique chest while I'm here in San Francisco. It will be packed and crated for me, but I'd like it delivered here to the hotel. I take it there's a service entrance somewhere?"

"Yes, the service entrance is at the rear of the hotel," the young woman said, indicating the direction with her hand. "Through the alley off Geary Street. Just have it delivered there, and we'll make arrangements to have it brought up to your room."

"Great," Michael said, nodding. "And how would I get out there from here? I'd just like to leave some instructions with the dock supervisor."

"Just past the security office, through the double doors and beyond the kitchen."

Michael thanked the young woman and headed in the direction she'd indicated. There was a chance, a slim one maybe, that his pursuers might have missed the loading dock. If they had, maybe he could slip out....

But that hope soon died when Michael passed the cluttered corridor outside the noisy room service kitchen and peered into the deserted alley at the hotel's rear. Parked at the curb at the end of the alley was a black Mercedes.

He slammed his fist hard against the rough concrete of the loading dock, bruising his hand immediately. Damn those filthy bastards. It didn't matter what he had done to his appearance; anyone leaving this alley on foot would look suspicious.

If only he had a car, or could hitch a ride out of here. If only he knew someone in San Francisco he could call for help....

Caitlin.

No, he told himself. He couldn't ask her to get involved again. She'd done enough already. She'd put up with him long enough. He needed to let her get back to her conference, back to her friends. But even as he gave himself one good reason after another as to why he should just leave the poor woman alone and stay out of her life, his feet were swiftly carrying him back through the littered corridor, out into the lobby and directly to the conference rooms where the booksellers' convention was being held.

There was so much confusion at the door that no one bothered to stop him when he walked casually past the registration desk. The huge conference room was packed, and the steady hum of voices and laughter was nearly deafening. The crowd had gathered for a lecture, but gratefully the program hadn't begun yet. People clustered around, talking noisily as PA sound checks caused occasional ear-piercing screeches that penetrated the drone of voices.

Michael's eyes canned the crowd as he made his way down the center aisle of the conference room. He knew what he was looking for—that precise shade of amber gold that was unique to Caitlin's long silky hair. Like a hunter on the scent of his prey, he stalked through the crowded passages past one boisterous group after another.

For anyone else, finding her in a crowd this size might have seemed like a hopeless venture, but Michael was a man obsessed. He'd made up his mind to see her again and nothing was going to stop him—even if that meant traipsing down every damn row in the entire room and searching every face. But as it turned out that wasn't necessary. Like a magnet drawn to an object of indisputable attraction, his gaze landed on the brilliant golden glow of her hair.

She was in the middle of a row of chairs close to the front of the room. Michael recognized Vivian sitting beside her, and several others of the group he'd been introduced to. It had been less than a half hour since he'd seen her last, since they'd said their goodbyes in the lobby, and he tried his best to ignore the odd constriction in his chest.

Before entering the row he hesitated for a moment. Did he really want to do this? She hadn't seen him yet. He could easily turn around and disappear into the crowd and she would never have to know. The woman made him uncomfortable in a way he hadn't felt in a very long time.

He didn't seem to have any control around her. It wasn't right that someone other than he should have authority over his private feelings. Especially someone who looked like her, someone who walked and talked as if she'd stepped out of a dream.

She was there—right *there*. Just a few feet away. He could almost feel the satiny silk of her hair, almost smell the delicate scent of her perfume, and already he felt himself begin to slip. Already controls were being relinquished and caution disregarded. Standing there watching her, he could think of a million reasons to turn around and walk away, but only one that made him want to stay. She was his only hope. She was his only port in a nightmarish storm.

He was torn, caught between the proverbial rock and a hard place. Those creeps outside the hotel would probably kill him if they got a chance. But as he started slowly down the aisle toward her, he wondered if spending any more time with this woman was any less hazardous.

He wanted her. But wanting a beautiful woman was nothing new to him. He just wished his fascination for the woman ended there. He found himself wanting more than just a quick and convenient roll in the hay with Caitlin MacKenzie. It troubled him greatly to realize that he actually wanted to spend time with her, to discover just what made her tick. He wanted to find out exactly what made her so honest and caring, what kind of life she led and the people who were part of it. But most of all he wanted to know what had happened to make a woman who looked like her so guileless and unsure of herself.

Damn! Did he know how to pick his moments or what? It was ludicrous. He had killers after him. He was fighting for his life for God's sake! This was no time to want to start delving into a woman's psyche—and most certainly not a woman like her.

It didn't take a genius to figure out that Caitlin MacKenzie was a woman who was used to permanence, stability, reliability. All the things he'd never had to offer a woman. And yet he found himself drawn to her—inexplicably and undeniably.

He made his way down the crowded row of people, stumbling over one person after another, excusing himself and apologizing. As he stepped and swayed, he took some comfort in telling himself he was desperate, that he was merely here to solicit her help and nothing more. After all, he hardly had time for anything else. If she would just help him give his pursuers the slip, help him get the tape, then he'd do them both a favor and get out—and stay out—of her life once and for all.

He had almost reached her now, but she still hadn't looked up, still hadn't noticed him. In a way he was grateful. He needed this time to think, to get matters clear in his head.

The tall, somber-faced man sitting beside Caitlin wasn't exactly thrilled when Michael suggested he move down a seat. Not that Michael could blame him. What man would want to give up a seat next to a woman who looked like that? When it became obvious that Michael wasn't about to give up, the man begrudgingly moved and Michael slipped quietly into his seat.

Caitlin was aware of the commotion beside her, but was too preoccupied to pay much attention. The program was finally beginning to start and her mind was too filled with images of blue-eyed strangers, dark hotel rooms and bare chests for much else to penetrate. Besides that, Vivian had kept up a steady stream of chatter since they'd sat down. So between her troubling thoughts and the idle chitchat she ignored much of what went on around her. That was why when she turned and found herself staring into those haunting blue eyes she was sure she was hallucinating.

"Michael!"

"Shh," he whispered, placing a gentle finger on her lips. With his other hand he reached for hers and entwined their fingers. "We can't talk now."

And they couldn't. The speakers were already seated on the dais, and applause broke out from the crowd.

"Why, Michael," Vivian called to him over the din of the clapping, "you decided to join us, after all."

"Yes," Michael said, sending Caitlin a deliberate gaze. "I came back."

Caitlin's heart leaped into her throat and a million thoughts raced through her mind. From the look on his face she could tell something had happened. Had he been recognized? Were they after him again?

No, if the man from the elevator was after him again, he wouldn't be calmly sitting here. But if that wasn't it, then why had he come back? She stared up into his blue eyes and warned herself about speculating.

Don't read too much into this, she told herself. Don't make any assumptions or theorize too much. Just hear him out. He probably needed help again. After all, what else would it be?

The loud burst of applause sounded like thunder, distracting her. She looked up at the stage and watched as the panel leader took the podium. Michael still held her hand, making it impossible for her to join the clapping. Not that it mattered. The hand wrapped around hers felt strong and warm, and she could feel the velvet of his corduroy pant leg brush against the thin jersey knit of her jumpsuit. Body heat penetrated through the fabrics at the point of contact, and the heat seemed to spread up Caitlin's leg, making her whole body glow.

As the opening comments were made by the speaker, Michael and Caitlin both stared down at their hands clasped tightly together. They watched as though some unique and unconventional method of communication were taking place at that junction, and in a way it was. Doubts mingled with desires in a message clouded with questions and doubts. They were still such strangers, but as strangers they had shared so much.

Michael looked around the room, unaware that his thumb was slowly stroking the soft knuckle of her forefinger. Introductions were still being made, and a few people continued to mingle in the aisles. This was probably a good time to leave. Trying to slip out with the program under way would only make them more conspicuous. So when there was a brief pause between introductions, he leaned over and whispered to her, "Let's go."

Caitlin was aware of the curious stares of Vivian and the others, but followed Michael out the row and up the aisle to the exit. Once outside he pulled her into an out-of-the-way spot just off the foyer of the convention area. He focused all his attention on what he needed to tell her. He didn't want to think about the way she looked, or how good it felt just having her with him again.

"Michael, what's going on?" she demanded in a loud whisper when they stopped. "What happened?"

"Caitlin, I'm sorry," he said, slowly dropping her hand. "I'm truly sorry, but I need your help again."

Don't feel bad, she warned herself. *You knew what to expect.* "Did they recognize you?"

"I'm not sure, but they're blocking all the exits," he told her. "Do you have a car?"

"It's in the hotel garage. Why?"

He grabbed her upper arms and looked down at her intently. "You'll help me?"

"Of course," she said without hesitation.

Of course, he thought to himself. He'd known he could depend on her, which was why he'd come back despite all his misgivings. She was the kind of person who wasn't afraid to get involved, who helped when she could and would never turn her back. He'd bet she hadn't run away from anything in her life. Unlike him, who'd made running a way of life.

"Get your car and drive around the hotel," he instructed. "There's an alley off Geary Street that leads to the hotel's loading dock. I'll be in that alley waiting."

Caitlin nodded slowly, taking in the instructions. Carefully she lifted her eyes to his once more. "Those men, they'll be out there?"

"They're only interested in me," he told her calmly, not blaming her for being afraid. "But if you'd rather not, I'll understand."

She *was* afraid, but it was nothing compared to her fear of what would happen to Michael if she didn't help him get away.

"No, no, it's okay," she lied, squaring her shoulders like a soldier awaiting further orders. "What happens after the alley?"

"If I can just make it to the BART station, I can handle things from there," he explained carefully.

Caitlin nodded slowly. "Okay, I'll get the car."

"Wait," he said, stopping her as she moved to leave. "I...I don't really know what to say. Thank you seems so inadequate."

"Then don't say anything," Caitlin said, uncomfortable with his gratitude. "I'll meet you in the alley."

As she walked across the hotel, Caitlin felt a hundred eyes on her. Of course she knew it was only her imagination, but the feeling unsettled her. Suddenly even the most innocent glance from a passerby seemed menacing and suspicious.

She stopped at the valet station and handed the attendant her claim stub, then walked outside to wait until her car was brought around. She saw no sign of the man from last night or his friend from the elevator this morning, but she kept a cautious lookout.

What was it about Michael that had her doing things like this? Who did she think she was, anyway? An aging Nancy Drew? She was a housewife, an ordinary person. What was she doing rendezvousing with handsome strangers in back alleys? Was she out of her mind?

Well, maybe she was, but despite the fear, despite the anxiety and suspicion, this was the most exciting thing that had ever happened to her.

She couldn't help but notice how ordinary and out of place her utilitarian minivan looked among the row of expensive European automobiles and plush limos that lined the valet parking area in the front of the hotel. She laughed, thinking how Chloe had called it her "suburban assault vehicle."

It did look pretty suburban now in the company of such sleek, classy companions. A real country mouse. Especially with all her junk scattered in the back—books, maps, even a heavy ceramic pot she'd forgotten to remove that kept rolling around the back.

She remembered how she'd had to cajole Brian to buy it for her. She'd wanted to fill it with their children—chauffeuring them to preschool, little league, ballet lessons and Boy Scouts. And in a way the van was a forlorn reminder of lost hope and abandoned dreams. The ticking of her biological clock got louder with each passing day, and the dream of a home, a husband and children faded more and more.

The valet signaled her, and she roused herself from all those bothersome thoughts. After tipping the young man, she slid in behind the wheel.

As usual, San Francisco traffic was a tangle. Cautiously she made her way out onto the street. She missed the alley completely the first time around, not seeing it until it was too late to turn. And getting around the block again was no small feat. With the maze of one-way streets and traffic snarls she had to go blocks out of her way.

But she persevered, refusing to be intimidated by honking horns or careening city buses. She was a woman on a mission, and nothing was going to keep her from it. Well prepared on her second time around, she was ready for the alley and easily pulled into it.

The alley looked deserted, and after a moment Caitlin began to wonder if Michael had changed his mind. Carefully she pulled up to the loading dock, drawing as close to it as she could.

Still no sign of Michael.

Had something happened to him? Had they caught him as he tried to enter the alley? Should she park the van and wait, or should she telephone for a policeman?

She was still trying to decide on a plan of action when she saw Michael step out of the shadows and slip into the passenger side of the car.

''Okay, let's get out of here,'' he said, sliding low in the seat.

Caitlin spun the van around and headed back to the street. "BART station?" she asked, purposely keeping her eyes straight ahead.

"BART station," he concurred. "The one across from the Embarcadero Center on Market."

Spotting a gap in the steady flow of cars, Caitlin pulled the van out of the alley. Dodging cabs, rapid transit buses and mobs of pedestrians, she skillfully maneuvered through the busy noon-hour congestion. It wasn't easy— the cars, the people and the million traffic signals made their course a slow one.

Finally Caitlin spotted the Embarcadero Center and the sign pointing to the BART station just in front. "It's coming up on the left," she told Michael, who remained low in the seat. "Get ready. I'll keep circling the block. Just wait for me on the corner."

Michael glanced across at her, but her eyes were fixed steadily on the street. She was no shrinking violet, that was for sure. She'd handled the nightmare traffic with the ease and confidence of a New York City cabbie.

He hadn't argued with her when she offered to wait for him and pick him up. He'd really only expected her to get him to the station, then beat it back to the hotel as fast as her minivan could take her. After all, she'd done all he'd asked her to do. Frankly, the fact that she was willing to wait surprised him.

It would be nice to have her waiting. Then maybe they could drive somewhere together. He could tell her how much he appreciated her help, and they could take their time and say goodbye. Because it would *really* be goodbye this time, and it would be nice not to have things rushed.

"Go!" she said, bringing the van to a sudden stop.

In one smooth motion Michael opened the door and slid out. Within seconds Caitlin was back in the relentless flow of traffic.

Circling the block was nerve-racking. The one-way streets again caused her to go blocks out of her way, and she was sure she'd managed to catch every red light possible. She approached the corner by the Embarcadero station with much anticipation and great relief, but Michael was nowhere to be seen. She scanned the crowded street, desperate for the sight of him. But he wasn't there.

The journey to circle back around was even more frustrating. She was extremely anxious and her mind filled with dozens of different scenarios to explain Michael's tardiness—none of them good. Had someone been waiting for him? Had he been hurt? Had he been kill—

No, she refused to think about that.

Red lights, pedestrians, slow-moving buses—it seemed as though the entire city had suddenly conspired to impede her progress. When the panel truck in front of her stopped suddenly and turned on its emergency flashers, it was the last straw.

"Move that thing, or I'm going through it," she screamed at the delivery man who rounded the truck and began to unload his cargo.

There must have been something about the expression on her face that told him she'd do it, for he quickly hopped aboard the vehicle and edged the big truck to the side of the street. Screeching her tires noisily, Caitlin cleared the delivery truck and proceeded on her way.

Finally she made her approach to the station again. Already her mind was working furiously, trying to decide what she should do if Michael failed to show this time. Should she go look for him, call the police or simply go back to the hotel as though none of this had happened?

She felt frightened and confused. It wasn't as though she hadn't believed he was in danger before. She'd seen the men who were after him. She'd looked into their faces. It was just that she hadn't been able to appreciate fully how real the danger was until this very moment.

He could be dying right now, lying in a pool of blood somewhere, and she had no way of knowing. She'd have to go back to the hotel, back to Stockton, without ever knowing, without—

Just then she caught a glimpse of something that caused her thoughts to scatter and brought all five senses to full alert. There, above the crowd, just for a moment, she saw something familiar—a fleeting streak of dusty blond, moving in and out of the mob of pedestrians on the sidewalk.

Hope soared, and when Michael finally stepped out of the crowd and up to the curb, Caitlin felt every muscle in her body go limp.

"Did you get it?" she asked as he climbed into the seat beside her. She was grateful she had her driving to concentrate on or she might have done something stupid like throw her arms around him.

"Right here," he said, smiling and pulling the videocassette out from beneath his bulky sweater.

"What took you so long?" She glanced in the rearview mirror and slowly merged with the traffic.

"The stall was occupied," he said, laughing. "Do you have any idea just how difficult it is to try to explain to someone why you prefer waiting for one particular bathroom stall and not use one of the other dozen or so that were empty?"

"What happened?" Caitlin asked, glancing in the mirror again.

"Don't ask. You don't want to know." He laughed again, and it was infectious. She laughed, too.

"Okay." She sighed, feeling just a little giddy. "Where to now? Could I drop you at the customs office?"

His laughter slowly died and his face stiffened just a little. He hadn't told her about Agent Mason being out on field assignment and having to wait until Monday to turn in the tape. He didn't want her to know. She might feel obligated to do something really nice like offer to help him find a place to hide, and he'd probably do something really stupid like let her. Best for them just to go someplace quiet, say their goodbyes and go their separate ways.

"Ah, no," he said vaguely. "That won't be necessary."

He was being evasive, but she decided not to push. After all, this was his business. If he didn't want to share it with her, she certainly didn't want to be accused of prying. Still, she couldn't help but feel a little hurt. Up until now she'd thought of this as "their" mission, something "they" shared and did together. Now she felt left out and in the way.

"Where should I drop you then?" she asked, glancing in the rearview mirror at the car behind them and frowning.

"Anywhere along here is fine," he said. He'd seen her frown, and the rigid lines around his mouth deepened. "Maybe you could park for a minute."

"Okay." She nodded absently. "Uh, that's funny."

"What?" he demanded, his whole body tensing. "What's the matter?"

"Oh, it's nothing." She shrugged, shaking her head. "Just that car back there. It just seems strange—"

"Damn!" Michael swore, turning around and spotting the black Mercedes behind them. "It's them! Step on it!"

"Step on it?" Caitlin repeated dubiously.

"Get the hell out of here."

It took a brief second for the danger to sink in, but when it did, Caitlin reacted immediately. With a loud screech of the tires she swung the van into another lane, almost hitting a lumbering city bus. Instantly, behind them, the menacing black Mercedes gave chase.

As their speed increased, Caitlin worked the wheel furiously, twisting and turning frantically to avoid the onslaught of cars and people. Horns honked in their wake, and a sea of angry fists and despicable curses trailed behind them. She cut across lanes, turning across traffic and changing directions, but the Mercedes continued to follow.

"Turn there," Michael barked from the passenger seat, keeping an eye on the car behind them. "Up that alley."

Caitlin turned, swerving to avoid a delivery truck, sending the books in the back seat flying and the heavy ceramic pot on the floor crashing loudly against the door. Behind them the Mercedes careened around the corner, jumping a curb and crashing a bumper along a solid concrete wall. But the chase continued.

Caitlin turned out of the alley, spinning the wheel and heading up a steep, narrow street. At the cross street the bottom of the van scraped loudly against the surface, and the rear bumper left deep grooves in the blacktop when they headed up another steep incline. Chinatown merchants yelled obscenities they were unable to understand, and pedestrians scrambled out of the way.

"Hang on," Caitlin warned, veering suddenly to the left.

On a straightway again she floored the accelerator and succeeded in putting some distance between themselves and their pursuers. But the black Mercedes was tenacious, stubbornly hanging on to their trail and refusing to give up.

Michael was amazed at Caitlin's ability. She was as cool as a cucumber, handling the steep streets and narrow thoroughfares with remarkable skill and gutsy determination, maneuvering the unwieldy van as though it were a Formula One racing car.

"Look out!" he warned, seeing a cable car heading straight for them. Caitlin deftly steered out of the way, swerving just in time to avoid a yellow cab. Michael glanced over at her, his heart in his throat. "You sure you've never done this before?"

Caitlin merely shot him a killing look. She had no time to answer, no time to think or consider, only react. Adrenaline was pumping through her veins like a strong, intoxicating drug—exciting and dangerous. She felt detached, removed, as though she were watching these events on the giant screen of a theater, and it made her feel invincible and strong.

With tires smoking she turned sharply, plunging headlong down the impossibly sharp turns of Lombard Street. "Damn," she cursed, hearing the brick retaining wall scrape along the full length of the driver's side.

The van was awkward on the twisting curves, and the Mercedes began to gain on them. As soon as she could, Caitlin spun the vehicle around, heading down a long, straight stretch, hoping to outdistance them again.

In a crazy, twisting, hair-raising route they traversed street after street. Finally passing through the hilly portion of the city, they sped along the flat boulevards, picking up speed and increasing their lead. Caitlin had no idea where she was going. They were passing through sections of the city she'd never seen before. The buildings began to change, businesses were left behind, and they found themselves surrounded by the huge warehouses and littered streets of the city's industrial section.

The distance between themselves and the Mercedes continued to grow, and both she and Michael began to think they might actually be losing them. But when she whirled around the corner between two large storage buildings, the flashing lights of a railroad crossing arm loomed ahead.

"Watch out!" she screamed as she hit the brakes and the van went skidding sideways toward the slow-moving freight train.

Michael braced himself for impact as they careened along the street and crashed through the crossing arm. Miraculously, though, the guardrail was enough to slow their momentum, bringing them to a stop just a few feet short of the tracks. Glancing back, Michael saw the Mercedes rounding the corner.

"Stay here," he ordered Caitlin, stuffing the tape beneath the seat and opening the door. His only hope was to draw those bastards away long enough to allow Caitlin to get away safely. He took off at a dead run across a crowded parking lot as the black Mercedes came screeching to a stop behind them.

Two occupants leaped from the car, and in the rearview mirror Caitlin recognized them as the men from the elevator. With her heart in her throat she saw the smaller one take off after Michael. And to her horror she watched the big, greasy-haired one start for her.

In an instant the situation had gone from exhilarating to terrifying. The adrenaline that had fueled her courage and quickened her abilities during the long, grueling car chase seemed now only able to incite her fears and contribute to her panic.

She tried to lock the door, but it was too late. Scrambling out of her seat belt and shoulder harness, she leaped into the back seat as the thick-necked maniac yanked open the door.

Terrified, she watched as he lunged over the seat toward her. With a strangled scream she fought him as well as she could. Braced against the back seat, she kicked and pushed at him with her long legs. But he was huge and easily deflected her blows.

Despite her struggles he grabbed her by an ankle. Caitlin clawed around her, desperate for a means of escape. She grabbed at the maps and books that lay on the seat and threw them at him, but they were ineffective weapons against this monster.

Then her hand brushed against the large ceramic pot that had been rolling back and forth on the floor in the back. Reaching for it, she picked it up and raised it high above her head. Then, with all her might, she smashed it down onto her attacker's head.

The pot broke into a million pieces, and the hulking, ugly giant gazed up at her with a dazed look. Caitlin quickly pulled her ankle free, but even a blow on the head didn't distract him for long. Mumbling something she didn't understand through dirty yellow teeth, he lunged for her again.

This time, however, he was grabbed from behind and hurled out of the car. Even before the lumbering thug was able to react, Michael placed several iron blows to his jaw, then one to his blubbery stomach that sent him sprawling unconscious across the pavement.

Michael climbed into the driver's seat, quickly turned and pulled Caitlin into the front with him. For a moment all they could do was sit and stare at each other. They were both relieved to see that the other was all right, but there was no time for full-blown inventories. Those two goons would regain consciousness soon, and Michael wanted to be out of there before they did.

Still gazing into her frightened brown eyes, he put the car into gear and sped off.

Chapter 5

Michael just drove. He didn't care what direction, nor did he care where they ended up. He just wanted to put as much distance as possible between them and their attackers. That had been close, way too close, and he wasn't about to let something like that happen again.

He glanced over at Caitlin, who sat rigidly in the seat next to him. Slamming his fist down hard on the steering wheel, he cursed furiously under his breath. He'd nearly gotten her killed today. Had she realized just how close she had come? Not only that, but those bastards had seen her. They'd be after her now, too.

Damn, he cursed again. What could he have been thinking? He should never have asked her to help him. Hadn't he put her through enough last night? Why hadn't he just said his goodbyes this morning and left it at that? He should have walked out of her life and kept right on walking. Instead he'd gone running back.

He'd told himself he'd needed her help, that his back had been against a wall, that he had nowhere else to run, no one else to turn to, but he knew now that wasn't the case. The simple truth of the matter was he'd wanted to see her again. Needing her help had been a convenient excuse, a way to soothe his conscience and put to rest all his uneasiness. That way he could keep telling himself he wanted to be free of her and still have a handy excuse that would justify his reasons for staying. God! He'd never had a woman make him nuts like this before. Not only had he been lying to her, he'd been lying to himself.

He was getting in over his head. Things were moving too fast, getting too complex. It seemed as if he had no control over what he felt when it came to this woman, as though the attraction was there whether he wanted it or not, whether he welcomed it or not. That wasn't the way he operated with women. Since Alaura, he'd always been the one in control—at least until now. Caitlin MacKenzie had a way of getting him to care, of getting him involved, of getting him committed, and he didn't like it.

Damn, just thinking about it made his old running instincts kick in. But he wouldn't run this time. He couldn't. Despite all his denials earlier he had wanted to go back and get her from that conference. In all truthfulness he could have come up with something else to get him out of that hotel. Instead he'd seized the first good excuse he could think of to see her again. But his self-indulgence and shortsightedness had put her life at risk, and like it or not, he couldn't leave now until he was sure she was safe.

"This isn't the way back to the hotel," Caitlin said, looking around her.

"We're not going back to the hotel."

"What? What do you mean?" she demanded. "Why not?"

"We can't go back there," he told her irritably. "It's the first place they'll look."

"Now wait a minute," she told him, sitting up even straighter in the seat. "You take me back to that hotel right now."

"No can do, lady."

"That's . . . that's kidnapping."

"Call it what you want. We're not going back," he told her reasonably.

"I'll call the police," she sputtered, furious and frustrated. "I'll . . . I'll have you arrested."

"Yeah, well, you try and do that."

Caitlin flung herself back against the seat. God, she hated that sarcastic tone of his. Who did he think he was threatening her and throwing his weight about? She used to think Brian was a bully, but this guy left her ex-husband in the dust.

She was still shaking, still reeling from the chase and those awful men. She just wanted to go back to her hotel room and the conference. She'd had enough of action and adventure. She wanted her old, dull life back.

She looked across the seat at Michael. His strong, handsome profile looked hard and rigid. Pushing him was impossible. She'd never met anyone so stubborn and unreasonable. She'd have to use a different tack.

"Okay," she agreed. "Maybe it isn't such a good idea to go back just yet. So we'll go to the customs office first?"

"Not exactly."

"Then what?" she asked impatiently, feeling her anger flare again. "Exactly."

"The agent I need isn't there right now," he offered simply. "We'll need to lie low until he gets back."

"Oh." Caitlin shrugged, thinking this sounded reasonable. Once they turned in the tape there would be no reason to stay away from the hotel. "Okay. So when is this guy due back?"

"Uh, Monday," Michael mumbled, bracing himself.

"What?" she cried. "What do you mean, *Monday?*"

"I mean we can't get rid of the tape until Monday."

"You mean..." Caitlin started, nonplussed, but her voice gave out. Clearing her throat, she stared across the van at him. "You mean you expect...you actually think I'm going to...I can't go back to my hotel..." This wasn't happening, she told herself. "What about the conference?" she demanded. "What about all my things?"

Michael suddenly swerved to the curb and brought the van to an abrupt stop, drawing loud honks and angry jeers from several passing cars. Angry and impatient, he turned and grabbed her roughly by the arms. Did she think he liked this any better than she did? "Mason won't be back until Monday. Now unless you're real anxious to meet up again with our buddies back there, you'll do as you're told."

"Do as I'm told?" she repeated, carefully enunciating each word through tightly clenched teeth. "How dare you? How *dare* you? Who do you think you are? Either you take me back to my hotel right now or I'll...I'll—"

"You'll what?"

Caitlin stared up at him. What would she do? His fingers were biting into the skin on her arms, but she forced herself to ignore it. "I hate you."

"Yeah? Well, I'm all broken up." He released her with a harsh shove and turned to the wheel again. The anger felt good. It made him forget the guilt for a while and kept him from thinking about how frightened she was.

"Look," Caitlin told him reasonably after they drove a little farther. Absently she rubbed at the sore spots on her arms. "Why can't you just drop me somewhere? You can keep the car. I'll find my own way back."

He looked at her and shook his head. "You just don't get it, do you? Or are you really that anxious for your fat friend back there to finish the job he started on you?"

"They're not after me," she argued, but inwardly she cringed at the thought of that awful-looking man and what would have happened to her if Michael hadn't pulled him off her.

"They are now."

He could feel her cold stare clear through to his soul. She hated him, and he couldn't blame her. He'd taken her life and turned it upside down. He'd taken her from her conference, her friends, and he'd very nearly gotten her killed.

Yeah, she hated him.

Caitlin crossed her arms resolutely over her chest. Rage warred with fear, but she was determined not to show him either.

She was furious with him. His high-handed tactics made her feel powerless and weak, yet when she thought of those men and that hair-raising chase through the city, she had to fight the urge to cling to him for protection.

She turned and looked out the window, batting back the tears that began to form in her eyes. Even though she felt herself precariously close to falling apart, she didn't want him to see her cry. She didn't want him to see that she was frightened, that she couldn't take it. Maybe her life was dull and drab compared to the excitement and adventure of a globe-trotting archaeologist, but she'd be damned if she'd let him see her break down.

If only she could stop shaking, if only she could stop thinking about those men. Her life had never been in jeopardy before. She'd never experienced that kind of terror. She hadn't even had so much as an obscene phone call.

But when she thought of that greasy-haired man—how he'd leered at her, the hideous sounds of the words he'd growled, the smell of his stale breath in her face—she'd understood the meaning of terror. She shuddered again, a chill running the length of her spine.

"You cold?" Michael asked.

"I'm fine," she snapped. Looking in the distance, she saw the sweeping arches of the Golden Gate Bridge ahead. "Do you have any idea where you're going?"

"Not really," he admitted, glancing over at her and smiling. The look she gave him could have frostbitten his lips, and the smile froze on his face. Apparently good, decent people had their limits, and she'd obviously reached hers. Not that he blamed her. She was more than justified, but he was going to miss her smile. "We need to get out of the city for a while."

"A while? Or until Monday?"

"Okay," he conceded, understanding her hostility. "Yes, until Monday."

The sound of the tires as they rolled onto the pavement of the bridge was hollow and loud, causing them to sing noisily. Caitlin looked out across the breathtaking view of the cold, turbulent bay, but saw none of it. Her thoughts were too troubled to notice and appreciate the beauty of such a vista. She was thinking too hard how she was going to make it all the way to Monday with this man who both infuriated and fascinated her.

After leaving the bridge, the traffic lightened considerably as they made their way up Highway 101. But they'd only driven a short distance when Michael suddenly braked hard and pulled the car off the highway onto a long gravel drive.

"What now?" Caitlin grumbled, proving to herself she could be just as sarcastic as he.

But to her complete fury Michael didn't even bother to answer. He simply followed the steep, narrow drive up a sharp incline to where it ended in the parking lot of a lovely inn. The rambling old farmhouse looked picture-perfect, with grounds that were neatly groomed and well tended. The brightly painted sign lazily swaying from the shiny wrought-iron frame pronounced the place Cliff House Inn.

The van's tires skidded on the gravel as Michael brought the vehicle to a stop. Caitlin peered curiously out the window.

"Hey, where are you going?" she called after him as Michael leaped from the van and sprinted toward the house. Again he ignored her.

Clenching her jaw, she made a face as he disappeared inside, then she slowly turned and gazed around. The setting was beautiful—there was no doubt about that. The old inn was secluded and out of the way, perched high on a hill overlooking Sausalito and the bay below. Geraniums blossomed in pots lined along the porch steps, and the white shutters looked clean and freshly painted. The wide front porch sported an inviting swing suspended from the beamed rafters. A birdbath sat in the neatly kept garden, and comfortable-looking wicker furniture was arranged in clusters around the lawn.

Inside, Michael bent over the check-in desk and filled out the registration card.

"You're quite fortunate," the young innkeeper remarked, eyeing Michael with some curiosity. "The cancellation came in less than an hour ago. Normally our rooms are booked weeks in advance. Most of the inns in the area are."

"Then I guess we really are lucky." Michael smiled and handed her the card. "It was a spur-of-the-moment trip for us."

"Well, I hope you and your wife will enjoy your stay," the innkeeper said, handing him the room key.

Michael took the key and stepped out onto the porch. He'd never registered as Mr. and Mrs. before, and he wasn't sure why he'd done it now. It certainly wouldn't have mattered to the innkeeper whether he and Caitlin were married or not. So why had he done it? What little game was he playing imagining her as his wife?

His wife? Pull yourself together, man.

He walked to the van and opened Caitlin's door. "Come on."

"What?" she asked. With his hand pulling at her upper arm she had no choice but to step out. "Where are we going? And—" She stopped and jerked her arm free. "Let go of me." She rubbed at the spot where he'd held her. "What is it with you and bruises? You got a thing for black and blue?"

"I'm . . . sorry," he mumbled, pushing back a surge of guilt. That Mr.-and-Mrs. thing still bugged him. "I've got us a room."

"A room? Here?"

"Yeah, why? What's wrong?"

"But this . . . this is a bed-and-breakfast inn."

"So?"

"So this is where people go for...for—" She looked up at him helplessly. "You know, for honeymoons and things like that."

"I know." He smiled and tossed the key into the air. "That's why I rented the bridal suite."

"What?"

"Look, calm down. It was all they had—just a fluke. There was a last-minute cancellation." Very gently he grabbed her by the arm and tried to get her to move, but she stubbornly refused.

"But why this place?" she asked, pulling herself free again. "And I want a room of my own."

He let out a long, slow sigh. "This is the last place those bastards would think of looking for us. And I told you, they only had the one room. They're booked solid."

"I want my own room," she insisted, unconsciously stomping her foot.

"Well, you can't have it," he told her, like a father addressing his spoiled child.

"Then I'm not going in."

"You're going in if I have to carry you," he warned.

"You wouldn't dare."

"Just try me."

"We are *not* going to share a room," she declared flatly.

His shoulder slumped at her bullheadedness. Why was she being so stubborn? Couldn't she see all he wanted to do was keep her safe? To get them both out of this in one piece? Her obstinacy made him furious, and his male pride stung to think that the idea of sharing a room with him was so offensive to her.

"This is ridiculous," he exploded. "Aren't we in enough trouble? Lady, we've got guys with guns after us. Believe me, I've got more on my mind than getting you into bed."

Caitlin stared up at him, his words piercing her heart clear through. He couldn't have made it any clearer how undesirable he found her if he'd tried. She must have looked pretty foolish to him, ranting and raving with indignant outrage. She was nothing more than a mousy little housewife to him. She was making some awfully big assumptions thinking he would want a dull little nobody like her.

Michael stared down at the look of raw pain on her face and felt his stomach twist into a knot. Didn't she know how hard he'd been trying *not* to think of her? How he'd been fighting himself to keep from imagining the two of them together—touching, caressing, kissing. Didn't she know he found her more fascinating and desirable the more time they spent together?

But he had no right to her. All he'd done was take from her, giving nothing in return. How could he ask her for more? He couldn't afford the luxury of fantasy and daydreams. Every moment he spent with her he had to face the temptation and resist it. And every moment it grew more and more difficult.

Yes, he had more on his mind than getting her into bed—but not much.

"I see," she said tightly, turning quickly away. She reached back into the van for her purse and slammed the door closed. "I guess we have nothing to worry about then."

"Caitlin, wait," Michael pleaded, catching her by the arm and stopping her as she started to walk away. At this moment he didn't care if he had a right to her or not; he couldn't stand to see her hurt. "I . . . I didn't mean it that way. I just—"

She turned to him, her shoulders square and her expression cool and controlled, and cut him off with the wave of a hand. "Look, it seems absurd to stand here and argue about what's desirable to you and what's not." And because she had her pride, too, she added, "Since it's impossible for us each to have our own room, I trust we'll have no trouble respecting each other's privacy."

Michael looked down at her. Maybe it was better this way. Maybe he should just concentrate on feeding her anger. The more she hated him, the easier it would be. It was like having a safety buffer around her. He didn't have to worry about slipping and doing something stupid; she wouldn't let him.

Maybe it hadn't left any bruises, but that thoughtless remark he'd made had hurt her nonetheless. He could take her fury, he could take her loathing, but he wasn't sure he could take her pain.

He watched her as she rounded the van and headed up the gravel drive toward the inn, then slowly started after her. He'd just turned to follow when he heard her gasp loudly.

"Oh, no."

"What? What is it?" he asked. Her hands covered her mouth, partially obscuring her horrified expression. "What's the matter?"

"My car," she moaned, pointing at the large, ugly scratches that marred the whole length of the driver's side.

Michael let his whole body relax with relief. "Don't worry. I'll take care of it."

Caitlin shook her head sadly, still surveying the damage, and started for the inn again, mumbling, "All those times at the mall and never a scratch."

Their room was on the third floor of the house, in what had once been the attic. Michael unlocked the door, then stood back and waited for Caitlin to pass. When she hesitated, he looked down at her and shrugged. "Should I carry you over the threshold?"

Her eyes narrowed menacingly as she stepped purposefully around him. "I'm still quite capable of making it on my own steam."

When she walked into the room, she marveled at the magnificent four-poster bed that dominated the room. The dark mahogany wood contrasted brilliantly with the snowy white Battenburg lace sheets, shams and dust ruffle. At the foot of the bed a matching white down comforter was folded neatly on the mattress.

The four huge sash windows were opened and covered with sheer lace curtains that billowed and moved with the ocean breeze. An elaborate, embroidered settee faced the windows, where one could sit and enjoy the scenic view outside, and a heavy iron lamp with a tiffany shade sat on the marble-topped table beside it.

A huge fireplace filled the wall opposite the bed, with andirons and a beautifully placed stained glass screen. On the coved ceiling above, Casablanca fans turned lazily, and the doors leading to the closets and bathroom were arched. An old-fashioned walnut vanity and stool filled one of the areas made by the dormers, and on it a shiny silver mirror, comb and brush set rested on a starched white doily. The subtle touches of antiques and collectibles added to the romantic ambience of the room, and Caitlin stopped in her tracks.

Fate had dealt her a very bad hand. This could only happen to her. Only she would find herself in a quaint old inn overlooking the bay with a man who admittedly found her less than desirable.

She turned around to find Michael watching her. Seeing her there, standing in the middle of this enchanted room, was almost too much for him. She looked like something out of a dream, like a priceless treasure he'd searched the world for. Maybe he could fool her into thinking he didn't want her, but there was no way he could fool himself. Finding her just might be the best and the worst thing to come out of this whole business.

Before meeting Caitlin MacKenzie he'd willingly settled for convenience and simplicity. But now... well, now he was getting a pretty good idea what he'd been missing all these years. He hadn't fully realized until just this moment how difficult these next couple of days were going to be.

Caitlin looked at him standing in the doorway and felt herself go weak all over. He treated her with such mocking tolerance some of the time and gruff indifference most of the time. Why then, if he had no desire for her, did he have a way of looking at her with those crystal blue eyes of his that made her so aware of him as a man, and herself as a woman?

"What do you think?" he asked, schooling his features as best he could.

Caitlin glanced around the room again quickly. "Nice."

Nice? Had she actually said that? What a ridiculously inadequate word to use to describe all of this. In her wildest dreams she never thought she'd ever be in a place like this with someone like him.

He was gruff, yet incredibly sensitive. He was rude, yet unbelievably thoughtful. His words seemed to communicate one thing, yet his eyes make her feel something else entirely. She was so confused, so lost. She didn't know what to think anymore, and hardly recognized what she was feeling.

Oh, if she could just close her eyes and wake up Monday morning. What she would give to be back in her comfortable little home in Stockton, back in the uncomplicated routine of the bookstore, and Wednesday night ceramics class and the children's story time on Saturday mornings. That was her world, what she knew and was comfortable with. Not incriminating videotapes, stolen antiquities, thrilling car chases and impromptu kidnappings. And especially not blond, blue-eyed strangers who left her confused and crazy with desire.

How was she ever going to make it through this weekend?

"Well," she said tightly, walking to the window and hoping the breeze would cool her down, "I guess we don't have to worry about unpacking."

"Guess not," he agreed, closing the door behind him. "We can pick up a few things when we go out for some lunch." Looking at his watch, he noticed it was nearly three and shrugged. "Late lunch."

"Lunch?"

"Yeah, you hungry?"

Caitlin could hardly believe, given all the horrific things that had occurred in the past few hours, that she was actually starving. She hadn't eaten since dinner last night. God, she thought, was it only last night that Michael Seger had slipped into her room and stormed into her life? It seemed like centuries.

"Well?" he prompted, watching the array of emotions play across her face.

"Huh? Oh! Yes, I'm famished."

He looked at her, understanding how the turmoil of the day had taken its toll. "Would you like to rest for a while, or do you want to go now?"

"Give me just a second to wash up, then we'll go."

They drove into the small community of Sausalito and stopped first at a small drugstore to pick up a few necessities—toothpaste, toothbrushes, deodorant. As they stood in the short line waiting to pay, Caitlin tossed numerous extras into the small old-fashioned hand basket they carried.

Michael watched as she tossed candy bars, chips and peanuts into the basket and couldn't help but smile. Then, as he handed the basket to the clerk, she reached for a package of Twinkies.

"Hors d'oeuvre?" he asked as she opened the package and bit into the spongy cake.

"Better." She laughed, held up the other half of the Twinkie and popped it into his mouth. "When was the last time you had one of these?"

"I think it was sixth grade," Michael answered dryly, reaching out and wiping a dab of gooey cream from her lips.

Caitlin could only stand and stare as his finger brushed her lips. It was such an innocent gesture, with all the easy familiarity of friend to friend. Yet when his fingertip swept the soft texture of her lip, innocence turned quickly to intimacy and two friends became a man and a woman.

Caitlin felt herself transported, up and away from the quaint little drugstore, out beyond the stars to a place where she'd never been before. Hunger had grown, but the appetite had changed.

"That will be twelve fifty-seven," the clerk said, looking up and smiling. "Including the Twinkie."

"Hum—oh! Twelve?" Caitlin stammered, flustered at finding herself catapulted back to earth. "What was that?"

"I've got it," Michael said carefully, handing the clerk the money.

They were quiet as they walked to the small deli-grocery down the block. Shadows were getting longer, and the winds off the bay were turning cool and brisk. Caitlin shivered.

"You okay?" Michael asked as he held the grocery store door open for her.

"Just a little chilly," she said, rubbing her hands over the thin jersey arms of her jumpsuit. "I wish I'd grabbed a jacket before leaving."

"You can have my sweater."

"No," Caitlin said, stopping him as he started to make good on his offer. "No, really, I'm fine. I can start a fire back at the inn. I'll be fine."

Having his sweater around her was out of the question, she thought as she started inside. It would have been too much like being in his arms.

Michael stepped back to let her pass and watched as she started up an aisle of the small market. This was definitely not going to be easy. If he lived to be a hundred, he wouldn't forget the look in her eyes when he touched her lips. What man could resist those soft, smoky eyes, those full lips?

In the past week he'd survived a smelly little cabin on a tramp steamer, attacks by those South American gorillas, a footrace up Market Street and a frantic car chase on some of the most harrowing streets in the country, but remembering the look in her eyes, he wasn't sure he'd survive this weekend.

The aromas inside the small market prompted their appetites to take control again. They gathered a picnic to take back to the inn, with huge deli sandwiches, a bottle of red wine, fat stuffed olives and spicy pepperocini, paper cups and a corkscrew.

Back at the inn Michael made Caitlin a fire while she spread a soft quilt on the carpet in front of the hearth and laid out their feast. Then, with little ceremony, they ate.

The familiar saying about one's eyes being larger than one's stomach was never more true than that evening. Caitlin got through the first half of her enormous sandwich, but just barely.

"I can't take another bite," she groaned, pushing her food away. Still on the floor, she leaned back against the footboard of the bed, holding her cup of wine with one hand and her stomach with the other. "Can you finish mine?"

Michael, moving from the hearth and sitting beside her on the floor, looked at what he had left of his own sandwich and shook his head. "Not without it being painful."

Caitlin gazed into the fire, feeling warm and comfortable now. It was only a little after six, but the sun was very low in the sky. Outside, across the bay, heavy fingers of fog had settled among the giant skyscrapers of the city, weaving through the skyline like colored fibers in a rug.

With her hunger appeased a heavy fatigue settled upon her. Leaning her head carefully against the delicately carved wooden bed frame, she closed her eyes.

When was the last time she'd slept? She hadn't been able to get more than a few snatches last night. She'd been too terrified of what was happening, and too uncertain of Michael to get much rest. But she wasn't ready to fall asleep just yet. She needed some downtime, some respite from the frantic emotions of the day, before she slept.

Opening her eyes, she gazed at Michael's profile as he stared into the fire. Not much had changed in the past twenty-four hours. She was still terrified of the situation, still uncertain of Michael.

"Why don't you try to get some sleep," he suggested, reaching over and taking the cup of wine from her hand. "You look beat."

"I am beat," she agreed, stifling a yawn. "But I just want to sit here for a while."

"Should I put some more wood on the fire?"

"Yeah, that would be nice."

Michael placed another oak log on the burning embers and worked at it with the poker. "Warm enough?"

She nodded, resting her head against the bed. There were a million reasons she should be cautious, on her guard, but she was too relaxed and comfortable to be worried about them now. She simply told herself she wouldn't think about this lovely old inn and the beautiful setting, the bridal suite or the blazing fire. And especially she wouldn't think about the man beside her.

Michael tipped the cup to his lips and took the last swallow of the wine in one long gulp. Its rich, smooth flavor tasted clean and dry, and he welcomed its warmth moving through him. He wasn't sure he could remember the last time he'd drunk wine from a paper cup, but then most of his digs were primitive and remote, and the team wasn't usually accustomed to having wine with dinner— even in paper cups.

He turned his head and looked at Caitlin. The room was almost dark now, save for the light from the fire, and he felt himself growing restless and uneasy. He'd never trusted the darkness, but never less so than now.

As Rick in *Casablanca* had lamented his luck concerning all the gin joints in all the towns in all the world, Michael bemoaned at having chosen her room to break into. What were the odds against his picking a room with a woman who had a way of getting under his skin, of making her way into his thoughts and staying there? Wouldn't it have been just as easy to have chosen the room of some kindly retired schoolteacher with sensible shoes who would have suffered through the intrusion, gotten rid of him as soon possible and been left with a story for the folks back home? But it had been Caitlin's room, and he'd been reeling from that choice ever since.

In the darkness last night they'd gone from enemies to strangers, and strangers to...to what? What were they now? He still didn't know. All he knew was that from the moment he'd met her, the woman had him questioning and testing every precaution he'd imposed upon himself. And now the night had come again, and he warned himself to be on his guard.

"Where's the tape?" she asked suddenly, her eyes half opened.

"In the drawer of the vanity," he answered. He was surprised that she was still awake. He could see the strains of the day in her face, the deep lines of fatigue and exhaustion. "Why?"

"I just wondered." She shrugged, lifting her head and looking at him. "Aren't you even a little bit curious what's on it?"

"I know what's on it."

"You've watched it?"

"In Lima one night before catching the freighter," he confessed. Turning his head, he met her gaze. "You think maybe I shouldn't have?"

"Oh, no, not at all. He was your friend. I think I'd have done the same thing. Jorge died getting that information."

It surprised him to hear her say Jorge's name, and he felt a surge of emotion rise from deep inside. Jorge was dead, and even though he'd held his friend's lifeless body in his arms, it seemed impossible to believe. There had been no time to grieve, no time to say goodbye. Rage mixed with sorrow, and he steeled himself against it.

"There was so much he could have done with his life," Michael muttered bitterly. "He had so much to live for."

Caitlin heard the pain in his voice and couldn't help but respond to it. She knew it took some very powerful emotions to penetrate that sturdy exterior of his. In the darkness she reached out and gingerly touched his hand. "I'm sorry about your friend. You're going to miss him, aren't you?"

Michael nodded, not trusting his voice. The feel of her feathery touch along his hand had loosened something inside. Biting back a surge of emotion, he closed his eyes. "Jorge never should have tried to take this on by himself."

"Maybe not," Caitlin mused thoughtfully, awkwardly pulling her hand away. Michael wasn't a man who would welcome that kind of comfort from her. "But from what you've told me about him, I think I can understand why he felt he had to do something. I mean, he didn't sound like the kind of man who could sit back and watch his people's heritage—their history—be stolen right out from under their noses."

Michael could only stare at her, amazed. She'd never met the man, and yet she was able to empathize and appreciate something very special about him.

"Did he have a family?" she asked. "Jorge, I mean."

"Wife, four kids," Michael mumbled, remembering Jorge's pretty wife, Elise, and noisy dinners in their cramped apartment. Long, hot nights sitting out on the small balcony with Jorge, smoking cigars and drinking late into the night as Elise and the kids slept peacefully inside.

Caitlin sat up, leaning a little closer and lowering her voice. "What's on it? The tape, I mean."

Michael thought about the grainy images on the tape—the deals being transacted, the money changing hands, the goods being delivered. Jorge had paid too high a price to capture those images, but if the bastards involved in the smuggling were ever hauled into court, a prosecutor could hang them with what Jorge had recorded.

"Payoff, bribes, prominent officials—pretty powerful stuff," he told her. "Those creeps who are after it have reason to be worried."

Caitlin was quiet for a long time. She thought about Jorge's wife. She was a stranger, someone who lived a different life in a different country thousands of miles away. Yet Caitlin felt a curious kinship with the woman. She would never forget the way she'd felt when Brian left her alone. But Brian had merely left her for another woman. That paled in comparison to what this poor woman in Peru was having to face—alone with four children to raise.

"Good," she said emphatically.

"What?"

"I said good," Caitlin repeated. "I'm glad they're afraid of the stuff on the tape."

Michael studied her for a moment, curious. "Why?"

"I want to get them." She turned her head and looked up at him. "I want to get them good."

Chapter 6

Michael got up suddenly and walked to the window. He drew a shaky hand through his hair and stared out at the hazy lights of the city across the bay. Fog made the lights glow eerily in the night, and that only seemed to contribute to his growing restlessness.

Her words had surprised him. *I want to get them,* she had said. *She* wanted to get them. Not she hoped *he* would get them, not she wanted the *authorities* to step in and get them. *She* wanted them caught. *She* wanted justice.

Michael wasn't used to sharing—not his findings, not his causes and most certainly not his grief. He'd learned a hard lesson from Alaura, but he'd learned it well. At his digs he'd guarded his current projects jealously—trusting only those few hand-chosen assistants he'd worked with for years. He didn't engage in open discussions or speculations with his colleagues, preferring instead to complete his research quietly, keeping a firm control over the release of his findings. And his reticence about sharing affected more than just his professional life.

When it came to his private life, he trusted no one, and in the past twenty years he'd made damn sure he never had to. He'd never allowed a woman close enough to worry about trust and betrayal. The ground rules had been simple, and he'd come to rely on them. There was always give and take, consent and denial. He'd never taken any more from a woman than she was willing to give, and he'd always stopped short of giving too much of himself.

Those were rules he knew. Those were the rules he understood.

But with a few impassioned words the rules had suddenly changed. He wasn't used to someone picking up the torch for him, making his fight their fight, forging the way beside him.

And the real irony was that the restlessness, the uneasiness he was experiencing, had nothing to do with those rules or the fact that she'd managed to break every one of them. In an odd sort of way he felt comforted by her support. He felt stronger and justified in his duties now that she'd become his port in the storm, his candle in the window.

His restlessness and discomfort stemmed from something far more basic than her thoughtful and touching empathy. It was rooted firmly in something deeper and more menacing than the men who were after them, and it was far more perilous than darkness.

He wanted her. He wanted to take her and touch her, explore and discover all there was of her. His hands fidgeted, wanting to reach out to her. His legs moved restlessly, wanting to run to her. He wanted to be with her and find out what it was about her that made him so willing to turn his back on a lifetime of caution and concern. What buttons had she pushed, what instincts had she followed that had him wanting to reach out, to touch, to share?

Caitlin sat quietly before the dying fire and watched his dark silhouette at the window. He was restless and uneasy, and she knew she was responsible for it.

What had ever possessed her to get so carried away? He clearly didn't welcome her support or her zealous interference, and she wasn't entirely sure herself what had prompted her to offer it. She had no business poking her nose into his affairs, and it was obvious he felt the same way. Undoubtedly she'd stepped over the line somewhere along the way, and she still didn't know when it had happened. But after a day filled with incredible adventures, warring emotions and confusing feelings, the lines had become blurred. The harrowing experiences of the day had only moved to reinforce her misconception that they had somehow become a unit. She continued to think of things in terms of ''their'' safety, ''their'' friend, ''their'' loss, and now she understood what a dangerous mistake that had been.

She was still little more than a hostage to this man, even though she'd willingly helped him this morning. It was imperative she keep things in perspective and never lose sight of the truth again.

''Where did the pot come from?''

''What?'' Caitlin jumped, ousted from her musings and surprised by his sudden question. ''What pot?''

Michael turned and walked to the fireplace. Putting another log on the fire, he stirred up a flame. Thinking about her only made his restlessness worse. He needed something—anything—even if it was just a little inane conversation to get his mind off touching her. ''The one you used to bash in the head of our friend this afternoon. Where did it come from?''

"It was, uh, just one I'd made. I'd forgotten to take it out of the car before leaving for the conference." She laughed just a little. "I'm kind of glad now I did."

"So you're a potter, then?" he asked, imagining her hands molding the soft, wet clay.

"Hardly," she scoffed. "It's just a hobby."

He reached for another log, working with it until the flames leaped and grew. "So what do you do?"

She looked up at him and laughed again. "I work in a bookstore. That was a booksellers' convention I was attending."

Michael smiled, turning his face away from the hot flames. "I guess I hadn't noticed." He couldn't help notice, though, how her hair matched the color of the flames. "So tell me, how long have you worked in a bookstore?"

"Just a couple of years," she murmured. "Since the divorce."

"Ah, I remember now," he lied. He'd never forgotten. "Brian, right? Didn't like to hear about shopping."

Caitlin cringed, remembering how she'd rattled on about her shopping this morning. "Right."

"You didn't work outside the home while you were married?"

Caitlin shook her head. "No, Brian never wanted me to." She shrugged. "He didn't think anything I could do would be as important as being his wife."

"Sounds incredibly selfish."

She looked up at him, nodding. "Yeah, it does, doesn't it?"

"Kids?"

She hesitated only slightly, but it was enough for Michael to notice. "No, no children. What about you? Do you have a family?"

"No." He shrugged. "The time never seemed to be right for that sort of thing."

Caitlin smiled.

"You find that amusing?"

"No, it just sounds very familiar."

"Brian?"

She nodded. "Starting a family was something he always wanted to do *next* year."

"And you saw things differently."

"Well, it was fine when I was twenty-five to think about having a child 'next' year," she told him. "But I'm thirty-five now. That old biological clock keeps ticking louder and louder."

"Oh, my, you are ancient."

"Oh, don't give me that," she argued in the same good-natured tone as his. "A man can afford to be patient and take his time. You can be sixty, seventy even, and still father children. With a woman it's a different story." Without her being aware of it her tone changed and her voice took on a serious note. "I waited twelve years for Brian to decide when the time was right. Now he's gone and I've blown my only chance for a family."

"Oh, come on," he scoffed. "Aren't you being a little dramatic? There are other men, you know."

"I'm being practical," she clarified. "Sure I'd like to think there's a chance I'll meet someone else, but the odds of that happening are very slim. Men don't exactly line up to marry thirty-five-year-old divorcées, you know."

"No, I didn't know that." He was finding this conversation more and more interesting. "Why do you suppose that is?"

Caitlin gazed at him skeptically. "Don't give me that innocent look."

"Innocent look?" he repeated. No one had accused him of looking innocent in a very long time.

"Yes, that innocent look," she repeated shrewdly, eyes narrowed. "That 'I don't have the faintest idea what you're talking about' look."

"Well, I don't," he claimed honestly, smiling.

"Because if you're not twenty years old and built like a...well, *built,* you might as well be invisible. Let me enlighten you a bit on what a fun-filled adventure life as a 'mature' single woman is in our society," she offered with a good-natured cynicism. "Let me tell you about my first date after my divorce." She neglected to add that it was also her *only* "date" since her divorce. "This man came into the shop with his son one Saturday. I lead a children's story circle on Saturday mornings, and he and the little boy decided to stay for story time. They seemed to like it and started coming regularly after that. Eventually, after several weeks, we struck up a conversation. He told me he was divorced and how difficult things had been.

"One week, after story time, he asked me to join them for lunch afterward. I went and we had a pleasant time." She paused and shook her head slowly as she remembered. "He wasn't particularly good-looking or anything, but he was nice and polite. I started thinking...okay, maybe I could do this. Maybe I could actually survive a *date.* I mean, it had been so nice just to go someplace with a man again." She stopped, the smile slowly fading from her face. "The next week he came in really anxious to see me. I was flattered. At first, when he asked if his little boy could stay at the shop for a few hours with me, I thought maybe he wanted us to get to know each other better or something like that. Then Bambi walked in."

"Bambi?" Michael asked dryly. "Flower's friend?"

"Hardly. This Bambi was eighteen, and...well, I think you get the picture. It seems they were desperate for a baby-sitter. Would I mind?"

"You didn't," Michael said, wondering what kind of morons she was meeting. Were they all blind?

Caitlin shook her head. "Are you kidding? Besides, Chloe would have killed me. She practically threw them out as it was."

Michael laughed. "I think I like this Chloe."

"But it proves my point."

"It proves nothing," he scoffed. "You had a bad experience. You can't judge all men by that one loser."

She thought for a moment before responding. "This wasn't exactly my first experience in this area."

Michael looked at her. "Your husband left you for a younger woman?"

"Almost a textbook case," she said dryly. "You know the scenario—young secretary at the office, husband suddenly starts working late, wife is the last one to know, et cetera, et cetera."

He gazed back into the fire, wondering what kind of idiot could have walked away from a woman like her.

"So you have to admit," she went on. "I have some background on which to base my theories."

"I still say you can't generalize people," he argued, picking up the poker and jabbing aimlessly at the blowing logs.

"Men prefer younger women," she stated again. "It's as simple as that."

"I'd say that depends on the man," he murmured in a low voice, turning to her. "And the woman."

Caitlin lowered her eyes to her lap. She couldn't look at him, didn't dare let him see what effect his words had upon her.

He slipped the poker back into its holder. "Not every man is like your ex-husband or that jerk at the bookstore. Believe it or not, there are actually men out there who think there's more to a woman than a big chest and a tight butt. And besides," he added, sprawling on the rug and watching the shadows along the ceiling. "Women don't have the market on being the injured parties in relationships, either. They've been known to play dirty."

Caitlin looked over at him. "And is this a conclusion drawn from personal experience?"

"Maybe," he hedged, feeling a taboo coming dangerously close to falling.

Caitlin had to fight her curiosity. "So you're saying it's impossible to generalize. Men have to be judged on a case-by-case basis. Is that it?"

He turned his head and gazed up at her. "Exactly."

"And what about women?"

Michael turned back and stared up at the ceiling. He'd done a fair amount of generalizing himself after his experience with Alaura, but it was funny that he hadn't realized it until now. "Case by case."

Case by case, Caitlin repeated in her mind. Is that what he did? Then what did he make of her case? Did he find her horribly provincial? Did he find her experiences dull? Uninteresting? How did she compare to the women he knew, or to the one who had hurt him?

They were both quiet for a long time after that, lost in their individual thoughts. As the fire slowly began to die, Michael got up and added another log.

"Tell me about your work," she asked as she watched him coax the fire to life again. "How did you get interested in archaeology?"

Michael never discussed his work with anyone, but in the comfort of the darkness, watching the shadows of the fire dancing along the ceiling, that long-standing taboo seemed easy to ignore. His mind drifted back, thinking about a kid whose imagination had been piqued by the writings of a true adventurer. "When I was in high school, I read a book by Hiram Bingham. Ever hear of him?"

Caitlin shook her head. "No, was he an archaeologist?"

"Actually, he taught history at Princeton in the early 1900s. But he was a wanderer at heart and grew bored with academic life. He was married and had something like seven kids, but he set off for South America in search of adventure. In Peru he became fascinated by the ruins of the Inca fortress of Sacsahuaman above Cuzco. He heard tales of lost cities with hidden Incan gold and treasure, so he put together what's come to be known as the Yale expedition and set out to discover them."

Typical, Caitlin thought cynically. Men always had enjoyed a special freedom. Where was this man's poor wife while he was exploring Peru and doing all the wonderful and exciting things in life? No doubt she got to stay home, left alone to care for their seven children. "Did he ever find his treasure?"

"Something like that. In 1911 he made about the greatest archaeological discovery of the century."

"You're kidding? What was that?"

"He found the famous 'Lost City' of the Incas."

"Machu Picchu?" she asked.

"Right, Machu Picchu." He turned his head slowly to look at her. He knew the dramatic ruins of that ancient city were famous, but it still surprised him that she'd come up with the name so easily. "You know about that?"

"Not really." She shrugged matter-of-factly, but she couldn't help feeling just a little pleased she'd surprised him. "You know, just pictures, a couple of documentaries on PBS." She stopped, remembering the haunting images of the lush mountain landscapes and magnificent settings. "It must be so beautiful there."

"It is," he said, but thinking of being at the remote, ancient site suddenly felt strangely desolate and bleak compared to the cozy warmth of their little inn. Normally he welcomed the isolation and remoteness of his dig sites, like his current dig high in an isolated region of the Andes near the famous Machu Picchu he'd become so fascinated with as a boy. But in the past twenty-four hours even his most tried and true habits seemed to have fallen into question. He thought what it would be like to have Caitlin with him at the dig. Somehow the long hours of back-breaking work wouldn't seem so bad if she were there to share the sunsets and long, cold nights. "Actually Bingham thought it might be the ancient Incan city of Vilcapampa, which was supposedly where lost Incan gold had been hidden."

"Was it?"

"More than likely it wasn't, but the ruins alone were quite a treasure. Probably because it was so isolated Machu Picchu was spared the fate of other Incan cities that were totally destroyed by the Spaniards. That's why it was such a find. The city had been abandoned for nearly three centuries, but it was still pretty much intact."

"So after reading about Hiram Bingham you decided to become an archaeologist?"

He smiled. "Not exactly. Reading about the Incas is what got to me. I could understand Bingham's fascination with them. I was intrigued, too. They were such a mystery, a—what's the word? Ah . . ." He closed his eyes, then snapped his fingers and pointed. "A conundrum, that's it. You know, a riddle, a puzzle." He looked at her and flinched just a little. "But I must be boring you to death. You don't want to hear this."

"No, not at all," Caitlin insisted. "Please go on. I'm becoming pretty intrigued myself."

He grinned almost boyishly. "It's just that, I mean, here was a race of people who built an entire civilization, were advanced in agriculture and irrigation and science, were able to organize and mobilize huge numbers of workers, erect huge stone edifices with only the simplest of tools, and yet they had no written language and no wheel. Amazing."

"That is amazing," Caitlin agreed, fascinated by the man as much as by the ancient race of people. "And have you found your treasure?"

He shrugged. "I guess you could say that. Reading about the Incas got me reading about the Mayans, and I just went on from there. I like what I do, so I guess that's worth something."

Caitlin turned to him, thinking how different they were. "Your life must be very exciting."

"My life?" he scoffed. "I don't think so. Remember, I don't always have a band of outlaws on my trail. This is something new for me, too."

She laughed. "No, that's not what I meant. I mean your work. It must be very exciting."

"Mostly it's just a lot of hard, dirty work," he said. "It's exciting to be on the track of something, to feel as though you're on the verge of uncovering something really important," he admitted. "But mostly it's just a lot of painstaking work—sifting through tons of dirt and debris for even the tiniest clues, long days, sweltering sun, freezing nights, hard cots, cold food, no running water." He turned to her again and smiled. "But then I guess adventure doesn't come without a price."

She laughed again. "You seem willing to pay it."

"Sometimes I wonder," he said, coming slowly to a sitting position and stretching a cramp in his neck. "The older I get, the harder the work, the hotter the sun, the colder the nights, the narrower that damn cot gets."

"Now who sounds ancient?"

He looked over at her and smiled. "But antiquities are my specialty."

Caitlin felt her face flaming again. Quickly she looked away and changed the subject. "Did Jorge visit you at the dig?"

"Jorge?" he repeated, watching as she carefully diverted her eyes. "No, not usually. Cuzco is too far away. His office is...uh, his office *was* at the government building in Lima. My research is partially funded by a grant from the University of Peru in Lima. I liked to accompany personally any shipments from the site to the museum at the university. It's safer that way, and it gives— it gave—me a chance to see Jorge from time to time. He'd usually pick me up at the airport in Callao and we'd have dinner and drinks." Michael stopped for a moment, remembering that last night in the cantina. There had been no laughter that night, no joking around, no kidding. Jorge had been frightened, and he'd handed Michael the videocassette as though it were one of the national treasures he was trying to preserve. "I'm going to miss him."

Caitlin shook her head. "I know. Good friends are hard to come by. Chloe saved my life. I don't know what I'd do without her."

"After your divorce?"

She nodded. "She made me get out and face the world again. She cared about me when a lot of my other so-called 'friends' just wanted to gossip about Brian MacKenzie and his pregnant girlfriend."

"Pregnant?"

"Yeah." She laughed humorlessly. "I guess Brian decided the time was finally right. He and his, uh, 'friend' have a thirteen-month-old daughter."

Michael turned to her when she paused. She stared into the fire, lost in thought, but pain was clearly visible on her face. That had been a bitter pill for her, he concluded to himself as he watched the reflection of the fire in her eyes. Her husband had given his younger girlfriend the child he'd denied her all those years. What a jerk this Brian MacKenzie must be. After a moment, though, Caitlin seemed to rouse herself from her troubling thoughts and gave him a weak smile.

"But Chloe stuck by me," she said, giving her head a little shake. "She made me want to start living again."

Michael picked up the poker and jabbed at the fire. "I think I'd like your friend Chloe."

"Most people do. But she's not going to believe me when I tell her about all this." Caitlin stopped and laughed a little. "Especially since it was Chloe who talked me into attending this conference in the first place. She thought I needed a little excitement in my life."

Michael and Caitlin looked at each other, and both started to laugh.

"I'm sorry I've made you miss your conference," Michael said in an uncharacteristic apology.

Caitlin shrugged. "There'll be other conferences."

But there would never be another experience like this, she added silently. In her whole life she would never forget this weekend, or Michael Seger. This was definitely a once-in-a-lifetime affair.

Affair?

They both watched in silence as the fire slowly died, lost in their own thoughts. Then Caitlin excused herself and went into the bathroom.

Michael wandered back to the windows. Checking his watch, he was surprised at how late it was. They'd talked for most of the evening. Across the bay the fog had lifted from parts of the city, and where it was gone the lights shone bright and clear. Caitlin was in the bathroom preparing for bed, and for the second time in two nights he stood in the darkness and listened to the sounds.

It was black—as dark and inky as midnight. The moon outside sent a pale glow of light pouring in through the windows, but it was enough for her to see him. He was standing there beside the bed, staring down at her with those intense blue eyes. She couldn't see the color of his eyes in the blackness, but she could feel the heat of their flames.

He lowered his hand and let it skim the surface of the smooth, cool sheet that covered her. Then he lightly traced the curves of her body.

"Michael," she murmured, feeling restless and uneasy. "Michael, please."

But he didn't say a thing. He just stared down at her, his dark eyes burning, his hand gently tracing. Couldn't he see how much she wanted him? Didn't he know how much she cared?

His hand dashed briefly over her breast, almost a whisper.

"Touch me," she whimpered, feeling the pressure building inside. "Please, Michael, touch me."

She was burning up, burning inside, but still his hands only drifted and skimmed. He lightly stroked the surface, never stopping, never staying. His fingers moved above her breasts to the edge of the sheet. He played with the edge teasingly. She was naked beneath.

"Michael," she murmured again, almost a cry.

Slowly his fingers grasped the edge of the sheet. Slowly it began to move lower, and lower.

"Yes," she said, smiling at last. This was what she wanted. This was what she'd been waiting for.

But something was wrong. Something had changed. His hand wasn't drifting any longer; it was clutching and clawing. His eyes weren't fiery any more, but as cold as black ice.

"Michael?" she gasped, seeing his form change and re-shape. "Michael, where are you?"

But he didn't answer. He only stood there, his dark, menacing shape frightening her.

"No," she screamed, no longer feeling protected and safe.

The dark, hulking shadow took shape and form. This wasn't Michael. This was terror. This was fear.

Caitlin opened her eyes just as the bloated, foul face of the man from the van vanished into the darkness. She was gasping for air, and her body was drenched with perspiration.

"A dream," she whispered into the darkness. She sat up slowly, letting the room take shape around her. "Just a dream."

Across the room she could see Michael asleep on the settee, the steady, even rhythm of his breathing sounding comforting and reassuring. Slowly she lowered her head back onto the pillow.

It had only been a dream, she reminded herself again as she stared up at the shadows on the ceiling. But still the image of that ugly face made her shudder.

"Michael," she whispered into the darkness, listening to the soothing sounds of his sleep.

She watched the shadows until her heart returned to its normal beat and her breathing had slowed, then she turned onto her side and closed her eyes. But sleep was elusive, and it was a long time before she found it again.

Michael turned, and a wrenching pain moved down the length of his spine. Swearing, he readjusted his weight and wedged his shoulders more deeply into the hard cushions of the narrow settee.

The sun was just rising. He'd been so exhausted last night that he would have been able to fall asleep anywhere, but now, after six long hours on the narrow sofa, every muscle in his body protested.

Checking his watch, he could barely make out the hands. Almost six-thirty. Slowly he shifted his weight again, bringing his arms up and bending them beneath his head.

Across the room Caitlin slept peacefully on the bed. From where he lay he could just make out her honey-colored hair spread out on the pillow. She'd washed it again last night before going to sleep, and now it was a soft array of curls on the bed. He was glad she was still asleep. She needed the rest.

He'd slept pretty well himself after finally drifting off. There had been so many things on his mind. He'd lain awake long after Caitlin had fallen asleep, thinking over the things they'd talked about. He knew her better, and now he was that much more fascinated.

He hadn't enjoyed hearing about her marriage, discovering how much she'd suffered by losing her husband to a younger woman. As irrational as it might be, he felt protective of her and didn't like to think about her being hurt.

Still, listening to her tell about it had helped to explain a lot, and he understood a little better now.

What he didn't understand was himself. He'd talked about things last night he hadn't discussed with anyone else before. It seemed there was nothing off-limits when it came to this woman, nothing he felt compelled to hold back.

Well, that wasn't entirely true. There was something very important he had held back.

He let his gaze travel the length of the bed again, following her form beneath the lace-trimmed sheets. Then he shifted his weight in an effort to quell the gnawing ache in his loins.

It had felt good to talk and share and make a connection with someone else—well, not just with someone else. With Caitlin. He'd searched his conscience for any trace of regret, but could find none. It hadn't been a matter of merely her reaching out, or him. They'd reached out together. There had been something in the chemistry between them that had made it feel almost natural. What had been impossible with all the other women he'd known seemed so easy with her.

Nearly seven. He was wide awake now. Swinging into a sitting position, he stretched his cramped muscles and reached for his slacks. Slipping them on, he glanced over at the bed again. Caitlin still hadn't stirred.

When he went into the bathroom last night after Caitlin had gone to bed, he'd discovered she'd washed out all her undergarments and left them draped on the towel rack to dry. While she'd prepared for bed he'd discreetly gone out to check on the car to give her some privacy, and by the time he'd gotten back, she was in bed with the sheet drawn up to her chin. But all night he'd wondered what she slept in. The images of those little lacy panties and sheer bra hanging over the towel rack in the bathroom burned in his brain. He imagined her naked beneath those sheets, and he'd fought his body's reaction late into the night.

It was so still in the room, so quiet, and she slept so peacefully in the bed. After so many hours of lying there and wondering, his curiosity threatened to get the better of him and he took a few hesitant steps toward the bed. The wooden slats beneath the rug squeaked noisily, and guiltily he froze. Holding his breath, he waited to see if she moved.

Nothing, just the steady, even sound of her breathing.

Gingerly he took another step, then another, and another. After each one he'd pause and carefully check to see that she was still asleep. At the foot of the bed he stopped, and his heart began to thunder so loudly in his chest that he feared she would hear.

She was sleeping on her stomach, and sometime during the night she'd turned, causing the sheet to move. Though it still covered most of her, the sheet had shifted, revealing a narrow sliver of flesh stretching from knee to shoulder.

She was naked beneath the sheet.

Michael felt the air slowly desert his body, leaving his lungs empty. His body tensed and roared to life, and the deep ache of longing almost became a rage. He moved around the bed, heedless of what sounds he might make. His mind was filled with her beauty, and his body cried out in desperation.

He was no voyeur looking for a quick glimpse or brief thrill. He worshiped her with his gaze, like a devout follower beholding something holy.

She stirred, her body shifting lazily beneath the thin veil of bedding. Like a long, languorous cat, she stretched, finding her way to consciousness slowly.

Her lids cracked, barely open, seeing only the faint, blurry light that came in through the windows. But then she saw him standing tall and bare-chested, staring down at her.

He looked huge, towering above her, and her eyes opened wide. He didn't flinch or look away. He made no attempt to move or seek to explain. He simply stared at her, his sapphire eyes like blue flames. The heat from his gaze turned her blood to fire and threatened to burn her alive.

As she watched, he leaned down slightly, enough for the back of his fingers to touch the small column of skin exposed by the sheet. Her eyes followed his hand as it made its slow journey from her knee to her shoulder. When he finished, he straightened, pulled his hand away and looked into her eyes again. "You're beautiful," he said in a low, rough voice.

"Michael," she whispered as she'd whispered in her dream.

The moment held…suspended…beautiful…fragile… then it shattered into a million pieces when a harsh knock on the door reverberated through the room.

Chapter 7

In an instant everything changed. They were no longer two people together in a romantic inn, two people on the verge of reaching out to each other. They were two strangers hunted by the same madmen, on the run, isolated and alone.

Caitlin watched as Michael moved toward the door. His whole body was tense, protective. She gathered the sheet around her, fear tasting strong and bitter in her throat. Had the thugs found them? Was another nightmare about to begin?

The knocking sounded again as Michael silently approached the door. Bracing himself against the wall of the entryway, he waited for a moment. "Who is it?" he called out.

"Your breakfast," the voice of the perky innkeeper replied.

Michael looked across the room to Caitlin, who was perched rigidly on the bed. In unison their bodies sagged with relief.

"Breakfast is served," he announced drolly as he opened the door and greeted their smiling hostess.

Relieving the young woman of the huge, elaborately laden tray, Michael thanked her and kicked the door shut with his foot. Carefully balancing the tray, he carried it across the room.

"I forgot I told her we wanted breakfast served in our room," he confessed sheepishly as he slid the tray onto the bed. "I thought we'd be less conspicuous that way."

"Well, it certainly got the adrenaline pumping this morning," Caitlin said, taking a deep breath and feeling her heart slowly return to normal. She perused the array of muffins, scones, jams, fresh fruit and eggs and inhaled deeply. "This smells delicious." She pinched off a piece of bran muffin and popped it into her mouth. "I didn't think I'd ever be hungry again after last night." She swallowed the muffin and smiled up at him. "Wrong again, I guess."

Michael felt as though he'd been struck hard in the chest. The sight of her wrapped in the sheet and sitting Indian-style on the bed literally took away his breath. She hadn't mentioned anything about what had happened earlier, so he'd take her lead. If she was interested in having him continue touching her, she'd find a way of letting him know. If not, ignoring the incident might be a convenient way out of it for both of them.

He couldn't help but remember, though, and his mind turned over the possibilities of what might have happened if the innkeeper hadn't arrived at just that moment. There were other appetites he was more interested in appeasing at the moment, but he wouldn't let himself think about that now. He settled himself on the bed opposite her, and they feasted on their breakfast hungrily.

As they finished eating, an awkward silence seemed to develop. They didn't talk about what they should have, and it created a cloudy tension in the room.

"How did you sleep?" he asked finally, playing with the last little piece of scone on the tray. It was a stupid question, only slightly better than commenting on the weather, but it was all he could think of. "You look as if you got some rest."

"I feel much better this morning," she confessed, running a nervous hand through her hair. She probably looked like something out of a nightmare. Had he forgotten about what had happened earlier? Was she just supposed to ignore it? She gestured with her chin. "Was that settee all right?"

"Fine," he lied. "Compared to the dig, it's high living."

They were empty words, exchanged in awkward circumstances and had nothing to do with what either of them really wanted to talk about. The tension made them both edgy and uncertain.

"Well, I . . . I guess I should get dressed," Caitlin mumbled, sliding to the edge of the bed. "I, uh, I suppose we'll just be staying here today."

"That would probably be safest," he told her.

Wonderful, she thought as her stomach tightened. She secured the sheet around her and headed for the bathroom. The thought of being confined in the room hardly seemed pleasant, especially since the tension was so thick one could cut it with a knife.

"I've got some books in the back of the car," she suggested, turning at the bathroom door and looking back at him. "I suppose we could read."

He smiled. "Sure. You're the expert. I'll let you recommend something."

In the bathroom Caitlin looked at herself in the mirror. He'd said she was beautiful, but the woman looking back at her in the mirror was hardly a picture of beauty. She looked more like a battle-weary veteran with her puffy eyes and tiny laugh lines.

She'd talked too much last night, way too much. The wine, the fire, the darkness had all worked to undermine her inhibitions, and she felt embarrassed now. She'd been a fool to confess to him what a blow to the ego it had been to lose Brian to a younger woman. Did he feel sorry for her now? Did he feel compelled to try to repair some of the damage to her self-esteem? She cringed with humiliation.

But gazing at herself in the mirror, she thought back at the look in his eyes, the sound of his voice. Just remembering, she felt herself grow weak and warm all over. The way he had looked at her almost made her believe he'd meant what he'd said. Almost.

Since Michael had decided it would be wise to "lie low," they stayed sequestered in their room. But it seemed as though time decided to pick this particular day to come to a dead stop. Minutes passed like hours, and hours seemed to stretch out until forever. And with each painstakingly slow minute, each century-long hour, the tension in their quaint, secluded room seemed to grow more and more intense.

Caitlin had gone to the car and picked out several books from the various ones she'd found scattered in the back, but it hadn't taken long to go through them. None of them had held her interest for long, but then she hadn't exactly been in the mood to read. Her mind was filled with too much—their talk last night, her dream, waking to find him staring down at her.

But she could have handled the distracting thoughts and the awkward silence. What she couldn't handle was Michael. It had been obvious he hadn't been in the mood to read, either. He hadn't even bothered to open any of the books she'd brought in for him. Since breakfast it was as though he'd undergone some sort of transformation. She thought he'd been restless and tense that night in her hotel room, but it was nothing compared to this. He paced the room incessantly, making her more and more nervous, and he'd barely given her so much as a brief glance all day.

From the settee she watched him pace fitfully back and forth in front of the windows. What was he so restless about? It seemed unlikely those creeps would find them in this secluded old inn. Why was he so uptight?

He'd barely spoken to her all day, giving her only curt, one-syllable answers when she attempted to ask him anything. That hadn't been bad, but what she really hated was when he lapsed back into that mildly sarcastic tone she found so irritating.

He was a different person from the man who'd talked and teased with her last night. He was troubled and brooding now. What had brought about the change? Did he find her so boring that conversation was out of the question? Couldn't she even provide a mild distraction from his restlessness?

She banked her anger and reached for one of the books again. Whatever was bugging him, it was obvious he would have to work it out for himself.

Michael thought he was going to explode. If only there was a television, or even a damn radio, *anything* to help keep his mind off the woman sitting just a few feet away.

The books she had given him offered him little distraction when all he could think about was the sight of her soft golden flesh against the creamy white sheets.

He couldn't ever remember getting so hung up on a woman before. After all, this hardly went along with his policy on women. Finding this woman on his mind all the time wasn't what he'd call comfortable, and it was getting damn inconvenient.

Yet on his mind she was. Her hair, the scent of her perfume, the sound of her voice—there seemed to be no escape. He'd managed to give those South American gorillas the slip, but this woman wasn't going to let him escape.

He wondered what she would do if he just walked across the room and grabbed her. He wanted her, damn it—why not just take what he wanted? They were stuck together. Why not make the best of it? Why not pass the time a little more pleasantly, blow off a little steam, indulge in a little harmless sex?

He let his gaze wander back across the room to where she sat reading on the settee. He knew why. He knew and it scared the hell out of him. He didn't have to touch the woman to know that being with her would be different. He wouldn't be able to take what he wanted and walk away. Somehow, even without touching her, he knew if he was to take what he wanted he wouldn't want to walk away.

They'd decided to skip lunch, neither of them very interested in food. They munched instead on what remained of the chips, olives and Twinkies from their dinner the night before.

By two in the afternoon, Caitlin thought she was literally going to succumb to either the boredom or the underlying tension in the room. She had just tossed one of her books aside, wondering how she was ever going to make it through the rest of the afternoon, when suddenly Michael turned to her.

She blinked in surprise as he stalked across the room toward her. Something must have snapped in him, because his eyes looked fierce and angry and his breathing was deep and labored.

"I've got to get out of here," he growled, charging for the door. On his way he reached down, grabbed her by the wrist and hauled her to her feet. "Come on, let's go."

Caitlin didn't care what it was that had caused his sudden outburst, nor would she ask. It was enough for now that they were up and moving and out of the confines of their room for a while.

She followed him down the staircase, sometimes having to run a bit to keep up with him. He stalked through the old house, nodding curtly to the curious innkeeper as he passed, and he stomped out onto the porch.

Stopping, he looked out over the grounds. The quiet, serene setting was in stark contrast to the tempest that raged inside him. The wind rustled through the treetops, the porch swing creaked quietly as it swayed in the breeze, and the bay was blue-green and calm in the distance.

Caitlin stepped onto the porch and slowly walked up beside him. Her eyes scanned the panorama, and she drew in a deep breath. "Beautiful," she said on a sigh, looking out across the bay. Turning to him, she looked up. His face was still rigid and tight, but some of the fierceness had left his eyes. "Now where?"

"This way," he said gruffly.

Without waiting for her he stepped down from the porch and crossed the wide lawn. At the cliff they picked up a small footpath that led down to the water. At the water's edge was a small dock, its planks weathered and warped from the water and wind. A creaking boathouse made of rusted green corrugated steel rested low in the water. Across from the old structure on the other side of the dock several small rowboats were tied to their moorings.

"Let's take out one of the boats," Michael suggested, starting down the dock toward the rowboats.

"You mean one of those?" Caitlin asked, horrified.

He turned around and looked at her. "Yeah, why not?"

"You mean take one of those tiny little boats out there?" she asked, pointing out across the great expanse of San Francisco Bay.

"What's wrong with that?"

Caitlin looked at him as though he'd suddenly lost his mind. "Nothing. Fine, go," she said. "But I'll wait right here."

"You don't like the water?"

"I love the water, but I'm not going out onto that bay in one of those puny little things."

"But it's calm," he pointed out. "It'll be okay."

"You're not getting me into one of those things," she stated flatly.

"Caitlin," he said impatiently. "Look, it's perfectly safe. I've rowed boats in rough waters before."

"Then go. I'm not stopping you."

"I want you to come with me."

"I'll wait right here."

"Please."

"I'm not the adventurer, remember?"

"Please?"

Caitlin just looked at him. He was stubborn, and pushy, and . . . and he'd surprised her by saying please.

"Oh, for heaven's sake," she said with an angry shake of the head. She stomped down the dock toward the boat. "I don't understand why it's so important that I have to go, too," she muttered as she gingerly stepped into the wobbly vessel and sat on the small seat.

"Get up," he ordered as he untied the boat and stepped inside.

"What?"

"We have to switch places."

"What for?"

"Because I have to sit at that end of the boat if I'm going to row." When she didn't move, he carelessly shrugged his shoulders. "Unless, of course, you'd like to do it."

"You know you could have said something before I sat down," she sputtered, coming slowly to her feet. The small boat swayed furiously, and she put out her arms for balance, then looked up at Michael helplessly. "I don't think I can move."

"Sure you can," he told her easily, taking her carefully by the shoulders and slowly edging his way around her. "Just ease a little to the left. There, that's a girl."

He helped her down onto the small bench opposite the one she'd been sitting on, then sat down himself. "Hand me that oar."

Caitlin struggled with the ungainly oar, knocking the end against the edge of the dock. "What am I supposed to do with this?"

Michael merely gave her a deliberate look. "You really want me to answer that?"

"Never mind."

"Hand it to me," he said, a slight smile cracking the rigid lines of his mouth.

Despite her ill temper Caitlin hadn't missed the smile. It was the first time he'd smiled since breakfast this morning.

"Won't we get into trouble for boat theft or something?" she asked, hanging on to the edge of the small craft for dear life.

"They belong to the inn," he explained, guiding the small boat away from the dock. "The innkeeper told me about them when I checked in." He noticed her death grip along the sides of the boat and smiled again. "Relax, will you? This will be fun."

"Fun," she mumbled.

Michael set their course to follow the bank. The unusually warm temperature made the water calm, with only a gentle wind buffeting them. But despite the temperate conditions Michael insisted Caitlin take his sweater and slip it over her shoulders.

Gradually she began to relax, slowly becoming accustomed to the even, steady sway of the little boat. It felt wonderful being out after having spent the morning cooped up inside their room. Michael was far less tense and actually seemed to enjoy the physical demand of the rowing. Caitlin began to think he'd worked through whatever had been eating him earlier, but she remained leery. They were still a long way from the easy conversation and good-natured teasing of the night before.

Michael leisurely pulled the oars of the little boat back and forth with ease. The strain on the muscles in his neck and shoulders loosened the tension that had been building in them all morning. But the physical exertion did nothing to stop him from noticing how the sun glinted golden in Caitlin's long hair, or how the breeze caused the nipples of her breasts to pucker and show through the cotton jersey jumpsuit. Only a cold shower would do that. Still, anything was better than the slow torture he'd endured in the room. How he was ever going to make it through the night, he'd never know. But he would cross that bridge when the time came. For now it was enough just to be outside and moving again.

He gradually led them back toward the docks. Caitlin seemed to have forgotten about her initial objections to the boat ride and appeared to be enjoying their little journey now. She looked around with interest, pointed out birds, dragged her hand in the icy water and actually seemed disappointed as they slowly approached the inn's dock.

Michael considered turning the small vessel and taking it out again, but the wind had picked up and the bay was getting a little choppy. Caitlin had done wonderfully on the calm waters, but he wasn't so sure how she'd fare in rougher weather.

At the dock Michael stood and stepped out of the boat. He secured it carefully to its mooring and reached down to help Caitlin as she warily made it to her feet.

"That wasn't so bad now, was it?" he said.

"No, not bad," she admitted begrudgingly, pushing the hair away from her face. Actually she'd loved it, but was hardly ready to admit that to him. She started back up the dock toward the path when she suddenly stopped. "Do we have to go back right now?"

Michael watched as she pulled a golden strand of hair across her deep, full lips, and felt his stomach tighten. "No," he said, shaking his head. "No, let's not go back yet."

Instead they walked along the narrow, sandy beach and climbed around the large rocks that had fallen from the cliffs and littered the shoreline. The afternoon was nearly over, and the breeze had turned cool. Michael refused Caitlin's offer to return his sweater, insisting instead that she take the sweater from around her shoulders and slip it on. Of course, it was many sizes too big and hung down past her bottom, but it felt warm.

As she balanced carefully, jumping from one rock to another, Caitlin stopped. "Hey, look at this." She bent down and picked up a smooth gray stone she'd spotted next to the cliff. "What an unusual rock."

Michael easily hopped from one smooth rock to another until he reached the spot where she stood. He took the rock from her and perused it carefully.

"There are shells embedded in it," she said, pointing at the white shell fragments wedged in the dull gray of the rock.

"They're not just shells," he corrected her, looking into her excited eyes. "They're fossils."

"Fossils? Here?"

"Sure." He turned and pointed to an area at the base of the cliff. "See this colored line of rock running along the cliff? This piece probably came from along there somewhere. Probably broke off from the cliff during a storm or something and it's been smoothed out by the water." He moved closer to the cliff and examined the line in the strata a little closer. "If you look here very closely, you can see other fossilized shells in this layer."

Caitlin stumbled over to where he stood and studied the spot he pointed to. "Amazing," she mumbled absently.

"They're probably clam fossils," he said, examining the rock in his hand. "This might have been an ancient sea floor or clam bed at one time."

Caitlin took the stone again and looked it over once more. "I found a fossil. I can't believe it."

He watched her as she scrutinized the stone carefully and felt his heart constrict at her almost childlike wonder. He understood those feelings of awe at pulling something from the earth and exposing it to the sunlight for the first time in centuries.

"Do you think I could keep it?" she whispered, looking around suspiciously.

"Why are you whispering?"

She looked up at him and smiled sheepishly. "I don't know," she confessed, looking back down at the rock. "But I feel as though I've found a little treasure of my own."

"I don't think anyone would mind if you kept your fossil."

They slowly started back, and as they climbed the path back up to the inn, Caitlin looked up from her fossil and turned to Michael. "Is this the kind of thing you do?"

"Fossils? They're a little out of my line," he said, smiling. "Archaeologists usually stick to the study of ancient people and artifacts, stuff like that."

She gazed at the silvery impressions of the clam shells in the rock. Then, slowly, she shook her head. "It really must be something to do what you do."

Michael stood on the path and watched as she made her way up to the lawn. He didn't need anything more to find fascinating about the woman, and yet his mind was alive with images. He could picture her exploring the ruins, discovering the evidence of an ancient people. How she would love a dig, working the earth, coaxing it to reveal small bits and pieces of its rich and colorful past. He could take her places and show her things she'd only dreamed of, show her a side of life she never even knew existed. He could . . .

He could get hold of himself, that was what he could do, he told himself irritably. He could stop thinking about her, stop making plans with her and stop wanting her.

She was sitting on the porch swing waiting for him by the time he reached the inn.

"You have the key," she said, holding the fossil rock in her lap.

Michael stopped on the steps and looked up at her. The muscles in his neck and shoulders began to tighten up again. She looked like a kid in his big, bulky sweater. It hid every swell, every soft curve of her lovely figure, and yet he knew all too well what lay beneath the thick confines of that sweater. He knew it because it had been burning in his brain like a fever all day long.

He glanced up and looked through the front door of the inn and to the steps that led to their room. He wasn't ready to go back up there. Not yet. His emotions were too raw, and the thought of returning to that slow form of torture made his entire body tense.

"Let's go for a drive," he suggested tersely.

Caitlin looked at him. A boat ride, a walk, now a drive. She was getting the distinct impression he wasn't anxious to go up to their room again. But that was all right with her. Obviously he'd been as uncomfortable with the tense morning as she had been and was willing to do anything to break the monotony.

She stood and followed him to the van, pulling off the sweater and handing it to him as she slipped into the seat beside him. She put the fossil on the floor of the back seat, brushing aside the broken pieces of her ceramic pot.

Michael drove into Sausalito in stony silence. Caitlin watched him out of the corner of her eye, but made no attempt to engage him in conversation. He was moody again, and whatever it was that was troubling him, he apparently wasn't interested in sharing it with her.

"Hungry?" he growled, pulling into the parking lot of a small restaurant.

"I could eat," Caitlin answered carefully.

He turned to her as though he was going to tell her something, then changed his mind. "Let's go, then."

Dinner was rich and delicious, if not a bit unusual. It was one of those quirky California cuisine types of meals that featured goat cheese and sprouts, but they both ate hungrily. Unfortunately the food failed to improve Michael's disposition. He sat through most of the meal in troubled silence. As he sullenly paid the bill, Caitlin started for the van.

"Feel like walking for a while?" he asked when he caught up with her in the parking lot.

Caitlin shrugged, a little surprised by his suggestion. "Sure, if you'd like."

"It's not too cool? Would you like the sweater again?"

"No," she said, looking at him a little suspiciously. This was more than he'd said to her all through dinner. "No, I'm fine."

They strolled quietly side by side down the narrow streets. It was dark, but the streetlamps and shop signs clearly lighted the way. The streets were still busy, with people rushing in and out of restaurants, shopping in the small stores, sipping espresso in coffeehouses. They walked for many blocks, content just to watch and listen to the others around them.

They passed a quaint-looking bookstore with a small coffee shop in the rear. Michael glanced at Caitlin and raised a brow. "Want to check out the competition?"

"Sure, why not?" There was still a long evening ahead, she thought, and it might be wise to try to find some new reading material to help pass the time.

When they opened the door, they were met with the savory aroma of freshly ground coffee. "Would you like some coffee?" Michael asked, inhaling deeply.

"No thanks," Caitlin said, shaking her head. The bookstore was charming with its hardwood floors and paneled walls. "I think I'll just wander around."

Michael nodded and started for the coffee counter at the rear of the store. "I'm going to grab a quick cup. Be back in a minute."

Caitlin browsed lazily through the aisles, noting the various displays so she could tell Chloe about them later. It was a lovely store, and she was impressed with the variety and volume of their stock. After a while she noticed Michael sipping cautiously on a steaming cup of coffee as he perused the books on a shelf a few rows down from her.

As she started to wander over to where he stood, she spotted a beautiful hardbound edition of a book with a large dramatic photo of Machu Picchu, the ancient Incan city Michael had talked about last night. Interested, she picked up the book and leafed through the pages. It was filled with beautiful photographs of the ancient Peruvian site, and she marveled at the breathtaking scenery and haunting beauty of the ancient city. She was particularly intrigued by a photo of a female archaeologist.

"What did you find?" Michael asked, coming up behind her.

"This book has some beautiful photos of Machu Picchu," she said, proudly displaying the pictures. "Have you ever heard of..." She paused, glancing down at the caption beneath one of the pictures. "Let me find the name again. Here it is. Alaura Anderson?" She looked up at him quizzically. "Do you know her?"

Michael's jaw clenched as he looked over Caitlin's shoulder into a face that he remembered all too well. The photo was one he'd seen before. Alaura's smiling blue eyes and short-cropped blond hair gave her a timeless and ageless beauty. He'd been over his hurt and anger for a very long time, and his own career had eclipsed hers years ago, but seeing her face never failed to draw a reaction in him.

Until now. Standing so closely behind Caitlin, with the delicate fragrance of her hair filling his senses and her soft body only inches from his, he found Alaura's face smiling back up at him merely a distant memory.

"Yeah, I know her," he acknowledged casually.

"That's quite a coincidence," she remarked, slowly closing the book and putting it back on the shelf. Was this the kind of woman he found appealing? One whose life was as adventurous and exciting as his own? "Have you ever worked together?"

He shrugged, taking another sip from the small foam cup. "Once, a long time ago."

Caitlin regarded him carefully. The woman in the picture was very beautiful, and she couldn't help but be curious. "At Machu Picchu?"

"No, her research ended there a long time ago." He finished his coffee and crushed the small cup in his palm. "Look, are you through in here? Want to walk some more?"

"Sure," Caitlin said cautiously, letting him lead her to the door. She had the distinct impression there was much more to this story than he was willing to admit, but she knew getting information out of him would be a little like pulling teeth.

Michael ushered her out onto the sidewalk. They crossed the street and passed lovely boutiques with their engaging window displays, a variety of unique shops carrying everything from antiques to handmade kites, and charming galleries displaying the works of local artists. Passing a small bakery, Michael stopped at the window and pointed at the display case with its neat lines of thick homemade cookies and rich chocolate brownies. "How about it?"

"Oh, I don't think I could," Caitlin protested, holding her stomach. "Dinner was so rich."

"How about for later?"

She looked up at him. He was such a mystery, every bit as challenging as any of those ancient ruins of his. His moods had ranged from brooding to boyish during the course of the afternoon, and she doubted she'd ever understand him even if she had all the time in the world. "Okay, but much later."

They went inside and bought a small bag of cookies, which Caitlin slipped inside her purse. They had just stepped back onto the street and taken only a few steps when Caitlin came to a dead stop.

"Oh, my God," she gasped, pointing at the noisy group of people who had just left a restaurant down the street and were headed their way. "It's Vivian."

Chapter 8

Michael glanced up and recognized Caitlin's robust friend from the conference. With her were several others from the group whom he'd been introduced to at the hotel yesterday.

"Quick, back here," he ordered in a harsh whisper. He pulled Caitlin with him into a narrow alley between the two buildings.

The alley was dark, and they stood listening as the voices from the street gradually grew louder. Caitlin's heart was in her throat, but it had nothing to do with the fear of being recognized. Michael stood closely behind her, so close she could feel his hot breath in her hair, feel his body heat fusing with her own.

The group was getting closer now, their laughter and conversation becoming more and more audible. Slipping his hands lightly onto her hips, Michael drew her more deeply into the shadows. Caitlin was galvanized with sensations. She could hardly breathe, hardly concentrate on anything other than his hands on her.

Heat seemed to spread through her veins like molten fire, and passions and desires glowed and sparked like embers as they burst into flames and were tossed around by the wind. She wasn't thinking of the group when his hold on her tightened. She didn't hear their laughter or their noisy dialogue when his hand slipped from her hips and slid slowly around her waist. And by the time he pulled her tightly against him and she found herself leaning back into his inviting warmth, she'd forgotten all about Vivian and the others from the conference. They were from a different lifetime, a distant land.

When his lips touched her neck, Caitlin's world tilted violently and careened out of control. Nothing else mattered, nothing else existed. Reason had vanished, fear became nonexistent and caution had been thrown to the wind.

His kisses started low at the soft, velvety juncture of her neck and shoulder, but slowly, tortuously, they made a lingering journey upward. One sumptuous kiss followed another, on and on until she was weak with desire. His hands moved over her, molding her to him, pressing her more closely into his warmth. He touched her hips, the indentation at her waist, her belly, her breasts. Behind her he felt so strong, so powerful, and he wanted her so badly.

Instinctively her hips moved, her bottom stroking against that part of him that was hard and ready. She heard his breath catch in his throat, heard a low groan deep in his throat. His hands moved down past her stomach and hips, lifting and fitting her more completely to him. His face was buried in her hair, and his breaths came in hot, heavy gasps.

"Caitlin," he whispered roughly into her ear.

Helpless, Caitlin let her head fall back against his shoulder. Her arms dropped to her sides, and her hands clutched recklessly against his thighs.

There was such power, such strength in the rock-hard muscles of his legs. She'd never been so aware of a man, had never taken such relish in sheer masculine strength. Until now she'd never known what it was to want a man. She'd only been with one man before, but being with Brian had never been like this.

Michael inhaled deeply, taking in the sweet scent of her silky golden hair, feeling her softness stoking the fire in his loins. Yes, he thought dizzily, this was what he wanted, this was what he'd been unconsciously waiting for from the very start. This was what had been building from the moment he'd gotten the first glimpse of her in the morning light. He'd wanted her since then—in his arms, her taste in his mouth. He'd wanted the sight, the sound, the taste and the touch of her filling his senses.

He'd tried to talk himself out of it, tried to tell himself to get out, to run. She was no one-night stand, no quick tumble in the sheets. Involvement with her wouldn't be uncomplicated and convenient. This was a woman who was used to security, who would demand permanence and stability from a man—things he could never hope to offer. He had no business starting something he knew he never could finish.

But it hadn't stopped him from wanting her. There had been no hope of escape since the moment he'd made her his captive. She'd been in his head and under his skin from that instant on.

He hadn't meant to touch her, hadn't meant to reach out, but in the quiet darkness of the alley he'd been helpless to stop the feelings. He'd breathed in her delicate scent, felt the brush of her body against his. He'd resisted for so long—all those long, lonely hours last night, all those endless, empty hours today. His emotions were raw, his nerves on edge.

So, despite his best intentions, despite his uncertainty and misgivings, he'd reached out…and she'd melted in his arms.

Neither could have said what it was that happened to break the spell—a car horn, a squeaky door hinge, a squealing tire. But something caused them both to stumble back to awareness at the same time. His hands stilled, she straightened, and for a moment they didn't move or attempt to speak.

Vivian and her group had long since gone. The world had returned, and with it doubt and uncertainty.

"I, uh, I think we can go now," Michael mumbled in a hoarse, gravelly voice.

Caitlin could only nod, staring straight ahead. They walked back to the van in awkward silence, both careful to avoid touching or making any eye contact. Michael stopped only once on their way back to the Cliff House Inn. He pulled the van into the parking lot of a liquor store, pausing only briefly before getting out. "Can I get you anything?"

"No," she answered barely above a whisper. She gave him a brief, embarrassed smile. He hesitated for a moment, staring at her profile in the darkness, then yanked the van door open and got out.

Caitlin watched as he crossed the parking lot and entered the small store. She felt so awkward, so stupid. He'd said nothing about what had just happened. Just like this morning when she awoke and found him standing over her. Was she supposed to forget those things? Pretend they never happened? Did he just feel sorry for her, or was his male ego curious to see what her response would be?

Michael was back within a few minutes, carrying a bottle of chilled wine. He made no attempt to say anything
more to her on the drive back to the inn, and Caitlin followed suit.

They climbed the narrow staircase to their room, their
footsteps echoing loudly on the hardwood stairs. Moods
had altered and stakes had changed. There were no clear
lines of demarcation keeping them apart, yet no approved
perimeters had been established to stay within. They were
adrift, lost somewhere between stranger and compatriot,
adversary and lover.

Michael unlocked the door, reaching inside to flip the
light switch by the door. The Tiffany lamp glowed on the
table by the settee, its colors radiant and bright.

Caitlin tossed her purse onto the hard cushions of the
small sofa and walked to the windows. As lovely as the
room was, it felt like a cell tonight, and the thought of being confined with Michael so distant and remote was
nothing short of slow torture.

From the door Michael watched her as she stared out
into the night. He wasn't sure how much more of this tormenting silence he could take. The scent of her hair
whirled in his memory, and the taste of her skin was still
on his lips. She hadn't slapped him away in outraged in-
dignation; she'd melted into his arms. She'd touched him
and let him touch her. And yet they were so awkward now.
There seemed to be no middle ground, no means of tran-
sition, nothing between callousness and intimacy except
this agonizing, clumsy silence. Why was it so difficult now
and how could he make it change?

At the window Caitlin rubbed her arms.

"Are you cold?" he asked gruffly, coming into the room
and tossing the wine onto the cushion next to her purse. "I
can make a fire."

"No," Caitlin said, turning around and starting for the bathroom. "I think I'll just get ready and go to bed. I'm a little tired."

"Caitlin," he said, stopping her midway across the room. He'd let the incident this morning drop and fade, but he couldn't let that happen again. He couldn't just let it end. "About what happened tonight...in the alley."

Caitlin felt color moving up her neck and into her cheeks. She wasn't up for some clumsy apology. She didn't want to hear any long, drawn-out excuses why it had been such a mistake. "Don't worry about it," she scoffed with forced lightness. "I've read about things like this happening. When people have dangerous experiences, are thrown together, their emotions go a little haywire, that's all."

"Caitlin—"

She looked at him and forced a smile, cutting him off. "Look, you don't have to apologize. I know someone with your...your experience wouldn't be interested in a person like me. I'm nobody, just ordinary, nothing special. What happened back there was just reflex. It was just a normal reaction to everything that's happened. Forget it. Really."

Michael stood there dumbfounded. The woman was driving him nuts. Maybe her ego had taken a beating when that jerk she'd married had walked out on her, but was she blind? Couldn't she see he was nearly half-crazy wanting her? Was she so unsure of herself she couldn't see what she was doing to him? Furious, he strode over to where she stood and grabbed her arm.

"Get over here," he ordered, pulling her to the vanity and forcing her to sit down on the small stool. "What do you see?" he asked, pointing at her image in the mirror. Bending down, he stood behind her and talked to her reflection. "This is beauty."

"Let me up," Caitlin cried, struggling. She was too inhibited and embarrassed to look at the images staring back at her.

"No," he insisted, taking her by the shoulders and turning her to see. "You *look!*" His voice softened as he met her gaze in the mirror. His hold on her shoulders loosened, massaged, and he stroked her long hair back. "You're beautiful. My God, can't you see that?"

She stopped struggling, and slowly her gaze lifted to him, then to herself in the mirror.

"Look how beautiful you are," he said again, his hands slowly caressing her shoulders, her neck. Reaching down, he carefully unbuckled the wide belt of her jumpsuit, ready to stop if she protested.

But Caitlin had become spellbound by his eyes, those fiery blue flames that were filling her with liquid heat. She watched as he slipped the jumpsuit down from her shoulders, offering no protest as the cool black jersey slid to her elbows, then past her wrists, freeing her arms. His hands moved over her slowly, over the lace of her bra, over the creamy silk of her skin.

"So beautiful," he murmured hoarsely, meeting her misty brown gaze in the mirror. "See my hands on you."

Caitlin wasn't sure she could bear the sight. It did look beautiful. Watching as he touched and caressed her was a beautiful thing.

Slowly his hands slid behind her, freeing the clasp on her bra and slipping the straps off her shoulders. Inch by inch the lacy material fell, exposing more and more of her full, round breasts to his hungry gaze.

His breathing became ragged, and sweat beaded on his forehead. His heart thundered, pumping blood furiously through his veins. In one smooth motion he lifted the bra from her, freeing her beauty.

"Oh, Caitlin," he groaned in agony. With hands on her upper arms he lifted her from the stool to face him. "I can't stand it. I want you so much." His voice was raspy, and he buried his face in the smooth satin of her neck. "Tell me it's all right. Tell me..." He brought his head up and looked into her eyes. "Tell me you want me, too."

"Oh, Michael," she breathed out in one long sigh, barely able to form the words. "Michael, I want you, too."

That was all he needed, all that was needed to be said.

He ground her lips to his in one long, crushing kiss. She tasted warm and rich—like woman and life and desire. With his lips he opened her mouth wider, his tongue bold and determined, drinking deeply from the very depths of her soul.

His hands moved up to caress her perfect breasts. He heard a small whimper from somewhere deep in her throat, felt her body tremble. He wanted this woman. Two days ago he hadn't known she existed, yet now he felt as though he'd been waiting for her forever.

He couldn't stand it, couldn't wait any longer. He tore his lips from hers, leaving a trail of wet kisses down her neck, down the smooth, ripe fullness of her breasts to their hard, aching centers. With lips, tongue and hands he paid homage to their beauty.

Caitlin couldn't think, couldn't reason or make sense of anything. All she could do was feel, and she'd never felt like this. He was desperate, and he made her desperate, too. She was discovering she had needs and desires she'd never known existed. She not only wanted—she needed, she demanded!

Michael pulled the rest of the jumpsuit from her, taking her panties and stockings along with it. She was naked in his arms, and he dragged her to him tightly. His hands were restless, seeking and searching. She was softer than velvet, smoother than silk, more precious than the most precious treasure he'd pulled from the earth. He'd been searching his whole life, and it had taken a lifetime to find her.

"I knew you were naked last night," he rasped against her lips. Lifting her, he carried her to the bed, and with strong arms he lowered her onto the smooth, cool sheets. "I nearly went crazy thinking of you lying here naked," he said, his eyes raking her body. He pulled his sweater off, tossing it onto the floor. Then his shirt, shoes and slacks followed. "Now I want to make you crazy, too."

This whole thing was crazy, but the way she felt she hoped she'd never find sanity again. He was magnificent, his body strong and sleek. He made her feel as no man ever had. She was breaking new ground with every look, every touch.

Reaching up, she let her hands slide over his chest, feeling his power and strength. He was strong and in control, like a huge, hungry cat—predatory and staking his claim. He watched her—his prey—with cool, steady eyes. He allowed her no time for restraints or denials. There was no room for inhibition or modesty between them. He wanted her too much for that. But when her hands moved over him, from broad, straight shoulders down the smooth, muscular chest to the very center of him, his eyes closed tightly and control threatened to shatter.

"Caitlin," he breathed, her name torn from him like a cry, a plea. His body throbbed and pulsated beneath her touch. Commands over body and soul were driven by instincts and needs.

With a deep groan he lowered himself onto the bed beside her and pulled her beneath him. Capturing her mouth with his, he pushed into her with one powerful thrust.

Caitlin's eyes opened as her body filled and accepted him. Never had it been like this before. Needs seemed to rise from somewhere deep inside her, desperate and untamed, demanding satisfaction. She wrapped herself around him, wanting more and more. The force within her was savage and frightening, propelling her to the very edge of madness and beyond.

He looked down at her with eyes that were wild and primitive. He'd captured his prey, taken his hostage, only to discover himself taken captive. It had never been like this before. He'd never known such passion, such intensity. This was it—he'd discovered the unspeakable pleasures spoken of by the ancients, what men had quested for century after century. He'd found the cache he'd been searching for his whole life—his prize, his spoils, his treasure.

Caitlin had been catapulted into a dimension of time and sensation she'd never known existed. A place where there was only Michael, where he was ever-present, taking up the middle and both ends of all she could touch, taste, think and see. She was lost within him, and yet he hurled her forward, launching her from perception to oblivion, insight to blindness. She was helpless, caught up in an emotion too powerful to control, too strong to deny. Before her was a barren, empty landscape that was filled and given life with each forceful thrust of their bodies together.

Then, in one blinding moment of realization and culmination, Caitlin entered the secret void where reason and insanity, fire and ice, hate and love found peaceful coexistence. Bliss.

Michael held her, her body convulsing beneath him. He wanted to give her more, and still more, but he felt the reins of control slipping. The eruption within her reverberated in him, giving way to rapture and projecting him forward into a timeless realm of ecstasy.

He held her long after the trembling had stopped, long after needs had been met and sanity had been restored. Their bodies were still locked together as though reluctant to make the journey back. His hand stroked her hair away from her face as she slowly moved her hand lightly up and down his long torso. Their sweat-soaked bodies gradually cooled, and the room took on shape and dimension again.

He touched his lips to her neck. "Are you cold?"

Caitlin turned to look at him. "No."

He looked into her eyes and pressed a soft, gentle kiss against her lips. Pulling back, he looked at her again, seeing how the lambent glow in her eyes had altered. He pressed another kiss to her lips, then another, and another.

With each touch of mouth to mouth reason began to slip again even as energies were revived. Soon bodies were moving, thoughts were scattering, and they were on a journey back to madness again.

Later, much later, Michael lay on his back and stared up at the ceiling, trying to collect his thoughts. He had to make sense of all of this, of what had just happened and what he was feeling, but he couldn't get himself to concentrate.

He held Caitlin at his side, her head supported by his shoulder, her hair scattered on the pillow and down his chest. But as it had been from the very first, he found himself not wanting to think of why or how. All he wanted to think about was her. She was incredible. In his whole life he'd never met anyone like her.

Over the years he'd been with countless women, had shared countless beds, but nothing, *nothing* had prepared him for what had happened tonight. Nothing had prepared him for her. At forty-one he felt like a virgin—ravished and seduced beyond thought and control. Even now, lying with her in his arms, all he could think about was having her again, taking her and following her to that magic place they'd discovered together.

Caitlin lazily stroked her fingers through the short mat of hair on his chest. She still could hardly believe what had happened. It felt too much like a dream, too good to be true.

There had only been Brian in her life, yet she'd felt anything but inexperienced in Michael's arms. He'd unleashed needs and desires in her that were all new, all unique. He'd been so decisive, so sure that it had made her sure, as well. He'd touched her, and kissed her, and made love to her with a single-minded determination, as though he'd tolerate nothing interfering with his having her. No one had ever wanted her like that, and never had she wanted someone more.

They still hadn't talked, still no words had passed between them. But that only seemed to underscore the way it had been with them from the beginning. So much of what there was between them was unspoken. They seemed to respond to each other instinctively, relying more on feelings and intuition than on words and explanations.

He'd burst into her room and into her life, demanding feelings and emotions from her and changing her life forever. She wouldn't kid herself into thinking she could ever have more from him than she had right now. But right now it was enough.

Men like Michael Seger didn't settle down to ordinary lives in the suburbs. They roamed the world, they tilted at windmills, they had adventures. She was just one stop along the way. But lying in his arms she could find no regrets. There would be time later—after the tape, after he went back to Peru, after she returned to Stockton—for lamenting her dreams and thinking about what might have been. He was here with her now, and that was all that was important.

"Let me get the light," Michael said after a while.

He crossed the room unabashedly naked and walked to the settee. As he reached to turn off the Tiffany lamp, he spotted the small bakery bag and the wine. Grabbing them, along with two of the paper cups left over from the night before, he headed back for the bed.

"Look what I found," he announced, holding up the bottle and the small bag of cookies as he climbed in beneath the fluffy comforter.

Caitlin held the cups while he opened the wine. Then they leaned against the pillows, sipped the light, dry Riesling and shared the cookies.

"Yum, good," Caitlin said, biting into the soft rich cookie. "Much better than the Twinkies. I'm glad now that we stopped for them."

"I'm glad, too," Michael murmured, turning to place a kiss on her bare shoulder. "Otherwise we might not have seen Vivian."

"I thought that was the idea," Caitlin pointed out, remembering their quick duck into the alley.

"I know," he whispered, grinning at her. He kissed her again on the shoulder and slid a line of kisses up her neck. "I could have taken you in that alley tonight. I wanted you that bad."

Caitlin looked down at him, feeling herself flush all over. "I wanted you, too."

The moment held, and they forgot about their wine and cookies. Slowly Michael raised his head and kissed her deeply on the mouth.

The kiss was long and fraught with all the things they'd left unsaid. Pulling away, Michael felt weak and a little light-headed.

"No, no," he said, shaking his head. "I'm not going to let you start that again."

"I wasn't starting anything," Caitlin denied, laughing. She let her thigh brush that part of his anatomy that had reacted most to the kiss. "I think you already started something on your own."

Pushing himself against her leg, he leaned down and gave her another kiss. "Well, not exactly all on my own."

She laughed again and pushed him away. "Drink your wine."

Michael chuckled softly as he leaned against the pillows and emptied his cup. Then he grabbed the bottle and re-filled both their cups.

Caitlin sipped the cool wine. "Do you feel a little strange? I mean, you and I together like this in bed?"

"No," he scoffed easily. "Do you?"

"I don't," she said in amazement. "And I find *that* very strange."

"What's so strange about it? No! Don't tell me. It's a woman thing, right? You're worried because you're not worried."

Caitlin giggled. "No, it's just I thought the first time I'd, well, you know, the first time I'd...since my divorce... I didn't think I'd feel so...so comfortable. I mean, I thought I'd be embarrassed or awkward or something."

Michael fought hard to control his reaction to what he'd just learned, and he had to fight the urge to pull her into his arms again. In two long years she'd been with no other man, and yet she'd chosen him. Deciding to end two years of abstinence obviously wasn't a decision she would have arrived at lightly, and he couldn't deny how special it made him feel. Old habits told him to be cautious, but a hard knot of emotion twisted in his chest.

He'd had enough experience with women to know she wasn't the kind who would fall into bed with a man on a moment's notice, but still it surprised him to know she'd denied herself for so long. She'd been wildly impulsive and spontaneous in his arms, in every way a woman, exciting and incredibly sensual, and suddenly he felt as though he'd been given a very special and precious gift.

He *didn't* love this woman—he couldn't. He wasn't capable of feeling that way anymore. He was too old, too jaded, too set in his ways. Still, as he reached up and let his knuckles graze the softness of her cheek, his throat was thick and tight with emotion. She was so beautiful, and he had to admit she made him feel as no other woman had. He wasn't sure what her motives had been in selecting him as her first lover since her husband, but if she'd been holding back because she was unsure of her ability to please a man, she had no reason to worry any longer.

Looking into her smoky eyes and smiling face, his heart lurched suddenly. That simpering jerk she'd married had hidden her light long enough. She shined now after twelve long years in captivity. She was free of worry and doubt, like a little bird testing her wings for the very first time.

"That's one of the things that's so nice about not being twenty anymore," he said, purposely keeping his tone light for both their sakes. "You don't have to sit around afterward and make stupid conversation. You know, really intelligent things like 'was it as good for you as it was for me?'"

Caitlin waited for a minute, then a grin broke across her face. "Well, was it?"

Michael purposefully took her cup of wine from her hand and set it beside his on the nightstand beside the bed.

To hell with caution, he decided. Rolling onto his belly, he found her beneath the sheet. "Sweetheart, you can't get much better than this and live to tell about it."

Caitlin felt herself go weak as his hand journeyed slowly up the inside of her leg. And when his lips followed the path blazed by his hand, her head fell back and her eyes closed at the sudden surge of pleasure that rocketed through her. Sure, decisive and totally uninhibited, he brought her to the very peak of ecstasy.

She looked at him when he rose to pull her beneath him. He was breathless and desperate with his need for her.

"Aren't you afraid this might be life-threatening?" she murmured, her flushed face presenting the challenge.

"I never said I wanted to live forever," he growled, crushing his mouth on hers and pushing fully into her waiting warmth.

And that was the way he kissed her, as though nothing else mattered. And at that moment nothing else did. If it would have meant his last breath, his last ounce of strength, he wouldn't be denied.

Caitlin reveled at the breadth of his desire for her and felt herself caught up in his desperation. Like a giant funnel cloud snatching up everything in its path, Michael grabbed her and carried her with him over the edge and into the void once again.

Chapter 9

"Michael?" Caitlin mumbled sleepily, tossing her head to one side.

"Shh," Michael soothed, laying her head back down on his shoulder and running a calming hand through her hair. "I'm here. Go back to sleep."

He'd been lying awake for hours, content just to hold her, satisfied with the steady, even rhythm of her breathing as she slept beside him. He still held her, their arms and legs entwined, reluctant to let her go.

"Michael," she murmured again, her lips moving against his neck. "Michael, I love you."

Michael's whole body went rigid. She loved him? Did she really? Was she willing to take a chance on him? He turned to her. But looking down into her quiet face, he realized she was deeply asleep. He pushed the hair gently from her face and lowered his head onto the pillow again.

Love. He'd been stumbling over that one small word all night. He'd been jumping around it, walking past it and trying to avoid it. But there it was right in front of him. Love.

He'd told himself over and over again he didn't love her. It was too late for him, they were too different, they'd only just met, he had nothing to offer her. But the more he tried to get away from it, the more he kept coming face-to-face with it. Love.

He wanted to take her away, take her to all the places she'd never been, share with her all he'd seen and all he was about to discover. But even as he pictured it in his mind he realized how futile those dreams were. She didn't need some jaded archaeologist who would drag her from one end of the earth to another. Her husband had given her enough turmoil and uncertainty in her life. She wanted stability—a husband, a child, a family. She needed some straight, upright sort of guy with a nine-to-five job. Someone who was home every evening—dinner on the table, car in the garage.

For the first time he began to regret never having taken one of the many offers he'd received for positions with various universities or museums. Then he could have offered her the kind of life she needed. He'd have given her all the stability and security she wanted, and he'd have given her the child she deserved. Hell, he'd have given her one every year if she wanted.

He pulled her more closely to him. The thought of her carrying his child, of it suckling at her breast, of her caring and nurturing the life created by them both was almost more than he could bear.

Her murmured whisper sounded over and over again in his brain. *Michael, I love you.* Words in the night, wistful and beguiling, but nothing more. How ironic life was. The very life-style and freedom he'd insisted on all these years were the very things keeping him from her now.

* * *

Caitlin slowly opened her eyes and stretched. Long, unused muscles protested, but she smiled, anyway, remembering the night of furious lovemaking. Sore muscles were a small price to pay for a night such as that.

It was still dark in the room, but morning was on the verge of breaking. Beside her Michael slept, his low, deep breathing regular and even. But even asleep he held her, and Caitlin snuggled deep into his warmth.

Her heart swelled with emotion, bringing a sting of tears to her eyes. Michael Seger was like no man she had ever known. With every look, with every touch, he'd shown her how foolish and unimportant age really was when it came to the desperate desires of a man and a woman. She'd been shallow and unrealistic to think only youth was appealing, that men had no need for intimacy and substance. He'd demonstrated very thoroughly just how wrong her theory had been.

But it was more than just his lovemaking. He was attentive to her, protective. He talked to her, not at her, and he hadn't smothered her the way Brian had. He'd listened to her, given her space, freedom. Respect.

And what woman could resist a man like that? He was everything a woman could want. He looked at her as though she were the most beautiful creature on earth, he made love to her as though there was no tomorrow, and he made her believe in the impossible.

After all, the impossible had happened. In two short days she'd fallen hopelessly in love. If someone would have said to her before leaving Stockton on Thursday that by Sunday morning she'd be lying in bed with the man of her dreams, she would have laughed in that person's face.

And yet here she was.

But happiness had a time limit and hers was just about up. Tomorrow reality would come crashing back into this fantasy existence she'd been living the past two days. They would deliver the tape to the customs official and they'd go their separate ways. She only had today—one day to create memories to last her a lifetime. She had one day to try to collect all the keepsakes, all the mementos of him that she could—enough to last all the long, lonely nights of a life without him.

She would go back to Stockton, back to the bookstore and the normal routine of her life. But things were different now. *She* was different now. The insecure, self-doubting Caitlin was gone, dead and buried. The new Caitlin no longer settled for compromise or second best. She'd experienced what it was to love a real man, and there was no way she could go back to the way things had been before.

And she knew Michael would leave. There had never been any doubt in her mind about that. He would go back to Peru, back to an exciting and challenging career he loved. He'd move on to other adventures, other exploits, other quests.

A tear slipped down her cheek and onto the soft mat of hair on his chest. Soon she would be nothing more than a faded memory to him. But this inn, this room, their time together would live in her memory forever.

She refused to feel sad. She simply wouldn't let herself. She would be lying if she said she didn't want more. Of course she wanted more. She loved him, and what woman wouldn't want a lifetime with the man she loved? To have his love, his children, share his life? But she had to be realistic—for her own sanity if for no other reason.

Michael Seger was a man of the world—successful, dynamic, sophisticated. Encounters like this one wouldn't be uncommon for him. She couldn't afford to fool herself into believing this one with her was any different than the rest. Men like Michael didn't settle down with ex-housewives from suburbia.

So, like it or not, she'd let him go when the time came, but in the meantime she'd make what memories she could.

As carefully as she could, she freed herself from his hold and slipped from the bed. If this was to be their last day together, she didn't want to waste the time sleeping. She found his shirt lying on the floor where he'd carelessly discarded it. Slipping it on, she savored the feel of it.

Outside, the fog hung low over the bay, giving the morning a dull, heavy look. The dampness misted against the windowpanes, causing the moisture to gather and drip down. The room was cold, and the hardwood floor beneath her feet felt like ice. She tiptoed to the fireplace. The innkeeper had set a fire for them yesterday when she brought fresh towels and made up the bed, but they'd never gotten around to lighting it last night.

Caitlin smiled again, remembering the events of the evening before. But heat hadn't been a problem between them last night, considering what they'd done. The aid of a fire simply hadn't been necessary.

Using one of the long wooden matches from a box on the mantel, she lit the small strips of fat wood at the bottom of the grate. They caught flame immediately, and soon the large logs were smoking and threatening to burn. Turning around, she was surprised to see Michael awake and watching her.

"Come back to bed," he said, his blue gaze raking the sight of her in his shirt.

"I'm sorry," she said as she stepped back to the bed. "Did the noise wake you?"

"Not having you beside me woke me up," he murmured, pulling the sheet back and reaching for her arm. He pulled her down onto the bed and begun unbuttoning the shirt. "And let's get rid of this thing."

When she was free of the shirt, he tossed it back onto the floor just as carelessly as before and pulled her into his arms.

"Are you always this bossy in the morning?" she teased, settling into his embrace and resting her hand on his shoulder. "Or is it just something about me that brings out the commandant in you?"

He smiled. Just what would she say if he told her the truth? If he told her he'd never taken pleasure in lingering in bed before, that he'd never felt the need to fondle and caress before today? It would probably make her uncomfortable, just like it would no doubt scare the hell out of her if she knew how he really felt.

"I don't know. I think it's you," he said dryly. "Must be a chemical thing between us."

She rose on her elbow and gazed down at him. "Chemical, huh? It wouldn't be anything like plain old chauvinism, now, would it?"

"What, me a chauvinist?" He shook his head. "No, I don't think so."

"No?" she asked skeptically. "Then let's see how you do taking a few orders yourself." She sat up. "Roll over onto your back."

"What? My back?"

"Roll over," she ordered with an impatient wave of one hand.

Begrudgingly he rolled onto his back. "All right, all right. I'm on my back. Now what?"

"Now," she cooed seductively, lowering her lips to his neck, his chest, his torso, "you're at my mercy."

Closing his eyes to an undescribable surge of pleasure, Michael knew she had no idea how true those words really were.

Mercy. She showed him none.

Inspired by needs and motivated by the constraints of time and circumstance, she was dauntless, exploring him with her hands and her lips with both drive and abandon. Her long hair trailed in her wake, bursting across his chest like golden sunlight breaking the dark shroud of night.

She ventured with the skill and expertise of a seasoned courtesan, yet with the innocent curiosity of one just realizing her full potential as a woman. She didn't rely on design or program but rather instincts that dated back to the beginnings of woman herself, the instincts of a woman well versed in the intuitive art of pleasing her man.

"Caitlin," Michael groaned when agony became too sweet to bear.

Rising up, like a goddess rising from the depths of the sea, Caitlin tossed her hair back and gazed down at him. "Mine," she murmured, taking possession of what belonged to her. She straddled him, lowering herself and taking all of him that there was to take.

Nearly blinded by rapture Michael came forward, sitting up and burying himself in the soft, fragrant valley between her ripe, perfect breasts. With lips and tongue he revered their beauty until the building tension could no longer be denied.

Then, as bodies demanded release and minds discovered harmony, they clung to each other, riding wave after wave of a violent, turbulent sea until all that was left was calm.

Michael collapsed back onto the mattress, taking Caitlin along with him. Holding her close, their overheated bodies damp and wet despite the cold morning, he let his lips find her ear.

"Maybe you're right," he managed in a gruff, exhausted whisper. "Maybe you should give the orders from now on."

Caitlin didn't know where it came from, but somehow she found the energy to laugh. Rolling her over and reversing their positions, Michael joined her.

They were still in bed an hour later when the innkeeper delivered their breakfast. Unlike the day before, when the knock sounded on the door, they were prepared. Still cautious, however, Michael made sure who it was before opening the door.

The breakfast was wonderful—fresh fruit, coffee, croissants, English muffins, currant jam and a sausage and egg frittata. They'd worked up healthy appetites and ate with relish.

"I suppose I should get in the shower," Caitlin said, finishing the last of her coffee and looking at the clock. It was nearly ten.

"What's your hurry?"

She looked at him over the rim of her coffee cup. "We can't spend all day in bed."

"We can't?"

Grinning, she put her cup down. "You're terrible."

"You love it," he murmured, pushing the tray aside and pulling her into his arms.

Yes, she thought to herself as his warm embrace surrounded her, she did love it, just like she loved him.

They lay back on the bed. Arms, legs, sheets, pillows intertwined in tribute to a lazy, relaxed morning.

Relaxed. For the first time in days they were both relaxed. There were no questions any longer, no ambiguities as to whether they were strangers or hostages. They were lovers now—lines had been clearly marked last night. It was as if Peru, or the book convention never existed, as if there was no tape, no bad guys, no danger.

Of course, the calm, easy morning was an illusion, and neither of them wasted time trying to convince themselves that it was anything other than a fantasy. But right now they wanted the fantasy. They needed it. Reality had been carefully held at bay, tucked securely away at a deeper, subconscious level, held there to be dealt with at a later time. For now they'd relax in a virtual archipelago and not think about the danger or the goodbye.

"I don't believe it," Caitlin gasped, throwing her head back onto the pillow and bursting into laughter. She'd never had a day like this before. They'd lain on the bed for hours, laughing and talking. They'd hopscotched from one topic to another—families, politicians, movies, growing up, high school, anything that popped into their heads. He seemed to want to know everything about her, and she marveled at what she discovered about him. She'd thought what had fascinated her about him was the mystery that surrounded him. But the more they talked, the more of the mystery she solved and the more fascinated she became. "You were a jock?"

"I was not," Michael denied, rising on one elbow. "I played football, that's all."

"Oh, forgive me." She laughed, gazing up into the blue gleam in his eyes. "I didn't know there was a difference."

"Look," he said, pointing a finger. "Just because I played football didn't automatically make me a cretin with no neck who barely made grades."

She brought her hands up and shifted his head from side to side, surveying him carefully. "Well, I must admit you definitely have a neck."

"And I made honor roll every year in high school."

"Hmm, interesting combination," she said after a moment. "A jock...*and* a nerd."

"Ooh, you're asking for it." He reached over and gave her ribs a tickle.

Caitlin looked up at him and felt her breath catch in her throat at how handsome he was.

The emotion in her face clawed at him. Feeling welled up from deep inside him, moving and gaining strength, wanting nothing more than to burst forth. He turned his face into her hand, kissing her palm. "Caitlin," he whispered in a voice filled with all the emotion churning inside him. "Caitlin—"

But she wouldn't let him finish, wouldn't let him say what was on the threshold. She pulled him down to her, kissing him with a depth and strength that matched his own.

Inspired by the limits of time, and fueled by desires to make the most of it, energies and stamina seemed to be in endless supply. Each time their bodies joined as one they reached a high plain, achieved a richer texture, secured a deeper love.

Michael knew how close he'd come—so close to blurting out what was in his heart and in his head. But he knew once the words were out there would have been no way to take them back. He didn't want to spoil their short time together with heavy scenes and awkward confessions. Still, the feelings were there, and they demanded release.

So instead of words and phrases, instead of disclosures and declarations, he'd used his body and his abilities to tell her how he felt. With every brush of his lips, every touch of his hand, every thrust of his body into hers, he demonstrated what she meant to him.

Caitlin felt herself powerless to do anything but follow his lead. His fierceness surprised her, his intensity swept her away. They'd started out so slowly, so relaxed, like the morning they'd just shared. But soon that changed. He wasn't content to coax the responses for her; he demanded them. She followed him, through the fury, through the fire storm, beyond doubt and uncertainty, tumbling into the abyss.

Afterward Michael collapsed onto the pillow beside her. For the time being those savage feelings had been appeased, content this time at having vented themselves through action rather than words. Turning his head, he gazed at Caitlin, who lay watching him in dazed silence.

"You know," he panted, his breathing labored and deep. "You're dangerous."

"I'm not the dangerous one," Caitlin argued, breathless. She pointed a weak finger at him. "You! You're the one who's dangerous."

He grabbed her outstretched hand and brought it to his lips. Then an idea struck him as he turned to her. "Let's get out of here."

"Out of here? Leave the inn, you mean?"

He nodded. "What do you say? Go for a drive with me?"

She hesitated for a moment. "You think it's okay? I mean, do you think it would be safe?"

He shrugged. "I don't know why not. We've been careful. I don't think those creeps have a clue where we are, and I suspect they're not thinking about a leisurely drive up the coast about now, anyway. They're probably scrambling to cover themselves." He lifted himself off the bed and pulled her up with him. "Besides, you and I can't be trusted together. If I don't get you out of this bed, I can't guarantee your safety with me, either."

They took a long shower together, the warm water and slick suds bringing them very close to "trouble" again. Then they dressed quickly.

Two hours later Michael pulled the van out of the parking lot of the Cliff House Inn and down the drive to the highway. Caitlin watched the passing scenery, feeling as though she were looking at the outside world for the first time in a very long time. Even though their odyssey had begun only a few days ago, it felt as if they'd been secluded at the inn for much longer—as though it had been weeks, months even, since there had been anything in her life but Michael.

They headed north, stopping at a small market off the road and putting together a picnic lunch. The early-morning fog had burned off, and even though a chill still remained in the air, the afternoon was sunny. When they passed the sign announcing the exit for Muir Woods, Michael turned to Caitlin. "What do you think?"

"Sounds perfect."

And it was. The age-old redwoods towered high into the heavens, their majestic beauty more breathtaking than even the most wondrous skyscraper constructed by man.

Finding a place for their picnic, Michael pulled the minivan into the tourist parking lot and they carried their lunch to a quiet spot. After eating, they strolled through the ancient forest, hand in hand. Beneath the canopy of the trees the air was cool, and Michael wrapped his sweater around Caitlin. They met others walking the paths through the historic woods—tourists, families, teens, but there were no signs of dangerous thugs. In this tranquil setting it was hard to believe that kind of danger existed.

After they had walked for some time, Michael sat on a large boulder and pulled Caitlin down to sit in front of him. With his arms wrapped around her from behind they rested and listened to the wind whistling through the giants. The afternoon was wearing on, and the sun began to sink lower in the sky. The shadows grew long and the number of people trekking the paths had diminished. They sat alone and watched darkness come to the woods.

"They're so beautiful," Caitlin murmured, leaning her head against Michael's chest and watching as the rosy hues of the setting sun made the redwood trunks appear that much redder. "Imagine all they've lived through. If only they could talk."

"That would certainly make my job easier," Michael said, resting his cheek against her hair. "To have the mountains and the trees give up their secrets instead of having to uncover them bit by bit would be wonderful."

"But then there'd be no discovery, no digs," she pointed out.

"And maybe there'd be no forgeries, no smuggled antiquities . . . no tape." The stiffening her body had been slight, but he'd felt it. Reality had stuck its ugly head in the doorway.

"You'll be rid of it tomorrow," she said cautiously.

He nodded slowly. "Yes, tomorrow."

She turned to him and looked up into his clear blue eyes. "Then Jorge's killers will be caught, the smuggling will stop, and it'll be over."

"Yes," he whispered sadly. "It'll be over."

Caitlin couldn't stop the tears from welling up in her eyes any more than she could stop the heavy feeling of melancholy. There was no way she could have hidden her feelings at that moment.

She couldn't believe that after tomorrow she would never see him again, never see the clear blue brilliance in his eyes, never again feel the warmth of his arms around her, never again have him make long, sweet love to her. She couldn't make herself believe, she didn't want to, and yet it was true. She'd done a fairly good job all day of putting the realities of tomorrow in the back of her mind, but as the day began to end and the darkness began, she was no longer able to forget.

"Hold me, Michael," she whispered, barely able to hold back the tears. "Please hold me."

He did. He held her and kissed her until she was able to shove all the harsh realities below the surface once again.

But she hadn't forgotten. Neither of them had. It was right there between them—hanging over their heads like a dark, ominous cloud.

It was nearly nightfall when Michael lifted her from his embrace and pulled them both to their feet. In the gathering shadows of that primal wood he looked down into the quiet anguish in her face. "Let's go back," he murmured, cupping her face in his hands. "Take me to bed."

She nodded, and they made their way arm in arm back to the minivan.

The drive back to the inn was quiet. Caitlin tried her best to shake her solemn mood, but it was impossible. Reality had gotten a foothold in their lives, and there would be no going back.

As he drove, Michael played back their conversation at Muir Woods over and over again in his mind. He'd seen the look in her eyes when he mentioned the tape, when they talked about tomorrow and putting an end to all of this. There had been tears in her eyes. He'd seen them.

Michael, I love you.

If he thought for a moment that she'd meant what she'd said. If he thought he could give her the kind of life she wanted, that she deserved. God, if he thought...

But it was foolish to think that way. Of course she would feel bad. She was a kindhearted person who felt things for people. He knew she had *some* feelings for him. They'd formed a friendship these past few days. They'd shared experiences that had brought them together and helped form a bond between them. She'd helped him escape those creeps who were after him, and he'd helped bolster her confidence in herself as a woman. It had been a mutually advantageous relationship. Just the kind he liked. They would both walk away the better for it.

But tomorrow their experiences together would be over, and the bond that had formed would be broken. She would return to Stockton—back to her bookstore and her friends, back to the kind of life he could never give her. She would miss him as her friend, but in time she would forget.

Michael, I love you.

He knew he'd never forget those words, or the woman who'd said them.

At their room Michael unlocked the door but stopped Caitlin when she started to go inside.

"Wait," he said, sweeping her up into his arms and carrying her across the threshold. With a movement from his foot he kicked the door closed behind them and carried her through the darkened room to the bed.

"Michael—" she started, but he cut her off with a kiss.

"Shh," he said, lifting his lips from hers. "Don't talk. Don't say anything. Just love me, Caitlin. Love me now."

Love. Yes, long into the night they loved each other—touching, tasting, caressing. Words were difficult, so they didn't bother with them. In the silence of the darkness they let actions speak—no words, no excuses, no regrets.

Sometime before dawn they drifted to sleep. Holding each other close, they shared the same pillow, dreamed the same dreams and prayed that morning would never come.

Chapter 10

The sudden knock on the door sounded like thunder. Caitlin's eyes flew open. She sat up, confused and disoriented. The brightness streaming in through the windows blinded her, making her feel even more disoriented. That couldn't be sunlight; she'd only now closed her eyes.

Michael was already in his slacks and at the door. Opening it, he greeted the innkeeper and relieved her of the tray bearing their breakfast. As he turned and slipped the door shut with his foot, he saw Caitlin watching him from the bed and he stopped.

Caitlin stared at Michael standing at the door with their breakfast tray in his hands. A rolling wave of nausea swept over her. It *was* morning.

"Good morning," he said as he carried the tray to the bed. The expression on her face tore at him, but he steeled himself against reacting. Getting through this day would be hard enough. Knowing how difficult it might be for her, too, wasn't going to make it any easier.

"W-what time is it?"

"A little after eight." He poured her a cup of coffee—one sugar, a drop of cream just the way she liked it. He handed her the cup but carefully avoided her eyes. "We, uh, we should probably think about going."

"Yes, of course," she mumbled, taking the cup that he offered. Her hands trembled badly, and it took them both to keep from spilling the coffee over the rim.

No longer were they Caitlin and Michael—best friends and lovers. They were strangers—awkward and ill at ease.

"What would you like?" Michael asked politely, indicating the tray.

Caitlin looked at the strawberry breads, the fresh fruits and poached eggs and felt her stomach roll uneasily. "Nothing, thank you."

Michael glanced up, and for a brief moment their eyes met. Quickly turning away, Caitlin set her coffee down and wrapped the sheet around herself. On shaky legs she lifted herself from the bed. "I'll just... get ready," she mumbled, heading for the bathroom.

"You don't have to hurry," Michael said, hating the clumsiness between them. "There's time for breakfast."

She looked down at the tray and shook her head again. "No, I'm fine."

He watched as she hurried into the bathroom and shut the door. Pouring himself a cup of coffee, he carried it with him to the windows. Staring out at the clear morning, he sipped his coffee and tried to put things into perspective.

Why did it have to be so difficult? After all, it wasn't as if they couldn't see each other again. They were both free agents, both unencumbered. Maybe when all this was over, maybe after things had settled down, maybe...

Maybe what? Maybe they could get together for an occasional weekend? A quick fling at a hotel in some mutual city of their choosing?

Furious and frustrated, Michael turned away blindly from the window and hurled the thin bone china cup against the brick hearth of the fireplace. The cup shattered into a million pieces, and coffee darkened the bricks.

Caitlin bolted from the bathroom, staring at him with wild, frightened eyes. "What was that?"

"Uh, my cup," Michael explained, embarrassed now. "I, uh, dropped it."

Her gaze traveled from him to the stained fireplace across the room. "Oh," she said, her eyes moving back and forth once more. After hesitating for a moment, she stepped back into the bathroom and closed the door behind her.

"Damn," Michael cursed, turning back to the windows. He slammed one fist into the palm of his other hand. God, he hated this.

This was it, this was really going to be the end for them today. There would be no casual meetings, no hotel rooms, no blasé affair. She wasn't the type of woman who would blithely bid him farewell and tell him to call her next time he was in town.

But more than that, he didn't want an affair with her. He didn't want a relationship of casual encounters and countless goodbyes. Having her, and having to let her go time after time, would be impossible. It would tear at his insides, eat away at him, leave him empty. No, this was the only way. A clean break. Take his memories and run.

He heard the sound of the water running in the shower, and a harsh constriction seized his chest. She was there right now in the shower. The water was flowing down her beautiful body, the soap making her skin silky and slick.

Turning, he stared across the room at the solid door that stood between them. If he went in there now, would she turn him away? Or would she open her arms and perform her magic on him?

He closed his eyes tightly. No, he couldn't go in. It was too difficult, too painful. Each time he had her it made it all the more difficult to let her go.

He walked to the telephone on the table by the settee. It had sat mute and useless all weekend, but now it would serve as the instrument he would use to take his first step away from her.

Finding the number of U.S. Customs from the card in his wallet, he dialed it carefully. "Extension 369," he said in response to the nasal inquiry on the other end of the line.

After only one ring, the line was picked up. "Len Mason."

"Mr. Mason," he started, crushing the card in his hand, "my name is Michael Seger."

Michael cradled the receiver. The die was cast. It seemed hard to believe that only three short days ago he'd been anxiously awaiting this moment. Turning over the tape and getting those involved with Jorge's murder and the smuggling ring behind bars had been his central focus since the day his friend had died in his arms. He'd wanted revenge, but he'd been willing to settle for justice.

So why, then—now that the moment had finally come, now when it looked as though those things might really begin to happen—did he feel as though he'd just signed his own death warrant?

He listened to the sound of the running water coming from the bathroom. Caitlin, that was why. Losing her was like dying inside.

Michael looked at the nearly untouched breakfast tray. He didn't feel like smashing another coffee cup. It would take more than one small cup to vent all the anger and frustration pent up inside him. It would take more than the whole damn tray.

Customs Agent Len Mason had been waiting for his call. Even though Michael hadn't left his name when he telephoned the agent on Thursday, Mason had been hoping that it was Michael who had called. His office had been keeping a tight surveillance on curator Ernesto Balcolar since he had arrived in the United States last week after accompanying another shipment from the Peruvian National Museum. Balcolar had made contact with the Peruvians in San Francisco who were thought to be working with him. They were suspected of shipping and receiving antiquities that were being smuggled into the country hidden in the shipments of legitimate museum artifacts that were headed for tours throughout the U.S. Going on information fed to them by Jorge, Customs had been tracking their operation for months, waiting only for definitive evidence that would guarantee a conviction.

Jorge's tape was just the evidence they needed, and to say they were anxious to get it would have been an understatement.

In their last communication Jorge had informed Mason he would be sending the tape to him through Michael, but when Mason learned of Jorge's murder, he'd feared the smugglers had gotten to Michael, too, as well as the tape. His whole investigation hinged on getting his hands on that tape, especially now.

The Peruvians in San Francisco who were thought to be the two ringleaders of the operation were making plans to leave the country and return to Peru. If Customs had any hope of rounding up these individuals, they would have to do it before they left the country. If they were allowed to slip back into Peru, the chances of extraditing them to stand trial in the U.S. would be difficult and time-consuming.

But Mason had just about given up hope. Without Jorge's tape his investigation was dead in the water. So hearing from Michael this morning and discovering that he was still in possession of the tape gave Mason new hope. Even while he'd spoken to Michael on the phone he hadn't wasted any time. Judges were being consulted and warrants were being prepared. He planned to be ready to take action just as soon as the tape was in their hands.

Michael had refused Mason's offer to come to him, preferring instead to deliver the tape to the customs office himself. He'd been looking over his shoulder for so long that it was becoming second nature to him now, and he wasn't about to trust a voice over the phone. Besides, Michael would turn over the tape only on one condition.

Mason would get the tape only if he would guarantee Caitlin's safety. It was imperative that she be kept safe and out of harm's way until all those implicated in the smuggling plot and the murder were behind bars.

Of course, Mason had agreed, assuring Michael that Caitlin would be provided with security until the danger had passed. With that assurance Michael had taken down the directions to Mason's office and to the security entrance of the building's underground parking facility, telling Mason they would get there as soon as possible. Before Mason had hung up he had emphasized again that time was of the essence.

The water in the bathroom had long since stopped, and Michael knew Caitlin would be emerging soon. Slowly he began to gather up his clothes. He'd take time for a quick shower himself, then it would be time for them to go.

* * *

Caitlin stared at herself in the mirror. Turning her head from side to side, she tried for an objective opinion.

It was no use, she decided as her shoulders slumped in defeat. Whatever angle she tried she couldn't disguise the red-rimmed eyes and puffy lids.

She bent down and splashed her face with water again. The ice-cold temperature of the water heightened her color a bit but did nothing to camouflage the evidence of her tears.

How long had she stood in the shower and let the warm spray crash down on her? She had no idea, but it was there that she had stood and let the tears flow. Waking up so harshly and having to face the equally harsh reality of the morning had been difficult enough, but discovering how awkward things had become between her and Michael had simply proven to be too much. All the pent-up emotions had come flooding out in the severe spray of the shower.

But she was dressed and ready now. She might not have a firm hand on her emotions, but it was the best she could do for now. If only her eyes didn't look so red and swollen.

She'd given up trying to think about Chloe and the bookstore, about going back to Stockton and picking up her life. Every time she thought about those things a hard lump of sentiment would form in her throat and the tenuous hold on her self-control would loosen and threaten to give way. She'd left home only last Thursday, and yet it felt like years ago. How could so much have changed in just a few short days? But change it had. The safe, routine life she'd left only last week felt so far away now. It didn't seem to fit anymore. It was as though it belonged to a different person, to a different spot in time.

She sighed deeply and leaned closer to the image in the mirror. Who was this woman? she wondered, looking beyond the tearstained eyes and puffy lids. What did she want out of life? What would make her happy?

She was headed back to a life that had belonged to someone else; it wasn't hers any longer. She'd been a very different person a week ago, a person who was insecure and uncertain, a person who doubted her abilities and too easily accepted what fate had tossed into her path.

But she wasn't like that anymore. What had been slowly occurring over the past two years had culminated in this one short weekend. She'd blossomed, opened up, came into her own. She couldn't go back to that old life.

It was more than just she and Michael saying goodbye. She'd changed, and today, slipping back into a life and a routine that no longer fitted the person she'd become, simply didn't feel right.

Today.

She looked at the person staring back at her in the mirror and felt tears stinging her already smarting eyes. It was really going to happen today. *Today.* Today marked a beginning and an end. The beginning of a new search, but an end to what she'd begun with Michael.

No. No, she wasn't going to cry anymore. She was going to turn around, walk out of this bathroom and meet her fate head-on. He'd given her so much. The least she could do was spare him any weepy scenes or cumbersome goodbyes. The last thing she wanted was for this to end on a note of regret. She didn't want to do anything that would mar the memory.

Giving her damp curls a final toss, she left the bathroom. Michael sat on the edge of the bed, staring down at the floor in front of him. When he heard the door open, he got slowly to his feet. She looked as though she'd been crying and his stomach twisted into a knot. "You okay?"

"Yes, I'm fine," she lied, quickly diverting her swollen eyes. She crossed the room to the vanity and picked up her purse. Finding her mascara, she darkened her lashes. "I'm sorry I took so long."

"It's all right." He gathered up his things and started for the bathroom. "I'll just grab a quick shower. I won't be long."

"Ah...aren't you going to...don't you have to call the customs office?"

"I already have."

Of course, she thought. Did she think he would have forgotten? "I see. How...I mean, when—"

"They're waiting for us now," he cut in. This awkwardness was driving him crazy. Letting her go was difficult enough, but this tension was making it impossible. "We'll leave as soon as I'm through here."

Caitlin stood and watched him close the bathroom door behind him. She knew he'd had to call, knew how important it was for the tape to reach the proper authorities, but she still couldn't help feeling just a little wounded to know that he'd wasted no time in making the arrangements.

You're being foolish, she told herself. *Foolish and unreasonable. You've shared one weekend. Don't make this a tragedy.*

But it was a tragedy. It was an outright calamity for her.

She dropped onto the vanity stool and gazed around the room. She wanted to remember everything about it. The fireplace—in front of which they'd sat and talked for hours. The vanity—where he'd sat her down and shown her how really beautiful she could be. The bed—where she'd discovered and learned about love for the very first time.

She wanted to imprint it all deeply in her memory—every moment, every detail, every time.

She'd been so deep in thought that when she heard the bathroom door open she started just a little. Michael stepped out, his hair damp and his face clean-shaven. He scanned the room carefully. "I suppose we should get going."

Caitlin could only nod, not trusting her voice. Slowly she came to her feet. Michael pulled out the top drawer of the vanity and took out the tape. He turned and looked at her, wondering at that moment if he really had the strength to do what had to be done.

"I guess we're ready," he said, feeling anything but.

"I guess," Caitlin whispered.

She turned and started out, and Michael followed close behind. At the door she stopped and started to reach for the knob just as Michael reached around from behind her to open the door. Their hands met on the handle, and their bodies brushed front to back.

At contact they froze.

At first neither of them could move. They stood immobile, like mannequins in a window. Memories flashed like the frenzied night sky on the Fourth of July—a dark alley, a desperate longing and a long night of love. Slowly, as heat began to radiate from those areas where their bodies made contact, hands began to move and needs began to grow.

Michael slid his hand around her waist, pulling her to him. He buried his face in her hair, his lips finding the soft, delicate skin of her neck.

Caitlin couldn't help herself. She leaned back into his warmth, tossing her head to one side and granting his lips access to what it was they wanted.

His lips were on her neck, her ear, her cheek. Then, turning her in his arms, he found her lips. He pulled her to him and she clung tightly. They were no longer the strangers of the morning, no longer withdrawn in their insecurities and doubts. They were Michael and Caitlin. Lovers, and in love.

"One more time," he growled, tearing at her clothes in an effort to free her of them. "I have to have you just once more."

He didn't care about Mason or the tape, he didn't care about Peruvians or smuggled antiquities. Not now, not at this moment. He was holding Caitlin. She was in his arms, her taste was in his mouth, and nothing else mattered.

Her purse fell onto the floor, then the tape, then shoes, shirt, jumpsuit, stockings and slacks. These articles of clothing joined others and littered the hardwood floor from the door to the bed.

Caitlin drew in his warmth, drew in his flavor and savored each as the treasures they were. She knew this would change nothing. They would still leave this room and go their separate ways, but she didn't care. If it was wrong, she'd gladly face damnation. She'd been given a very special gift—the man she loved one more time.

They were on the bed. Their bodies were naked, hands seeking, legs tangled, lips hungry.

"So beautiful," he murmured, gazing down into her misty brown eyes. With his hand caressing her cheek he entered her, feeling the warmth of her body stretch and make room for him. "Beautiful Caitlin."

Their bodies moved together in an ageless motion of man and woman. The pace wasn't frantic, nor was it placid. It was strong, sure, determined. It broke down the barriers of tension and uneasiness, pulled back the shroud of doubt and insecurity.

And though needs of the flesh were significant, concerns of the heart were paramount. It wasn't important that this would be the last time, or that in a few short hours their time together would be nothing more than memories. What was critical was that it ended as it had begun— instinctive, impulsive and with the calming whisper of love.

It ended in a zenith of reason and sensation. A culmination of mind and body, heart and soul. They dressed in silence. No longer was there the awkward tension from before. What could be said, had been said, and what could be done, had been. Time and circumstance made true satisfaction impossible, but those needs had been satiated for the time being.

Caitlin waited in the minivan as Michael settled the bill with the innkeeper. It was a glorious day. The sun was shining brightly over the smooth expanse of water, with the scenic skyline of San Francisco in the distance.

From the van Caitlin gazed back up at the old inn, finding the windows of their room at the top. Despite the swell of emotion in her throat she smiled as she looked up. Like the day, she was going to shine. It may not have lasted forever, but in their few short days together she'd been given what most people never found in a lifetime of searching. She didn't regret a moment, and she would never forget.

They'd missed the morning commuter traffic by hours, and travel through the city was remarkably smooth. Not that Caitlin minded. Now that they were on their way she was anxious to have things over with. She'd made her peace with the unavoidable. In every way that mattered she'd already said her goodbyes to Michael. Leaving the secluded safety of Cliff House Inn had been her first big step away from him and back to putting her life together again. Prolonging the inevitable only made it that much more difficult. Being with him now was more like a slow form of torture. So when he pulled the van into the underground parking garage at the offices of U.S. Customs, she was almost relieved.

"Michael Seger," the tall, bulky man dressed in a dark suit said. He swiftly crossed the parking garage to greet them, flanked on either side by two similarly dressed men. He flipped open a leather wallet with an official-looking badge inside. "I'm Special Agent Len Mason. This is Agent Newcomb and Agent Lassiter. I guess you know how glad we are to see you."

Michael took Mason's extended hand and the two men shook. "Agent Mason, this is Caitlin MacKenzie."

"Ma'am," Mason said, giving her a polite bow. He indicated the elevators along the far wall. "We can go this way to the office."

The small entourage crossed to the bank of elevators, their footsteps echoing loudly off the concrete floor and walls. The elevators were rather small, and they had to crowd back in order for everyone to fit.

When they started across the parking area, Michael had automatically reached for Caitlin's hand, and now, with the crowded conditions in the elevator, he stood very close beside her. Caitlin closed her eyes, willing herself not to think about the contact. Her body wanted to sing in response to him, but this wasn't the place and there was no longer any time.

"You okay?"

Caitlin's eyes fluttered open as she felt the slight tug on her hand. "Yes," she whispered. "I'm fine."

Michael didn't look convinced but was given no opportunity to pursue his concern. Mason interrupted.

"You said two men were waiting for you as you left the dock on Thursday night. Do you think you could describe them?"

"Sure," Michael said, slowly lifting his gaze from Caitlin. "One was big, two-eighty or so. Maybe a little over six feet, dark skin, thick neck, greasy black hair. The other was small, wiry. Same coloring."

"Sounds like the two that accompanied Balcolar in last week." Mason smiled. "I think you've got a few people nervous."

"Well, they've given me one or two tense moments since Thursday," Michael said dryly.

The elevator doors opened, dropping them into the middle of a busy office. Rows of clerks and secretaries busily worked over computer terminals and typewriters at the neatly lined work stations. Stacks of files cluttered the desk space, people rushed back and forth and phones rang incessantly. Small cubicles lined a far wall, divided by fabric-lined partitions. Some of them were filled with what looked like other agents working at desks.

Stepping off the elevator, Mason began shouting orders while escorting Michael and Caitlin toward a large conference room at the end of a corridor. The other agents followed close behind.

"Collins, get Lieutenant Hollister at SFPD and Harold Dunross from the FBI on the phone for me," Mason barked at a man seated behind a desk in one of the cubicles. "And, Jennings, get those surveillance photos up here."

He showed them into a large room with a long, narrow table placed in the middle. Chairs surrounded the table, and a television set and a VCR sat on a rolling stand at the far end of the room.

Mason graciously pulled out a chair and offered it to Caitlin. When she was seated, he turned to Michael. "Let's take a look at that tape."

"You've made arrangements for what we discussed?"

Mason indicated the two agents with them. "Newcomb and Lassiter have been assigned to Mrs. MacKenzie and are to remain with her until Balcolar and the others are in custody."

Caitlin's gaze lifted in surprise. Those two somber-faced men were assigned to protect her? "Wait a minute. What's all this about protection?"

She got to her feet and looked over at Michael, but it was Mason who answered her. "It's just precautionary," the agent assured when she turned to him. "Just until we're sure all of Balcolar's people are rounded up. I assured Mr. Seger we could guarantee your safety."

Caitlin's gaze vaulted back to Michael, and she took a step closer to him. "I don't understand."

Michael looked uneasily around him, wishing things could be more private. "You didn't expect me just to walk away when there was a chance those creeps were still out there, did you?"

"But the chances are so small of them even finding me."

He walked over to her, heedless of the three agents watching them. "It's a chance I don't want to take."

She stared up at him, reminding herself that he was grateful for her help this weekend and that this was his way of paying her back. But the blue flames in his eyes made her want desperately to believe something else.

"Ah, if you're assured now of Mrs. MacKenzie's safety," Mason interrupted. "The tape?"

"It's all yours," Michael said, turning his gaze away from Caitlin's. He pulled the videocassette out from beneath his sweater and slowly handed it to Mason. "A very good man died getting what's on this tape. Don't blow it."

"If what's on here is what I think it is, we won't," Mason assured him.

Of course, the grainy images on the tape meant little to Caitlin. All the people were strangers. But Michael and Mason easily recognized the man in a white three-piece suit as Ernesto Balcolar, curator and director of the Peruvian National Museum—and plunderer of his country's national treasures.

Despite the unsteady hand and erratic camera angles it was easy to see Mason was pleased with what he saw on the tape. Besides placing Balcolar at the scene and in the company of known smugglers, the tape also gave them a clear picture as to how antiquities were being hidden inside the packing crates of the legitimately sent artifacts.

They were still viewing the tape when another agent interrupted them. "Mason, here are your surveillance photos, and Lieutenant Hollister from SFPD is here. Should I send him back?"

"Yeah," Mason said, not taking his eyes from the television screen. "Get him in here to see this."

As the tape rewound, they were joined by a portly police lieutenant who, after brief introductions, viewed the tape with interest. When the tape was finished, Mason showed Michael and Caitlin the surveillance photos they'd taken of Balcolar and the two men who'd accompanied him into the country.

Caitlin stared down at the picture and recognized the thick, ugly face in the photo. It was the man from the hotel, and the one who had accosted her in her car. Looking at his dark, beady eyes and long, greasy hair caused vivid memories to form in her mind. She could almost smell his stale breath in her face, and a wave of nausea swept over her.

"Recognize him?" Mason asked.

Caitlin passed the photo to Michael across the table from her and nodded. "Yes, that's him."

Mason turned to Michael, who agreed. "That's the guy."

As Mason turned to the others and began issuing orders for search warrants and backup, Michael fished through the pile of pictures spread out on the table. Pulling one out, he slid it across the table to Caitlin.

Glancing down at it, Caitlin recognized it as another photo of the same man but with one notable difference. Clearly evident in the print was a big, angry bruise on the forehead of the man.

Caitlin remembered the dull, hollow sound of the pot when it made contact with the low, wrinkled forehead of her attacker. She remembered the shower of fragments that had scattered in all directions at the moment of impact. They were still littering the floor of her car. At the time the blow had barely stopped the aggressor, but in the photo the injury looked swollen and sore.

Michael watched her as she studied the picture. Slowly her hand came up and covered her mouth. Her thoughts were clearly revealed on her face—shock, surprise, revulsion at what she'd done. When she looked up him, he smiled.

"Remind me never to make you mad," he murmured, his fingertips lightly grazing the top of her hand.

Caitlin glanced back down at the photo. It had been only a few days ago since all that had happened—escaping the hotel, the car chase, breaking the pot across the forehead of that big oaf—but so much had happened since then. She lifted her gaze back to Michael, who still watched her from across the conference table. It seemed as though she'd known those intense blue eyes all her life. How could so much have changed in so short a time?

But that was something she would have to ponder later. Mason and the others were ready to take action.

"I think we're all set here," he announced briskly as the agents began filing out of the conference room. Mason ushered Caitlin and Michael out, following the others, along with Agents Newcomb and Lassiter, to the outer office.

"Our agents and the FBI are in place at the airport," Mason explained as they walked. "If Balcolar or any of the others attempt to board their aircraft, we'll have them."

The crowded outer office was a mass of confusion—people, phones, shouts, orders. The whole office seemed to have been caught up in an atmosphere of speed and urgency.

Turning to Caitlin, Mason briskly smiled. "Mrs. MacKenzie, our agents are ready to escort you back to your home. Your car and things from the hotel are being arranged for. Please accept my thanks for your assistance."

As he turned to speak to Michael, the two solemn-faced agents took Caitlin by the arm. "Mrs. MacKenzie, if you'll just come this way."

There was so much confusion that Caitlin was at the elevators before she realized what was happening. She was leaving. They were going to take her back home. This was it, this was the end, and it was all happening so fast, so abruptly that she didn't know quite what to do.

There was so much chaos around them. She'd hoped for some time with Michael—a brief moment to say goodbye, to wish him well. One last moment alone that she could look back and remember for the rest of her life.

"Michael?" she called, turning around in panic. But Michael wasn't behind her. He was walking in the other direction, being hustled away by Mason. "Michael?" she called again, but the noise and confusion seemed to drown out her plea.

She looked up helplessly at the agents on either side of her. Couldn't they see how hard this was for her? Didn't they know what was happening here? Her whole life was ending—right here, right now. Didn't they know? But her two escorts only stared down at her with their perfect white teeth and saccharine smiles.

Was it really going to end like this? Was it just going to stop as suddenly and as unexpectedly as it had begun? Was she just going to walk away with no words, no wisdom, no looking back?

"The warrants have just come through for the warehouse they're using to store the antiquities," Mason was saying as he took Michael by the arm and led him toward the group of agents who had gathered in anticipation to leave. "We'd like you there to help identify some of the stuff, and Balcolar and his goons, too, if they're still there."

"Sure," Michael said just as he heard Caitlin's voice calling through the noisy bedlam.

Looking over his shoulder, he came to a stop. He forgot about Mason, about what they'd been discussing, about everything. Looking around him, he felt himself start to panic. Caitlin. Where was she?

"Caitlin?" he called. Had she gotten lost in the confusion? "Caitlin?"

Through the bustle of people racing back and forth he caught a glimpse just in time to see her step onto the elevator with the two agents assigned to protect her. What was she doing? Where was she going? She couldn't be leaving, he told himself in horror, breaking for the elevators.

"Wait!" he shouted as the doors began to close.

From inside the elevator Caitlin looked up. "Michael?"

"Caitlin," he shouted again, watching the narrow opening begin to disappear. He lunged for the doors just as they closed. "Damn it," he cursed, pounding the palms of his hands flat against the solid metal door. Reaching for the call button, he began frantically pushing it in a futile effort to summon the elevator back. Frustrated, he spun back around, finding Mason behind him. "Damn it, why didn't you tell me they were taking her?"

"I...I just assumed—" Mason stammered, but Michael wouldn't let him finish.

"Where are they going?"

"To the parking garage," he said as Michael turned back to the elevators. "They're taking her home."

Michael hammered the elevator button again, then turned in frustration to the stairs.

"Seger, wait!" Mason called after him. "Get back here."

No, he thought as he ran down flight after flight of cold concrete steps. He had to see her one more time. He had to say something—anything. It just couldn't end like this.

He leaped down the bottom half of the last flight in one bound and raced through the door leading into the parking garage. On the ramp leading to the street a brown unmarked government sedan sped quickly toward the exit, tires squealing on the slick pavement.

"Caitlin," Michael called, his voice echoing loudly off the hard walls of the garage. "Stop, come back." Leaping a chain barricade, he ran for the ramp. "Caitlin, wait!"

He raced across the smooth concrete toward the exit, but the car was moving too fast. By the time he reached it, the car had cleared the ramp up to the street and turned around a corner.

"Caitlin," he whispered as the taillights of the car disappeared around the side of the building. He stood in the empty darkness of the parking garage, staring after them. His labored breathing reverberated loudly and unevenly off the hollow walls. He'd been in some of the most remote regions of the earth—distant jungles, rugged bush, isolated mountaintops. But never in all his wanderings had he felt as lost and alone as he did at this moment.

She was gone. Gone, and he would never see her again. Never again would he hold her soft body, never again taste her lips, never again know her warmth and passion.

She had left, and he'd never even had a chance to say goodbye. There had been so much he'd wanted to tell her, so much he'd wanted to say. *Thank you...you're wonderful...I owe you so much...I'll never forget you...I'll never forget us...*

Now it was too late. It was over and she was gone. She was out of his reach and out of his life, leaving nothing but an empty space where his heart had once been.

Hearing the sound of the elevator doors opening, he turned around and watched as Mason and the agents stepped out. Jorge's killers were still out there. He'd promised his friend he'd get the tape to Mason and he'd kept that promise. But he'd promised himself he'd see to it that the bastards who'd killed Jorge would pay for their crimes. That promise had yet to be honored.

"You ready, Seger?" Mason asked impatiently.

"Ready," Michael growled.

Chapter 11

Caitlin leaned against the back seat and stared dry-eyed out the window at a landscape of twirling windmills. The winds whipped through the treacherous Altamont Pass, buffeting the car and spinning the hundreds of huge turbines that lined the pass and created an environmentally safe supply of power to the surrounding communities.

In the distance the San Joaquin Valley lay on the horizon. It was a sweeping expanse, a checkerboard of green and gold stretching out as far as the eye could see. Like the people who had settled it over a century ago, the valley was strong, and solid, and enduring. Gazing out across its formidable panorama, Caitlin felt a nostalgic tug. This was her home, had been her home for the past fourteen years. It was where she lived and where she belonged, and yet as the standard-issue government sedan carried her through the winding Altamont, as it carefully descended toward the valley that was her home, the feeling of hopelessness that swelled in her heart was almost overwhelming.

Caitlin shifted her gaze from the scenery outside to the front seat where her two stoic companions, Agents Newcomb and Lassiter sat in silence. They were all business—eyes forward, backs straight, never giving the dramatic view so much as a blink. She slowly shook her head. Cold fish.

Her head ached and her eyes felt tired and scratchy. She just hoped the red, swollen lids would be back to normal by the time she got to the bookstore tomorrow. Chloe was going to have enough questions as it was. After all, she was already a day late getting back from the conference, and that alone was enough to pique Chloe's curiosity. But arriving home escorted in the protective custody of U.S. Customs agents . . . well, Chloe wouldn't rest until she had the whole story.

She gazed down at the small fossil rock that she held in her hand. The delicate, smooth outlines of the shells looked brilliant and snowy white in contrast to the dull gray color of the stone. The memory of that small creature's existence had lasted the ages embedded within that small stone, much like the memories of these past few days had been implanted in her brain.

Caitlin closed her tired eyes, resting them from the harsh glare of the sunlight. Who was ever going to believe the story she had to tell? She hardly believed it herself. It sounded like something out of a movie—a wild, reckless adventure filled with intrigue, danger and romance.

Romance. She thought of Michael and her heart lurched in her chest. Michael—he most certainly was her one great adventure, her grand passion. There had never been anyone in her life like him, and no one else would ever be able to fill the void now that he was gone.

He was gone. Oh, God, she wondered as tears threatened to sting her eyes once again, how was she ever going to accept the fact that she would never see him again? How would she survive without the sight and sound of him, without his touch and tenderness? How cruel it was to have given her a hint, a brief glimpse of the glory and the passion that was possible between a man and a woman, only to have it snatched away just as her discovery was made.

And yet she had no regrets. How could she? To have known him, even for a few brief days, was better than to have never known him at all. In the short time they'd had together he had given her life color and meaning. With him she had known excitement and adventure, depth and understanding, desire and love. He'd burst into her life like an exploding bomb, shaking up her tidy little existence in a way no one ever had. Maybe she had only known him a few short days, but they'd been intense days. And they had shared more in those days than some people shared in an entire lifetime—more than she and Brian had shared in twelve long years of marriage.

No, she had no regrets. But she'd known that when those elevator doors closed between them that something very special had died inside her. She would always love him, always, and she would never forget.

But it was over now. Over, and it was time for her to go home. She was going back to her ordinary life, back to the colorless, routine existence she had known for more years than she cared to admit.

But not Michael. He wasn't the kind of man who would ever settle for anything commonplace or mundane. He would go back to his life of adventure and excitement, back to a career he loved in a place as exotic and wondrous as any dreams could imagine. He would go back, and in time their brief period together would be nothing more than a distant memory for him.

Caitlin squeezed her eyes tighter in an effort to block out the dark thoughts, but it did no good. There was no sense in trying to fool herself. He would forget her. It was bound to happen.

He'd very conveniently neglected to mention—and she'd very conveniently neglected to ask—anything about women in his life, but Caitlin didn't doubt for a moment that there were others. Men like Michael attracted women—God knows she could attest to that. This weekend might have been something completely out of the ordinary for her, something special and unique, but it would be a mistake to think it had been the same for Michael.

With all the different places he had traveled and all the new and exciting people he met and worked with, meeting someone and engaging in a brief…relationship with them was probably nothing unusual. Men like Michael Seger roamed the world. They would have wild, romantic adventures with women all over the world. She was merely one woman, mired in the commonplace, trapped in the routine, with only her dreams and her memories to set her free. To think he'd remember someone like her, one ordinary housewife from the suburbs, would be a little like believing in fairy tales.

"Feeling better, Mrs. MacKenzie?"

"Hmm, what?" Surprised, Caitlin opened her eyes to find Agent Lassiter looking at her. His precisely cut hair didn't have a strand out of place, and his cool gray eyes showed professionalism rather than concern. He and his partner had let her cry herself out earlier as they'd left the customs building, politely offering her tissues as they were needed. It was their job to see to her safety, and if that required offering comfort and solace as she sobbed her eyes out, then that was what they would do, according to reg-

ulations. Just part of the job. "Oh, yes, I'm fine. Much
better."

He smiled at her and nodded curtly. "Fine. But if you'd
like to stop or anything, just let us know."

Caitlin managed a weak smile. "Yes. Yes, I will. Thank
you."

Turning around again, Lassiter settled himself in the
front seat and assumed the position again—back straight,
eyes forward. Caitlin had to smile in spite of her heavy
heart. Compassion 101, by the book.

Caitlin gazed out the window again. The swell of emotion in her throat had eased a bit, making it easier to hold
back the tears. The highway had descended out of the pass,
and they made their way quickly along the straightaway.

She had a lot in her life, she told herself as the sedan
brought her closer and closer to home. After all, she was
a survivor. She'd managed to survive a messy divorce,
cruel gossip and a painful journey toward independence.
She'd survive this, too. Of course, the hollow, empty feeling inside would never fully go away, but she would go on
with her life. She had Chloe, and her job, and an adventure she could tell her grandchildren about.

Grandchildren? That would require having children,
wouldn't it?

Unconsciously Caitlin placed her hand over her abdo-
men. Suddenly warmth spread throughout her body, a
comforting golden glow extending down her chest and out
through her arms and legs as though she were sitting in the
sunshine. They'd taken no precautions, and as ridiculous
as it might sound, she hadn't given birth control or protection as much as a passing thought the entire weekend.
It had been such a long time since there had been someone in her life that she was unaccustomed to thinking in
terms of safeguards and security. God knows she hadn't

gone away with the intent of falling in love. It had just . . . happened.

What would it be like to have Michael's child? To feel his baby growing inside of her? To have a living, breathing part of him to keep with her always? Was there a possibility? Could such a miracle really happen?

No, she cautioned herself. She couldn't think about it—she wouldn't. It was far too early to tell anything for sure. Only time would tell, and getting her hopes up would only make her crazy. If it happened, it happened, she told herself philosophically. But even as she attempted to put the matter out of her mind, she found herself hoping . . . and praying.

"We'll need some directions," Lassiter called back to Caitlin, turning his head to the side.

"Of course," Caitlin readily agreed. The drive had been uneventful, but she was exhausted and looked forward to a shower and some fresh clothes. She looked down at the rumpled black jumpsuit she'd worn for the past several days. It would be a long time—a very long time—before she felt like wearing it again. "You'll want the March Lane exit."

She directed them to the house Brian had taken such pride in showing off to their friends and family. When it came to having it built, he'd wanted no part in its plan or design. None of that had been important to him, so he'd left all that to Caitlin. It was Caitlin who had worked with the architects and decorators. Brian had merely been interested in the end results. He'd wanted a house that would sufficiently impress both his clients and his colleagues.

This one had. But it was Caitlin's house now. Brian had fought her long and hard, but the court had awarded it to her as part of the settlement. Located on a man-made lake and secured behind the confines of a gated community, the five-bedroom wood-and-brick Tudor-style residence was far too big for just Caitlin. But it was hers, and she'd kept it, a cavernous memento of twelve long years of marriage.

Michael wedged the end of the crowbar beneath the lid of the heavy wooden crate and carefully gave it the full force of his weight. The wood groaned noisily as the three-inch nails were forced to release their hold. After working his way around the crate, he lifted the lid off and tossed it to one side. Reaching inside the mass of packing materials and sawdust, he pulled out several articles carefully wrapped in soiled white gauze.

"What's in this one?" Mason asked, looking over Michael's shoulder.

"Looks like some bronze tools," he said, slowly unwrapping each item. "A hatchetlike implement and several spades."

"How would those be listed on the manifest?" Mason asked, handing Michael the clipboard he was holding.

Michael scanned the list of items slated for museum display. "Right here," he said, pointing to their location on the list and handing the clipboard back to Mason. "Listed as tools used for agricultural purposes."

"Anything else?"

"We'll see," Michael said dryly, removing the remainder of the packing material and depositing it on the littered concrete floor of the warehouse.

The bottom of the crate was one solid piece of plywood. Michael edged the end of the crowbar against the spot where the plywood met the side wall of the crate. It took several solid blows before the bottom gave away, but it did, exposing a small, narrow space below.

"False bottom?" Mason asked, peering inside.

"Looks like it."

Mason shook his head. "At least they're consistent."

Michael shrugged. "I guess if it works you stay with it."

"How many does that make now? Twelve? Fourteen containers?"

"Fifteen, I think."

"What's inside this one?"

Michael pulled out the three small articles and slowly began to unwrap one of them from its gauze protection. When the first small gold object fell into his hand, his breath caught in his throat. Cautiously he unwrapped the second and then the third.

"Those bastards," he growled, staring down at the intricately carved solid gold Incan beakers. Without even considering the value of the gold in today's market their value just as part of the precious few gold artifacts that had survived the Spanish conquest over the Incas made them priceless treasures. To think those greedy sons of bitches were going to sell them to the highest bidder made his blood boil.

Mason whistled, gaping down at the highly polished ceremonial vessels. These were like none of the other artifacts they'd recovered since the raid earlier today. Most of the other pieces consisted of beautifully carved ceramics, stone sculptures and various tools made of bronze. Even to his untrained eye these three magnificent pieces were something special.

"Those aren't, I mean, that isn't real . . ."

"Gold?" Michael turned slowly and looked at him. "I'm afraid it is."

A slow smile spread across Mason's face. "Was that a cell door I heard slamming on Balcolar?"

Michael watched as Mason, still smiling, turned around and sauntered off with clipboard in hand to review the progress of the rest of his team who were carefully sorting through and cataloging all the items that had been confiscated in their raid. Ernesto Balcolar and several members of his smuggling ring were in the custody of U.S. Customs agents, and it was expected the entire crew would be apprehended very soon. Between these seized antiquities and Jorge's tape the government's case against them would just about be airtight.

The end had come surprisingly quick for Balcolar. He'd been picked up as he'd attempted to leave the warehouse earlier. It had looked as if they'd arrived just in time, though. They'd literally caught him with his bags packed, including the one containing over a million dollars in cash.

Of course, such a big operation between the joint forces of U.S. Customs, the FBI and the San Francisco Police Department hadn't gone unnoticed by the news media. As soon as word had gotten out about stolen antiquities and millions in cash, the warehouse had been swamped with reporters and television cameras. Local police were able to keep them at a safe distance, but the straining camera lenses and microphones outside had been an intrusion for a while.

Michael had felt a sense of relief with Balcolar's arrest. He'd kept the promise he'd made to Jorge, as well as the one he'd made to himself. Jorge's tape was safe in the hands of U.S. Customs and his killers were going to be held accountable. The nightmare was finally going to be over. Michael could return now to Peru and to his dig with a clear conscience, back to the work he loved and the freedom he craved.

Except, at this moment, his mind felt anything but clear, and freedom felt more like a life sentence.

Seeing Balcolar and his creeps taken into custody had been small compensation for the loss of his friend. Jorge was gone, and nothing was ever going to bring him back—

nothing, no matter how many were arrested or how many trials were conducted. There would be no more noisy family dinners in that cramped little apartment, no more laughing and joking, no more long nights on the balcony sharing bottomless bottles of tequila. But it was more than the loss of his friend that had him feeling empty inside. Much more.

Michael slowly reached down and picked up one of the gold beakers. It felt heavy in his hand, solid, and the overhead lights dangling from the ceiling of the warehouse reflected off the brilliance of its highly polished finish. They were probably from the central southern region, he thought, making an educated guess, or maybe even Lambayeque in the north. At the time of the Inca, gold vessels such as these would only have been used on festive occasions by nobility. What ancient Incan ruler had drunk from this finery, what would he have been celebrating?

Michael lightly ran a finger over the ancient image that had been artfully worked into the beaker's intricate design. The ageless, unchanging face of some long-ago Inca stared stoically back at him, maintaining its secrets in stony silence. How many times had he searched for answers? How many years had he looked for solutions to the mysteries of the past?

Maybe too long, he thought as he rubbed his tired eyes. He'd been searching for years, and yet all he had were more questions. It was the nature of the profession—he understood that. There was always the searching, the seeking, the speculation. Every new discovery, each new piece of the puzzle that was found, would invariably create new questions and spawn more reasons to continue searching. It was what kept him going, kept him returning for more.

He put the golden beaker back down with the other two and slowly stood, stretching his cramped and weary muscles. He was exhausted—both body and soul. His body needed rest and nourishment, but his soul cried out for sustenance of a different kind. It was in dire need of the comfort and succor that could only be found at one source, one that was lost to him forever.

Caitlin. The thought of her caused a swell of emotion to rise inside of him. He steeled himself against the wave of sorrow and self-pity that threatened to consume him, and once more he cursed the twisted acts of fate.

Fear for her safety was constantly with him. Those two animals doing dirty work for Balcolar were still on the loose, and until they were caught he wouldn't rest easy. Still, Mason had assured him their capture was imminent, and the two agents assigned to Caitlin would keep her safe until all threat of danger had passed.

Michael had little choice but to rely on those assurances, but he didn't like it. He should have insisted that they stay together—just a little while longer. Then he could have protected her. He would have personally taken apart with his bare hands anyone who tried to harm her. God, he would have died before he would have let anything happen to her.

Slowly he made his way over the littered floor past the mass of agents and police milling around the seized warehouse to the large loading ramp outside. It was nearly dark, and a biting wind kicked up off the water, cutting through his sweater and chilling him straight to the bone. The brisk weather felt good, though, refreshing. His head cleared as he shook off the weariness and felt more alert. But there wasn't much that could be done for his ravaged spirit.

He wandered down the ramp and through the debris-covered parking lot, which was jammed with government cars, local law-enforcement vehicles and field technician vans. He maneuvered through them over old, rusted railroad tracks that looked as though they hadn't been used in years and found a quiet spot beside a small maintenance shed. The television crews and the reporters had long since left. They'd gotten their story and had already moved on to something else.

Leaning against the cold concrete block wall of the shed, he gazed out at the lights across the bay. The air was thick with the smell of the sea, and gulls squawked noisily in search of any scrap of food that might have been left among the litter in the streets and along the wharfs. The darkness and the dazzling lights that reflected off the water made the dreary industrial waterfront look softer and more pleasant, but the fog that was starting to drift up from the bay would soon change that. It would soon cover the area in a heavy blanket of gloom, making the neglected warehouses and depressing buildings look that much more menacing.

But the dreary scene appealed to Michael tonight. It matched his mood, which itself was rather gloomy and depressed. Three days ago he would have thought he'd be flying high by now. There were no ties on him any longer, no little details that needed attending, no demands on his time or his conscience. He was free to get on with his life, to finish up his current research and look forward to planning new and more exciting projects. So why wasn't he rejoicing and jumping for joy?

He knew why, and it was the same reason that made him feel his whole world had been torn apart. He didn't have Caitlin, and without her nothing felt right anymore.

But it was better this way, he told himself. She would be home by now, back to the safety of her secure and well-ordered existence. Back to her bookstore, and her friends, and the kind of life she deserved. It was what she needed and where she belonged. There would be no more South American wise guys to frighten and terrorize her, no more need to hide or to keep watch over her shoulder.

He'd brought all those awful things into her life. That would be his legacy to her. He was the one responsible for introducing her to the darker, slimier parts of life—all those things someone like her would never need to know or experience. He'd brought her nothing but heartache from the first, and it was the very reason why it was better that she'd gotten out when she had.

He was no good for her. What did he have to offer? A dusty tent at a remote dig somewhere? A suitcase packed and ready to go on a moment's notice? Caitlin was a woman accustomed to stability and permanence—two things he was in short supply of.

If things had been different, if he could have given her the kind of life she deserved, he never would have let her go. He would have married her and given her all the babies she wanted. But things weren't different and he couldn't change his life now. She had her freedom, and he of all people knew how precious freedom was. How could he have asked her to give it up just to follow him?

No, he decided again, leaning his head against the cold concrete and letting the wind whip his hair. It was better this way. He could offer her nothing—nothing she needed. He was a gypsy, a wanderer, drifting from one place to the next. All he had were two arms that longed to hold her, and a tired old heart that had finally found love.

"You must be beat."

Michael turned his head slowly at the sound of Mason's voice. "A little."

"When you heading back?" Mason asked, pulling out a pack of cigarettes and offering one to Michael.

Refusing, Michael shook his head. "I'm not sure. In a day or two."

Mason lit the end of the cigarette and pulled a long draw into his lungs. "You know, things are pretty much finished here. You could leave anytime."

"I know," Michael admitted. "I just want to make sure..." He let his words drift, then turned to Mason. "I'd like to stick around a little longer. You have a problem with that?"

"No problem, no problem," Mason assured him. He took in another deep drag from his cigarette and released it, creating one long plume of smoke. Looking at Michael, he narrowed his eyes. "You know, she's going to be all right. My people won't let her out of their sight until those two goons are picked up."

Michael was taken aback. Was it that obvious? "I know," he said a little defensively.

"We've arranged for her van to be fixed in the morning," Mason went on. "She should have it back by Thursday, Friday at the latest."

Michael nodded, letting his gaze drift back to the lights and the thin fingers of fog making their way inland. "I need a drink. You know a place?"

"Follow me," Mason said, swinging around and heading for his car. "You buy the first round."

Caitlin checked the TV guide one more time. She was exhausted, but it was too early to think of going to bed. All she wanted was some mindless entertainment to stop her from thinking. There were plenty of mindless programs to choose from, but none had been successful in curbing her thoughts.

She'd been fighting a feeling of despair all evening. The house had looked warm and inviting when they arrived that afternoon. But tonight it felt like a prison, complete with guards. Agents Newcomb and Lassiter stuck together like a law-enforcement version of Rosencrantz and Guildenstern—indistinguishable and interchangeable. They prowled around, just out of sight, checking doors and securing windows. They were polite and professional, but they were driving her crazy.

She'd told herself a million times it was just part of their job, but now she was beginning to feel like a goldfish in a large glass bowl. She wanted her privacy back. Her life was falling apart, and she felt like ranting and raving and crying and screaming, and preferred not to have an audience to such a performance.

Picking up the remote control, she flicked through the channels again. She'd actually felt...happy when they arrived at the house. It wasn't because she was home; it had more to do with the hope that swelled in her heart. Despite her best efforts she hadn't been able to stop thinking about the possibility that she might be pregnant. She cautioned herself time and time again not to get her hopes up, but it had been useless. The thought that she might be carrying Michael's child was just too wonderful. Her mind marveled at the possibility. It wasn't until she'd unpacked and headed for the shower that she realized all those hopes were futile. She'd started her period.

Leaving Michael had been the hardest thing she'd ever had to do. But the faint hope that she might have his child had cushioned that pain just a little. But to have those hopes cruelly dashed just as they were blossoming had been a crushing blow.

Caitlin tossed the remote control aside and slammed her fist down hard into the soft cushions of the brushed corduroy sofa. There was no one but herself to blame. She'd set herself up for this fall. It had been a pipe dream, a hope born of desperation. And she had been desperate—desperate, alone and in pain. But it had been such a beautiful dream, a dream that was like having a wish come true. She knew it had been foolish to hope, but hoped she had.

She turned and looked at the small fossil rock sitting on the end table beside the sofa. Like that small shell trapped inside the stone, she would have to be content with only the memory of what once had been.

Her head sank back against the cushions and she closed her tired eyes. Pressure at her temples throbbed, and her head felt as though it were ready to explode. How long had she stood in the shower and cried? At the rate she was going she would have permanently swollen red eyes.

She had just decided to get up and get something for her headache when she heard a name on the television that caused her eyelids to fly open. She fumbled for the remote control, increasing the audio level.

The local news broadcaster looked as clean-cut and confident as always as he reported on the seizure of a warehouse in San Francisco by U.S. Customs officials and of the arrest of prominent Peruvian curator Ernesto Balcolar. A smuggling ring had been broken, and countless antiquities and priceless artifacts, transported illegally into the country, had been confiscated.

Caitlin sat in stunned silence as she watched the videotape of the handcuffed Balcolar being led away by customs agents. When she recognized several of the agents as some she had seen this morning, her jaw dropped open. Unconsciously she moved off the sofa and leaned close to the television screen. She was so shocked that it barely

registered when the picture switched from the tape of Balcolar's arrest to the warehouse where the smuggled goods
had been seized. It wasn't until she saw clear blue eyes and
dusty blond hair that she realized she was looking into the
face of Michael Seger.

He walked with Len Mason, making their way up the
ramp into the warehouse when they were stopped by reporters. The shot had lasted only a few seconds before the
camera quickly panned away to capture the many shipping crates that had been seized in the raid, but his image
had been the only thing she'd seen.

Caitlin stared at the television screen long after the story
had been reported and the broadcast had moved on to
other news events. She couldn't move. She could scarcely
breathe. She'd been so unprepared, so stunned, and yet
she'd seen him—actually looked into his face one more
time.

He was safe, and she quietly breathed a silent prayer of
thanks. Balcolar had been arrested and the smuggling ring
had been broken. Jorge's tape had worked, and Michael
had kept his promise to his friend.

One large tear spilled onto her cheek and made a slow
journey downward. The end had finally come.

Chapter 12

Caitlin's first day back at the bookstore was a hectic one. Customers were cranky, deliveries were late but she really hadn't minded. She was just grateful to have her mind occupied for a few brief hours.

Chloe had come by last night, and the two of them had stayed up quite late talking, Caitlin filling in her shocked friend on all that had happened since she'd been away. And Chloe had told an equally shocked Caitlin that Brian had come by last week, looking for her. He wouldn't say what he'd wanted, not that it mattered. Caitlin only saw him when he wanted something or he had something to complain about. She was grateful she had missed him.

It had been well after midnight by the time Chloe had left and Caitlin had gotten to bed. Even though she'd fallen asleep as soon as her head had hit the pillow, her sleep and been troubled and filled with dreams. In them Michael had been there, but just out of reach, just out of touch. She'd spent the night in a frustrated effort trying to get to him, trying to call out to him, but all her attempts had failed. She'd awakened this morning feeling discouraged and disenchanted. This marked her first day without Michael, and she just wanted to get through it.

Agents Newcomb and Lassiter had been vigilant and alert this morning, going about their duties with their usual detached professionalism. They'd ushered her to work and had kept a constant vigil in the bookstore all morning.

It was well after three before things finally seemed to settle down. Caitlin was able to help Chloe with some new displays and check on the new deliveries.

"How about some lunch? I'm starving," Chloe announced, popping her head out from around a large display stand. "I could go get us something."

"Why don't you go ahead," Caitlin suggested with a shrug. "I can handle it here. I'm not very hungry, anyway."

"Humph," Chloe snorted inelegantly, her gaze moving in the direction of the two agents who kept quiet surveillance of Caitlin. "I can see how having the Brothers Grimm lurking around could spoil your appetite."

Caitlin laughed. "That's not it. They're okay."

Chloe slipped her oversize poncho over her head and hooked her large purse onto her shoulder. "Sure I can't bring you back something?" she asked, examining her friend closely. "You look like you could use a little nourishment."

Caitlin needed nurturing, not nourishment, but she didn't want to think about that now. Instead, she shook her head and gave Chloe a tired smile. "No, I'm fine. Now get out of here."

Chloe had been gone only a few minutes and Caitlin had just stepped into the back room to open a new carton of books when she heard the quiet jingle of the little brass bell over the front door. Being interrupted by customers was just part of the routine, so when she looked up from the counter and saw Agent Len Mason walking toward her, she was caught off guard.

What was he doing here? Had something happened to Michael? Had he been hurt?

The small razor-sharp instrument she used to cut through the book cartons slipped from her numb hands to the floor, landing dangerously close to the soft leather loafers she wore. Her heart thudded loudly in her throat, and her lungs had suddenly forgotten how to function.

"Mrs. Mackenzie," Mason greeted personally as he walked to the counter.

"Agen—" Caitlin's voice failed and she cleared her throat loudly. "Agent Mason, is there something wrong? Has something happened?"

"No, no," Mason assured her. "Nothing like that. I drove in to tell you that Balcolar was arrested last night and the two men who accosted you at the hotel were apprehended at the San Francisco airport this morning when they attempted to leave the country."

"You caught them?" Caitlin murmured wondrously as she remembered how to breathe again.

"We caught them," he assured her, smiling. "You're safe now."

"You got them all?"

"We got them all."

"Well," she sighed a little easier. "That is good news then."

"That's very good news," he said. "And I wanted to thank you again for all your help. Your van is being repaired and should be back to you in a few days. I hope that won't inconvenience you too much."

"Oh, right, my van," Caitlin said with a small shake of her head. She'd completely forgotten. "No, no. That's fine."

"I've relieved Agents Newcomb and Lassiter of their assignment. They'll be returning with me to our San Francisco office."

"O-of course," she stammered as all the news began to settle in. "Everything went as you'd expected then?"

"With just a few minor exceptions."

"Exceptions?" she repeated tightly. "No one...got hurt, did they?"

"Oh, no, nothing like that," he assured her. "You try to plan for every contingency, but there are always unexpected things that come up in procedures like this. They were just small glitches. But, overall, the operation was very much a success. Balcolar and his friends have a lot of explaining to do. They're going to be spending a very long time in jail."

"So," Caitlin said, taking a deep breath and giving him a strained smile, "I guess it's really over now. Thank you for driving all the way out here to let me know."

"There was just one other thing," he hedged, putting his hand into the breast pocket of his suit coat and bringing out a small wrapped parcel. "Mike, uh, I mean, Mr. Seger gave this to me last night. He, uh, he asked if I would give it to you."

"Michael?" Caitlin whispered as he placed the small package in her hand.

"He left for Lima this morning just after Balcolar's people were taken into custody and wanted me to make sure you got it."

Caitlin stared down at the tissue-wrapped bundle and felt all the air leave her lungs. It wasn't very big, only about six or seven inches, and very, very slender. But despite its size it was a considerable weight in her hand.

Gently she ran a cautious finger over the smooth, cool surface of the paper. She marveled at it but not out of any curiosity as to what it was. Michael had been thinking of her, had gone to the trouble of seeing to it that Mason deliver this to her. It didn't matter what was inside. Knowing that he had been thinking of her was gift enough.

"Aren't you going to open it?" Mason asked, shifting his weight again.

"Ah, yes, I suppose I should," she stammered absently.

"He thought maybe you should in case you had any questions."

Caitlin's hands trembled so badly that they were clumsy and unwieldy, and she wasn't entirely sure she would even be able to make them function. Taking a deep breath, she did her best to slide the thin string securing the paper over the edge of the item. Slowly, slowly, she unwrapped it— fold after careful fold.

At the last turn a highly polished, bronze article fell coolly into her palm. It was pointed and sharp on one end, with a flat, hammered half circle adorning the other. Its highly rubbed bronze glowed, reflecting the lights overhead off its burnished surface.

"He said it's a shawl pin," Mason told her, peering over the counter at the magnificent artifact. "He excavated it from a cave near Machu Picchu."

Machu Picchu. The Lost City of the Incas, that stunning and mysterious place that had grabbed the imagination of a young Michael Seger and set the whole course of his life. Caitlin knew how he felt about those enigmatic and ancient people, and she cherished his gift to her for the treasure that it was.

Closing her hand slowly, she brought the precious object to her chest and looked up at Mason. "He's gone now, you said?"

Mason nodded. "This morning."

She felt the sting of tears but forced them back. She wasn't going to break down or lose control. Michael had thought of her—had thought enough of her to send her this treasure. There had been no note, no handwritten message, but she hadn't needed one. This beautiful Incan artifact had been message enough. He was thousands of miles away by now. They were a world apart, but she would have him forever in her heart. Just as this treasure had survived the centuries, so would her love.

"Thank you, Agent Mason," she said, extending him her hand over the counter.

Mason nodded, looking slightly embarrassed. She walked around from behind the counter and escorted him to the door of the shop. Just outside Newcomb and Lassiter stood waiting, both offering her stiff handshakes. She thanked them all again and watched as they drove away in their matching government sedans.

It was all over now—truly over. Once and for all. She gazed down at the shawl pin she held in her hand.

"Oh, Michael," she sighed out loud, feeling better just saying his name. She leaned her head against the doorframe and closed her eyes tightly. She remembered the pictures of Machu Picchu she had seen in the small bookstore in Sausalito. Such breathtaking beauty, such haunting mystery. Michael would soon be there—soon be among all that beauty and mystery. He was free now, his obligations to his dead friend had been met. He was free to roam, free to explore and free to investigate all the ancient mysteries of that strange and wonderful place.

Opening her eyes, she looked around at the rows of small shops that made up the commercial center that housed the bookstore. Its clean, uncluttered style and low-slung lines were a stark contrast to the majestic structures of that ancient people. Like the contrast between Michael's world and her own. His was mysterious and exciting, hers was commonplace and everyday.

But for a few short days, she thought, closing her eyes and clutching the brass shawl pin to her breast again, for a few short days she'd been pulled from her safe, sedate life. She'd been challenged and tested, she'd been made to react instead of reason, and she'd been given just a taste of what life had to offer.

Michael had touched her, had reached into her safe and sane world and changed it forever. She was different now, and never again would she look at the sun and only see light. She would think of Michael and wonder where the sun was shining on him.

Caitlin pulled the belt one notch tighter and fastened it securely. Frowning at herself in the mirror, she studied the image that looked back at her. She'd been back in her old routine for four days now, but her appetite was still on vacation somewhere. If it didn't return soon, her clothes would all be hanging from her.

Meeting her own gaze in the mirror, she slowly shook her head. She'd lost over ten pounds after Brian left, and in the two years that had followed she had never managed to regain it. The scales this morning had indicated she was down almost five more pounds. If any more men walked out of her life, there wouldn't be much left.

She put her hands on her hips. It seemed hard to believe now, but there had been a time in her life when she actually thought she had to watch what she ate. Little did she know...

She looked at the dark, tired circles under her eyes and at her pasty, pallid complexion. There had to be a better form of weight control than this. Thin was small compensation for what she'd been through.

Checking the time, she quickly finished getting dressed. Chloe was due anytime, and she wanted to have time to try to force down some breakfast.

Caitlin had just pulled the bagel from the toaster when she heard the door chimes. She glanced at the clock—8:45. If it was Chloe, she was a half hour early...and Chloe was never early.

Caitlin ran across the slick tile of the entryway and peered through the beveled glass window in the large front door. A man who looked to be in his mid-twenties stood holding a clipboard. He was dressed in starched white overalls and wore sunglasses à la Tom Cruise.

"Yes?" she inquired suspiciously, calling through the door.

The young man glanced down at his clipboard. "Ah, Caitlin MacKenzie?"

"Yes?"

He held up a set of keys and peered at her through the glass. "I have your van."

Caitlin turned the dead bolt lock and opened the door. "My van?"

"Yes, ma'am," the young man said, smiling broadly as she opened the door. "If you'll just sign right here."

He handed her his clipboard and pen when she opened the door. She scribbled her name on the line he indicated and he dropped the keys into her hand.

"It's in the driveway," he told her, nodding in that direction. "And you have a nice day now."

Caitlin watched as he walked down her front walk and into the waiting car at the curb. As he drove away, she carefully stepped out onto the porch and looked across the yard to the driveway. Her van sat there just as it had the day she'd brought it home from the showroom.

She stood staring, visions of the frantic chase through the streets of San Francisco running through her mind. She remembered Michael crouched in the passenger seat, the harrowing turns and near misses, the railroad crossing arm that had halted their mad dash and that horrible thick-necked man who had lunged over the front toward her.

But in the quiet serenity of her drive the vehicle showed no signs of any of the hard use it had endured. Even the awful scar that had marred the length of the driver's side had completely disappeared.

Caitlin slowly crossed the lawn and inserted the key into the lock. She lifted herself up into the driver's seat and carefully looked around. It was spotless, vacuumed and polished to a showroom shine.

On the back seat the books she'd left in the van had been neatly stacked and sat waiting for her. It was as though nothing had ever happened. The van was in the same condition—even better—than it had been before.

But it wasn't until she glanced down at the carpeted floor that the feeling seemed to seep into her consciousness and emotions rose to the surface. The floor was spotless. Not a trace of the pottery shards could be found. Nothing.

She hadn't cried in two days. Her eyelids had only now begun to lose their puffed, reddened appearance. But sitting in the sterile van, having had every shred of evidence of her encounter wiped away, seemed too much.

It was over. She *knew* it was over. Michael was gone, but she had her memories, and her shawl pin, and her fossil rock. She really didn't need anything else. But somehow, seeing her van, seeing how it had been wiped clean of everything, having it look as though nothing had ever happened, was more than she could take. With hands on the steering wheel she lowered her head and cried.

"Caitlin?"

Startled, Caitlin jumped, surprised to find Brian MacKenzie standing at the open van door.

"My God," he said, reaching for her and pulling her out of the van. "Are you all right? Is something wrong?"

Caitlin closed her eyes and wiped the tears from her eyes and face. This was great, just great. All she needed to make this a perfect morning was an encounter with her ex-husband. What was it this time? The house? The money? Another complaint?

"I'm fine, Brian," she insisted, pulling out of his hold. She looked up at him and took a deep breath. "Was there something you wanted?"

Brian MacKenzie looked down at her, his pale brown eyes looking troubled and a little uneasy. "Were you on your way to work?"

"No, no," Caitlin sighed tiredly, shaking her head. "Look, do you want to come inside?"

"Yeah," he said, nodding as he followed her up the lawn. "I'd like to talk for a while if you have the time."

Crossing the entryway and heading back to the kitchen, Caitlin checked her watch. "Will this take long? I need to be at the bookstore in about a half hour."

"That depends on you."

Caitlin turned around and looked at him. "Let me give Chloe a call. I need to catch her before she leaves."

Chloe was delighted to hear that Caitlin's van had been returned, but she greeted the news of Brian's arrival with much less enthusiasm. "That guy is such a lowlife. He's too chicken to come back here and face me. I swear, he's such a little worm. What's he doing there, anyway?'' she demanded over the telephone.

''Well, why don't you let me find out?'' Caitlin asked in a syrupy tone. She glanced at Brian to see if he'd heard any of Chloe's biting comments, but he seemed blissfully ignorant of the fact that he was being unmercifully maligned over the line. ''I'll see you in a little while.''

Gently replacing the receiver, she turned to her ex-husband. ''Okay, Brian,'' she said, cutting to the chase, ''what's all this about?''

Brian was clearly surprised by her abrupt tone. ''You sure everything is all right?''

''It's fine,'' she said, picking up the stone-cold bagel and tossing it into the trash compactor. Her appetite was gone again.

He walked across the breakfast room to sit on one of the high stools across the counter from where she stood. ''I'm glad I caught you before you left. Did Chloe tell you I came by the store to see you?''

''She mentioned it.'' Caitlin gestured to the fresh pot of coffee that had just finished brewing. ''Coffee?''

He nodded, then made a face, cringing a little. ''Chloe doesn't really think much of me, does she?''

Caitlin smiled, handing him a cup of coffee and pouring one for herself. He wouldn't have had to hear her biting tirade of him over the telephone to have come to that conclusion. ''I sort of thought the feeling was mutual.''

''Me? No,'' Brian denied. ''I always liked Chloe.''

The coffee cup paused only slightly on the way to her lips. Brian always did have a way of rearranging the facts in order to suit his purposes. Apparently he'd just been teasing all those times he'd cautioned her not to get too tied up with that *weirdo.* Caitlin sipped her coffee and smiled. "I'm sure she'll be delighted to hear that."

"She said you were out of town."

"Yes," Caitlin said, setting the coffee cup down on the counter. "Yes, I was."

"She didn't say where."

"Maybe you didn't ask."

Brian laughed, embarrassed. "Business trip?"

"Look, Brian," Caitlin said, losing patience. She checked the time on her watch again. "Was there something specific? It's getting late and I really should get going."

Brian set down his coffee cup and got to his feet. "Caitlin, I really think we need to talk."

"Talk," Caitlin repeated. She unplugged the coffee-maker and reached for her purse. "Isn't that what we're doing?"

"No, I mean really talk."

"Brian," she said purposefully, reaching for her car keys, "you and I don't have anything to talk about anymore."

"I think we do."

"Then maybe we should do our talking through the lawyers," she told him simply. He followed her as she walked to each of the doors and secured the locks and closed up the windows.

"This isn't about lawyers."

Midway down the hall toward the foyer, she turned to him, exasperated. "Then why don't you just tell me what it is about?"

"Caitlin," he said uneasily, putting his head down and sinking his hands deeply into the pockets of his sport coat. "Caitlin, things haven't been going too well for me lately."

Caitlin regarded him carefully. This was a side of Brian she'd never seen before. Gone was the cocky, know-it-all attitude. He looked like a man defeated. "Brian, do you need money?"

"Money?" He looked up at her, confused. "No, this hasn't got anything to do with money." Suddenly he grabbed her by the upper arms and kissed her roughly on the mouth.

"Stop that," Caitlin struggled, horrified. Furious, she pushed him away and straightened her clothes, running a shaky hand through her hair. "What in heaven's name has gotten into you?"

"Caitlin, I'm miserable," he confessed, taking a step closer. "Things...my life...everything is in a shambles." He reached for her again. "I want to come home. I want you back."

Chapter 13

"What are you doing? Stop that," Caitlin demanded again, struggling and pulling free of him. Then she stopped and stared up at him. "What did you say?"

"I want you back," he said again. He made no move to touch her but took a step closer. "I've been such a fool."

Caitlin was flabbergasted and stood there staring at him. Brian wanted her back? No, something wasn't right. She'd known him too long and too well to take things at surface value. Brian never did anything without clear motives. What were his motives now?

"Say something," he prompted her when she had no response.

"Brian," she said skeptically, "what's all this about? What brought all this on?"

"Nothing," he insisted. "Caitlin, I realize what a mistake this whole thing with Krissy was. I want you to forgive me. I want to come home."

Home? Certainly he didn't mean here. "What about your daughter, Brian? You and Krissy have a child. Have you forgotten about that?"

"No, I haven't forgotten," he mumbled, turning his eyes away. "Truth is ... well, the truth is this whole thing just isn't for me. Maybe I wasn't cut out to be a father. The baby is sweet enough, but she fusses all the time. And Krissy's got that damn stereo of hers blaring day and night, and she's got these ... friends who drop by all the time. All she wants to do is spend money—she has no regard for how hard I have to work for it. She couldn't get into any of her clothes after the baby, so she spent a fortune on new ones. She'd redecorated the house twice already. It just goes on and on." He shook his head and looked at Caitlin pleadingly. "This whole thing was a big mistake. I see that now. I know what I did to you was terrible, but say you forgive me. Say you'll take me back."

Brian wanted her back. He wanted her to go back to the staid and sterile life she had endured for twelve agonizing years. He'd had his fun, he'd played his games, and now he wanted to come back to the safe, secure marriage he'd left behind two years before.

What goes around inevitably came around, Caitlin thought as the pieces began to fall into place, and it looked as though Brian had come full circle. Revenge could certainly be sweet at times, but she wasn't interested in that. Despite all the pain and humiliation Brian had put her through she had no appetite for revenge. She had no reason to be vindictive or spiteful. Brian was part of the past, tied to her now only through memories.

Up until a week ago Caitlin hadn't known what it was to love a man. But now she knew. She knew, and she understood that she'd never loved Brian. Not in all the ways that mattered, anyway. Maybe if there had been no Michael, maybe then she would have been content to live her life in the emotional limbo that life with Brian would be. But not now. She was a different person now. She wouldn't be bullied or content to settle for anything short of perfection. She knew what it was to fly with the angels. How could she go back to mere walking again?

"Brian," she said uneasily. How could she explain everything to him? "Brian, I'm really sorry things didn't work out the way you wanted."

"But it clears the way for us now," he said, trying to pull her into his arms. "We can be together."

"Oh, Brian, please," Caitlin admonished, resisting his embrace. "Will you listen to yourself?" She turned and walked down the small hallway to the family room where she tossed her purse and keys onto the coffee table. "Brian, you and Krissy have a daughter. You owe it to that little girl to make the relationship work."

"But it's over," he insisted. "I can't take any more. I want our life back. I want it to be the way it used to be."

The way it used to be, Caitlin repeated in her mind. A barren marriage, a lifetime filled with insipid, empty years. How could Brian be so blind? He had a child, with all the riches and joys parenthood had to offer. Yet all he wanted was the vain, hollow life they had shared together.

"Brian, it can never be that way again."

"I know, I know," he insisted. "You have this nice little job now. You'll want to keep it. That's fine, that's great. I don't mind."

"Brian, you don't understand."

"You've kept the house," he continued, ignoring what she was saying. "I'll move back home and it'll be just the way it used to be. Even better. We—"

"No, Brian, you're not listening," she said firmly, cutting him off. "You won't be moving back here. We won't be getting together again."

He looked at her, clearly stunned. "I can't believe you're saying that to me."

"Why, Brian? It's been two years. A lot has happened in those two years. A lot has changed."

"You mean you've changed."

She shrugged, acknowledging that fact. "Okay, I've changed." She walked up to him and reached for his hand. "Brian, I think you need to go back to Krissy, back to your child. Work things out. For once in your life do the right thing."

"Is this your way of punishing me?"

"No," Caitlin denied honestly. "I don't want to punish you. Brian, it's over between us. You were right in ending it. Go back to Krissy. Go back to your baby. I'm not interested."

Angry, Brian stomped to the door. Once there he turned back to her. "There's someone else, isn't there?"

Caitlin's heart twisted painfully in her chest. "Yes. Yes, there is."

Caitlin stood at the door and watched as he stomped down the walk and into his car. Tires squealed noisily as he angrily drove off.

There was no satisfaction in what she felt, no triumph as she watched him drive away. There was just a heavy sadness in her heart, and the realization that somewhere along the way she'd put that old hurt to rest.

Michael tilted the canteen back and let the cool water flow down his dry, burning throat. Closing his eyes, he brought the image of her up again in his mind for the hundredth time today. He thought about the long, silky hair, the satin-soft skin, the full, wet lips. He thought about lying with her, of being inside her, of feeling her body moving beneath his. Just remembering had his body tensing up and reacting.

Michael, I love you. Those soft words in the night. He played them over and over again in his brain.

He stayed there for just a moment, in his head and in the memories, savoring the touch and the feel and the taste of her for just an instant longer—his own oasis away from all the dirt and the sweat of the day. Only...opening his eyes, he faced the harsh reality that his oasis was nothing more than a mirage. Reluctantly he let the image fade and steeled himself against the unpleasant sinking feeling in the pit of his stomach.

He climbed back down into the trench again. This wasn't the time for daydreams, and it was about time he remembered that. He worked until the light was exhausted, then made the long, slow trek up the steep incline to the open plateau where they'd made their camp. With the sun gone, the wind blowing down the mountain pass was cold, cutting through his shirt.

His body had been pushed to its limit, but he felt keyed up, restless. He'd been experiencing a lot of restlessness lately. At first he'd tried to tell himself it was just his old bones telling him he was getting close, that something was down there, just below the surface, just waiting to be discovered, but that hadn't been it. His restlessness, his uneasiness, had nothing to do with his work, nothing to do with the dig.

It unsettled him. For the first time he was having trouble absorbing himself completely in his work.

Michael, I love you.

The soft voice sounded in his head. Never before had anything been able to pierce his concentration when he was at a dig site. He'd always been completely focused on his work—single-minded and centered. Nothing—least of all a woman—had ever been able to penetrate that total absorption. Until now.

Michael, I love you.

From the beginning Caitlin had broken all the rules. She'd worked her way into his head and into his heart. She'd pierced his thoughts, destroyed his concentration and turned his whole life upside down. Even now, half a world away, her hold was as strong and as commanding as it had been on those glorious nights in their room at the inn.

Another cold gust buffeted him, chilling him to the bone. He'd made an important discovery today, and yet all he could think about was holding her, of losing himself inside her and basking in her sun.

Gratefully his friend and fellow archaeologist, Gerry Hanlon, stoked up the campfire, bringing it to a full blaze. Michael sat down for a moment, feeling the heat penetrate his cold, weathered skin.

"I thought you were exhausted," Michael commented as he watched Gerry pull out a large pouch of freeze-dried stew and set a kettle of water on the hot coals of the fire.

"I am," Gerry acknowledged, stifling a yawn. "But damn, don't you ever get hungry? We haven't eaten since breakfast."

Now that he thought about it Michael felt hunger pains gnawing at his stomach. "Toss one of those pouches over here."

He pulled a few cleansing breaths into his lungs as he waited for the water to heat. The air was thin, but it hadn't taken him long to adjust to the altitude again. Of course, that had been nearly six weeks ago, and he barely noticed the effects of the high elevation any longer.

Six weeks. It had been six weeks since Balcolar and his cronies had been arrested. Six weeks since the news had broke and the effects had ricocheted throughout the entire archaeological world.

The Peruvian press had been filled with accounts of Jorge's bravery in capturing the incriminating evidence on videotape, and of his tragic death. Michael had been hailed in both the media and in professional circles for the part he had played in stopping the deplorable practice of stealing antiquities. Of course, that wouldn't hurt when it came time for him to make the rounds again in search of financing future digs, but he had been relieved when all the hoopla had finally died down.

He looked down at the pouch in his hand and then at the pot of water in the coals. It hadn't even begun to simmer yet. At this altitude it would take forever. Impatiently he slung the pouch aside and rose to his feet. He paced in front of the fire for a while, then walked to the edge of their small camp and gazed up at the sky. The stars shone brilliantly overhead, and he rubbed the sore muscle in his neck.

Six weeks. It had been six weeks since he'd seen her. Six long, agonizing weeks since they'd spoken, since he'd held her, since he'd kissed her lips and taken her into his arms and made long, sweet love to her. They had been the longest six weeks of his life.

The days had been tolerable, but just barely. With time and money running out there was a lot to be done at the dig, and just a short time to do it. He'd thrown himself into his work, the kind of backbreaking, exhausting labor that kept his body occupied and his mind a blank. But even then thoughts of her would seep into his consciousness.

He would picture her at the site, exploring the ruins and marveling at everything. He imagined showing her their findings, telling her his theories and whispering his dreams. He remembered her awe and excitement with the shell fossil; she would have thrilled at their find today.

But even if the days had been tolerable, the nights had been tormenting. During the long, cold nights, he had lain in the darkness—remembering, remembering. He'd known it would be difficult getting over her; he just hadn't figured on how difficult.

A shooting star streaked across the sky, disappearing into the darkness. What would he wish for? Should he wish to see her again? What would that change? They would still be the same people. He still had nothing. Maybe he should wish that things were different? That they were different people, or had met at a different time in life?

Did she think of him? Did she ever gaze up into the night sky and think of him? Did she remember their time together? Would she want to see him again?

Maybe it was just old age, or some midlife thing. Or maybe it was just normal for him to start rethinking the decisions he'd made years earlier. Those decisions had molded a life-style, and his life-style had become habit. God knows, habits of a lifetime were hard to change, but was that what he wanted—a change?

He watched as a faraway star seemed to shimmer and grow brighter. He'd set his course a long time ago, and it was too late to do anything about it now. He was too old to change, but . . . damn, the way he felt right now, he was just too tired to think of moving on.

He turned and stomped back to the fire, dropping to the ground and picking up the stew pack again. The questions bothered him, and he didn't want to think about them any longer.

"Why so restless?" Gerry asked, watching as he fidgeted with the food pouch. "What's gotten into you lately?"

"Why?" Michael asked, feeling his defenses shoot up. "What do you mean?"

"I mean this," Gerry explained. "Ever since you got back you've worked like a Trojan all day and are as skittish as a deer at night. You're driving me nuts. What gives?"

"We're running out of time," he pointed out defensively. "Or haven't you noticed?"

"Of course I've noticed, but what's the big deal? It isn't like it's the first time this has happened, you know. It's all part of the game. You of all people should know that. You're not worried about getting another grant, are you?"

"Not really," Michael grumbled, picking up a stick and tossing it into the fire. Why was he worried? After the publicity he'd been given, offers should be rolling in.

He studied his stocky assistant. He'd known Gerry Hanlon for over ten years. Knew how old he was, where he'd studied, what degrees he held, what papers he'd published, what people he'd worked with. But in ten long years he couldn't remember ever having a personal conversation with the man. Michael didn't know, for example, how Gerry had gotten into the field, what he wanted for the future, if he had ever had any second thoughts. Had there ever been anyone special in Gerry's life, and did he ever get lonely?

How could he have worked with this man for the past decade and know so little about him? Had he been so obsessed with his work that he couldn't see beyond that?

He gazed across the fire at Gerry, looking at him as though seeing him for the first time. "Do you ever regret it?"

"Regret what?"

"This," Michael said, gesturing around them. "Tramping around from one place to another. Having no roots, no home base."

Gerry looked up at him, surprised. "We're archaeologists. It's what we do."

"I know it's what we do. But don't you ever think about...settling down? Don't you ever miss having a home? A woman?"

Gerry shrugged. "What could be better than this? No strings, no chains. If I want a woman, I go into the village and get one. What's the problem?"

Yeah, what was the problem? Michael asked himself. The problem was he wanted more. It had been fine for more than twenty years to bum around the world. It had been fine to eat, drink, sleep, walk and talk shop twenty-four hours a day. He'd surrounded himself with people—all kinds of people—to whom he was bound only by the work.

Gerry had been his assistant for ten years, and yet he could hardly call the man a friend. After all, a friend was someone you talked to, confided in, shared your feelings with. He and Gerry had never done that. He'd never done that with any of his crews or colleagues or assistants. He'd share theories and philosophies, but nothing of himself, not the way he had shared with Jorge, and not the way he had shared with Caitlin.

He missed her. He missed more than just the physical closeness, although God knows he missed that. He missed talking to her, missed the easy rapport, missed having her there to share and confide in.

He'd made a big discovery today. He and Gerry could talk endlessly about various technical aspects of the unearthing. They could discuss various theories, put forth a variety of hypotheses, kick around any number of complex conjectures. But that wasn't what he needed now. Not now on this dark, clear night beneath a canopy of magnificent stars. He longed to share the discovery, but not with Gerry or the rest of the crew. With Caitlin. He wanted to tell her what it had meant and how it had made him feel.

He stared into the fire and remembered how they had talked before the fireplace in their room at the Cliff House Inn. They'd talked about everything. Not dry, scholarly dialogues, but warm, rich, emotional conversations. He knew everything about her—her dreams, her fears, what made her happy, who her best friend was, what she'd wanted most out of life. In the few short days they'd been together he knew more about her than he knew about Gerry whom he'd known for ten years.

After Alaura he'd kept all those feelings, all those needs for intimacy, locked deep inside. He refused to share with anyone for fear of being betrayed again. But Caitlin, with her candid, almost guileless nature, had found the key. She'd unlocked within him all the needs he'd buried for so long. She'd unlocked the door and set the beast free. She'd created a need within him—a need to share, a need for intimacy, a need for her.

"Water's ready," Gerry said, gingerly reaching for the handle of the steaming kettle.

"Hmm—what? Oh." Michael started suddenly. He looked at the steaming kettle and then at the packet of dehydrated stew in his hand. "Never mind," he mumbled, tossing the packet back to Gerry. Standing, he started toward the tents. "I'm going to bed."

"You're not going to eat?" Gerry asked, surprised.

"I'm not hungry."

Smiling just a little, Gerry shook his head and called after him. "I don't know what happened to you in 'Frisco, but man, you're flipping out."

Ignoring him, Michael crawled into his tent and collapsed onto his narrow cot. He knew what had happened to him in San Francisco—every precise detail of it.

He rolled onto his back and watched the shadows from the fire dance crazily across the lightweight nylon tent. He thought of how she looked, the feel of her beneath him, the clean, sweet scent of her hair. There had been no one since her husband—no one until him.

He squeezed his eyes tightly again on a sudden rush of emotion. Having lost her husband to a younger woman had left her shaken. She'd been unsure of herself, uncertain of her ability to please a man, and so for two long years she'd held back, reluctant to get out and test the waters again. But with him she'd jumped in headfirst and pleased him just fine. So fine, in fact, that he hadn't been able to get her out of his mind for more than a few minutes in the past six weeks. Like a butterfly breaking free of its confining cocoon, she was free now—free to fly, free to try, free to start again. She wasn't uncertain any longer.

Opening his eyes, he slowly sat up. Would she start again? There was nothing holding her back any longer. No overbearing husband, no crippling inhibitions. There was nothing to stop her from starting a new relationship with another man, and nothing he could do to stop it. And wasn't that what he wanted for her? To be happy in a fulfilling relationship, to marry and have the child she'd waited so long to have?

Slowly he lowered himself back onto the cot. His eyes were heavy with fatigue and his stiff muscles ached. She'd already been forced to give up too much for the sake of one selfish man; it was her time now. She deserved to find happiness and finally get what she wanted out of life. He wanted her happy, and if that meant finding it in the arms of another man, then so be it.

Still, the thought tore at him. Long after the shadows had stopped and the fire had died out, long after the moon had risen high in the sky, long after there was nothing but the night sounds of the jungle, he lay there awake. The thought of Caitlin with another man tormented him. He pictured them caressing, kissing, tangled naked on a bed together. She deserved some happiness, he reminded himself over and over again, and yet a storm raged within him.

Finally, slowly, the tension began to ease from his exhausted body as he felt the blessed respite of sleep and darkness engulfing him.

Michael, I love you.

Caitlin, I love you, too.

Chapter 14

Caitlin leaned back against the door frame and gazed up at the night sky. It was cold on the small balcony off her bedroom suite, but she ignored the bitter chill for the time being. The velvet sky was alive with stars and planets, stretching across the valley in a glittering panorama.

She spotted Orion, big and focal in the sky, and wished now she had a better understanding of the constellations. There had been many long nights that she'd spent staring up at them lately.

She sighed deeply and rubbed at her itchy eyes. She was tired and should really go inside and try to get some sleep. Tomorrow was Saturday, and Saturdays were always hectic at the bookstore. The place would be filled in the morning with children attending the reading circle. She loved the story time, but it was by far the busiest two hours of the week. She would need every bit of strength and energy she had just to get through it.

But she didn't feel like sleeping just now. Every time she put her head on the pillow she ran the risk of having another dream, and she knew she didn't have the strength for that just now. So instead she braved fatigue and the brisk weather to watch as a distant star shone brightly in the sky. Did this same sky look down on Michael tonight?

It had been two long months since her trip to San Francisco. Her life had slipped back into its comfortable routine with hardly a thought of dark alleys or high-speed car chases. Her days were spent at the bookstore, and she continued her Wednesday night ceramics class. Of course, there were changes. Michael was never far from her thoughts. She thought of him throughout the days—where was he? What was he doing? She read books on the Incas, on archaeology, even on Hiram Bingham and Machu Picchu. The more she read, the more fascinated she became, and the more she would think of Michael.

And there were the memories. She remembered every moment of their time together—their lovemaking, their conversations. At first she'd thought her memories would be enough to sustain her over the years, but it hadn't taken her long to discover how wrong she'd been. The memories were both cherished and bittersweet. At times they were her salvation, giving her a place to escape to when the loneliness seemed unbearable. Yet, even as they comforted, they inevitably left her feeling empty and wanting. Still, she could handle the memories; it was the dreams that were tearing her apart.

Dreams had plagued her since she'd returned from San Francisco. Michael filled them. They were so real, and in them he was with her—touching her, loving her, never leaving her. They were such beautiful dreams, and yet waking to the bitter reality was becoming more and more painful.

There had been a brief period there when she thought the dreams had ended. After weeks of torment, they seemed to stop, coming only occasionally. But in the past week they had returned full force, stronger and more vivid than ever.

Another strong blast of cool air caused her hair to dance, sending long strands across her face. Brushing it out of her eyes, she sighed deeply. Her daily routine might not be much different since returning from San Francisco, but her life was far from the same. Even without all the memories and dreams a world of change had occurred within her.

She wasn't the same old Caitlin anymore. Somewhere along the way she'd shed that old skin of hers and grown a whole new one. She wasn't just Brian MacKenzie's ex-wife anymore. She was her own person. And this new Caitlin wasn't as afraid as she'd once been. She was stronger, more determined. No longer did she shy away or duck for cover. She'd discovered a confidence in herself she'd never known existed, and the feeling was intoxicating.

Michael had done that for her. He'd touched her and made her new. He'd believed in her and made her dare to believe in herself.

She could feel him. Even after her eyes were open, even with the sun streaming in through the French doors, even as the alarm sounded noisily beside the bed, she could feel him. There was a presence, an awareness, as though he were somehow close by. It wasn't a dream, it wasn't an illusion, it was a feeling—as real and as genuine as anything she'd ever experienced.

But it had to be a dream, she reminded herself as she slowly reached over to switch off the alarm, or at least the remnants of one. Michael wasn't close by. In fact, he was thousands of miles away.

She could still remember the dream. He was kissing her. Kissing her as though nothing else mattered in the world. It had been such a wonderful dream. No wonder she woke up feeling so strange.

"Get a grip," she mumbled to herself, swinging her feet out of bed and bringing herself to a sitting position. Her eyes were still heavy with sleep, but she reminded herself that there was no more dream. She was awake and the dreams had ended and this absurd feeling in her heart would fade soon enough. In the meantime, however, she had to get showered, dressed and to the bookstore. Every time children arrived before she got there, Chloe became a nervous wreck.

Caitlin hurried as fast as she could, but still there was a small crowd of parents and children waiting at the front door of the shop by the time she pulled her minivan into her stall in the parking lot.

"I thought you'd never get here," Chloe grumbled as Caitlin came in through a back door. "You know how I hate being here alone with those pesky little rug rats."

"Those pesky little rug rats buy a lot of our books, you know," Caitlin reminded Chloe good-naturedly as she slipped out of her coat and hung it on a hanger. "And I can't help it if they get here early. It's not even ten yet."

"I know, I know," Chloe admitted, flipping on store lights and preparing to open for business. "But they make me nervous." She smiled and gave an animated wave to the crowd outside the door, then turned, gritting her teeth and grimacing at Caitlin. "The little monsters are really champing at the bit this morning. Ready?"

Caitlin nodded and laughed. She'd come up with the idea of a reading group soon after she started work at the bookstore two years ago. Being an astute businesswoman, Chloe had welcomed the idea and had done her best to help promote the venture. From the beginning they'd developed quite a following, becoming a popular community activity among the preschool and kindergarten set. It had also boosted the store's sales of children's books, not to mention the books they sold to the parents who browsed through the store while waiting for their children. Which made it all the more ironic given the fact that kids made Chloe very nervous. She had wisely left Caitlin to deal with "the little rug rats," content to help the parents with their purchases while they waited.

There were a number of children who attended regularly, and they shrieked loudly when they saw Caitlin approaching. Of course, there were always one or two new faces, and Caitlin always made a point to welcome everyone. She led them all back to the rear corner of the shop that was marked off just for the group's purpose, and as the children settled themselves in the small gathering of chairs, she greeted and chatted with their parents.

As she visited, Caitlin looked around at the children. She loved their little group and looked forward to the weekly meeting. She took great pains preparing for it—often reviewing many books before finding just the right selections. She began to wonder if she hadn't missed her calling. Perhaps she should have been a teacher. She certainly loved the children, and loved opening their little minds to new ideas and experiences. But in her heart she suspected the time and energy she expended on behalf of the small gathering probably had more to do with her own frustrated desire for children rather than any real interest in the field of education. How she would have enjoyed reading to her own child. But since that was impossible, she was grateful to have these children to read to.

She always tried to introduce at least one story that might be new to the children, and one she considered to be a "standard." Today she had selected *Carl's Afternoon In The Park* along with the classic story of *The Giving Tree*.

When she took her seat in the middle of the small circle of chairs, the children quickly quieted. Of course, there were the inevitable interruptions. Someone always had a question or two along the way, and Caitlin would stop and make sure each one was answered. And someone almost always would announce loudly to the rest of the group just how urgently they had to go "potty." This would invariably send a red-faced parent rushing over to offer assistance. Then there was the usual array of sneezes and runny noses, but they were all par for the course. Caitlin had learned long ago to roll with the punches.

"Is there something I can help you with?" Chloe asked, eyeing the rugged blonde in front of her. He didn't exactly look like a robber. In fact, with those broad shoulders and lethal blue eyes he looked more like someone out of the pages of an adventure novel. But he'd been wandering around the store all morning, and she was fairly sure he wasn't waiting for one of the children in the story circle, even though he seemed to have a keen interest in the small gathering.

"Not really," he said, casually leafing through the book in his hands. Michael looked at her long paisley skirt and wavy, waist-length hair and smiled. This had to be Chloe. Caitlin had described her as an "aging hippie," and the description fit her perfectly. "I'm just browsing, waiting for a friend."

Chloe nodded but didn't look convinced. "Well, uh, if you need anything, I'll be right up front."

"Okay, thanks," Michael said. His smile grew wider. She'd be right up front keeping an eye on him, no doubt. Not that he could blame her for being suspicious. He'd been "browsing" for well over an hour. Enough to make even the most trusting storekeeper uneasy. And from the looks of things, he'd be browsing for a while longer.

He hadn't been able to keep his eyes off Caitlin since he'd walked in. She was even more beautiful than he remembered, and it had been all he could do to stop himself from barreling across the store and gathering her into his arms. He'd managed to control himself, however, but not just out of consideration for her job or the children gathered around her. He was discovering he was more of a coward than he'd thought.

He'd watched her with the children, listened to her lovely voice as she read the engaging stories. The children adored her, and she responded to them with a loving concern that was natural and instinctive. She would make a wonderful mother, and she needed a child of her own. How he longed to put his baby inside her, how he wanted to see her belly swell and grow round with what they'd created together.

For the past two weeks he'd turned his whole life upside down with just one thought in mind—seeing her again. Only now that he was here, now that just a few feet separated them, he found himself almost reluctant to take those last few steps.

He'd taken a big chance in just showing up, a bigger chance than he'd realized. He had no idea how she felt, what her reaction would be. He'd spent the past two months slowly going crazy with desire for her. But now he felt ridiculously reticent and uncertain. And it was this uncertainty that had him holding back, watching her, sneaking up on her blind side.

He couldn't remember the last time he'd been uncertain about anything. But then nothing had been this important to him before, either—not his career, not his digs, not his research. What if she'd forgotten him? What if she didn't want to see him? What if there was someone else in her life? What if he was too late? What if...what if...what if...? All those questions and uncertainties were driving him crazy.

But coward or hero, winner or loser, he would have to settle this thing one way or another. Either she would want him, or she wouldn't. He'd come too far to turn back now.

Despite the countless interruptions Caitlin managed to make it through both books and the children seemed to enjoy themselves. The stories were able to captivate regardless of short attention spans, and small imaginations were sparked. Even many of the parents had wandered back to listen and enjoy.

Afterward it was as hectic as usual. There were always a few children who insisted on sitting on Caitlin's lap, and she would try her best to oblige them. Parents would have questions about one book or another, and there was always a crowd at the registers.

Finally, working her way to the front counter, Caitlin began to help Chloe ring up the children's purchases. It was nearly noon before the crowd thinned. Most of the children and their parents had left, and Chloe had gone into the back room to check on some special orders she had written up. Caitlin had just finished with her last customer when she noticed a book lying on the counter in front of her.

Bed-and-Breakfast Inns of the Bay Area. Immediately images of Cliff House Inn loomed in her mind.

"Oh, ma'am, excuse me," she called to her departing customer. When the woman turned around, Caitlin lifted the book. "Did you want this, as well? I must have missed it here on the counter. Would you like me to ring it up?"

The woman squinted at the book, making a face. "No, I don't want that. Someone else must have left it. I guess they'll come back for it if they really want it."

Caitlin nodded and smiled, but as she gazed back down at the book, her smile slowly faded. She glanced around the store, but the place had emptied out. It wasn't like her to overlook something on the counter and to miss a sale. Hopefully someone would miss it and return to purchase it.

She leafed through the beautiful photographs, searching for and finding the pictures of Cliff House Inn in Sausalito. Memories flooded back, and she felt the sting of tears for the first time in weeks. The setting looked as beautiful and dramatic as she remembered, as quaint and romantic as any dream.

"Michael," she whispered, squeezing her eyes tightly against the deep ache inside. "Oh, Michael, I miss you so much."

Even before he heard her whisper his name, Michael knew he had to touch her, if only to prove to himself that she was real, that he hadn't just imagined everything that had happened between them.

As the pandemonium that had erupted after the reading circle began to die down and Chloe had left to go into the back room, he'd managed to slip around the counter unnoticed. Now he stood, leaning back against the back room door, and watched her from behind. He'd left the book on bed-and-breakfast inns on the counter on purpose. He'd wanted to see her reaction, but he'd gotten more than he'd bargained for.

When she whispered his name, he'd thought for a moment that she'd discovered him standing behind her. It had taken him several seconds to realize that she had actually been calling for him, missing him.

Soundlessly he closed the distance between them, taking those last few steps he'd been so unsure about. She was so close that he could smell the sweet scent of her perfume, the clean, fresh fragrance of her hair. So close he could all but taste her in his mouth.

He hesitated, savoring the sweet agony for one last, brief moment.

When Caitlin first felt those familiar, strong arms slide around her waist, she closed her eyes, certain she was dreaming. She knew she would awaken any moment only to discover she was in her bed at home, that it was dark and that she was alone. Only...for a moment, before it all would end, she allowed herself to be transported back in time and space, back to the darkness of a hotel room when those arms first held her. However, this time she wasn't consumed with fear. She was filled with sweet, liquid heat.

"I wondered if you could recommend any bed-and-breakfast inns you found particularly enjoyable," he murmured into her ear, inhaling her sweet scent even as his hands moved over her.

Caitlin's eyes flew open. When she felt the hard, warm length of a man's body behind her, and the low, dulcet whisper in her ear, she understood in a blinding crescendo of sensation and sound that this was no dream. She spun around, gazing up into the face she knew couldn't be real.

"Mich—" she started to say, but his lips captured the rest of anything she might have said.

She tasted so rich—far richer and more pure than even his dreams had remembered. He drank deeply from her, taking in her warm, rich flavor and feeling himself imbued with new life and new hope. She was like a potent, powerful drug, and he felt a heady, electrifying rush. If he'd had any doubts, they didn't matter now. She was in his arms, her taste was invading his system, and nothing else in this world or beyond mattered.

He pulled his lips from hers, drawing her more tightly to him and burying his face in the soft, sweet flesh of her neck and shoulder. Her arms had moved from his arms to his shoulders and then around his neck. Shock was wearing off, and she was coming alive in his arms.

Caitlin didn't care anymore if he was real or not, if he was a dream or an illusion. She'd deal with the consequences later. He was holding her, kissing her, wanting her, and all that really mattered was that he would never stop.

Michael kissed her neck, her jaw, her cheek, her eyelids. He was bolting forward at breakneck speed, needs becoming desperate, and desire threatening to go out of control. Purposefully he reined himself in. With his lungs seeking oxygen in heavy, labored gasps he leaned his forehead against hers and gazed down into her smoky brown eyes.

"Y-you're here," she murmured, blinking her eyes and still only half believing it to be true. "How...I...I mean...?"

Michael smiled down at her. "You don't mind?"

"Mind?" She closed her eyes tightly, taking a deep breath, then opened them again. "No, I don't mind."

"You didn't forget me?"

She breathed out a little laugh. "No, no, I didn't forget you."

His hands on her hips squeezed tightly, and he closed his eyes against the sudden surge of desire. "I missed you," he whispered, brushing her lips with his.

Caitlin's hands balled into fists as emotions swelled in her heart. "I missed you, too."

"I've made reservations at several of those places in the book. Come with me?"

"Yes." She didn't need time to think or consider. She didn't even ask if he meant for just a night, a weekend or even for just a few hours. This was Michael. He was actually here. She could see him, touch him, delight in having him touch her. It didn't matter why he was here, or for how long. She loved him, and she would gladly take whatever time he was willing to give her.

She'd agreed so quickly that it threw him a little. He'd expected her to want time to rearrange her schedule, lay out plans, set down the ground rules. Reaching up, he caressed her cheek with the palm of his hand. "You mean just like that?"

"I'm sorry. Was I supposed to play hard to get?" She smiled, turning her face to place a kiss against his palm. "Do you want to start again?"

He laughed, pulling her close and letting his hands reacquaint themselves with every soft, delicious curve on her body. "What I want is to drag you into that back room there and ravish every delectable part of you. I was trying to be subtle."

"I accept your invitation," she murmured against his lips. "Is that subtle enough?"

"To hell with subtlety," he growled, lifting her to his mouth again.

"Don't tell me. This has got to be Michael," Chloe said dryly, leaning against the doorjamb and folding her arms across her chest. "Either that or this is the kinkiest robbery attempt I've ever heard of."

Chloe's voice barely pierced Caitlin's cloud of contentment. She glanced over to her friend and stared at her as though she were trying to place the face. Slowly, as her faculties gradually made it through the haze, she pulled reluctantly out of Michael's embrace. He let her go but kept the fingers of his one hand entwined with hers.

"Ah, Chloe, this is Michael Seger," Caitlin said, ignoring her friend's devilish smile. "Michael, Chloe Mitchell."

"Yes, Ms. Mitchell and I have already met," Michael said, smiling and accepting Chloe's outstretched hand.

Chloe shook his hand and turned to Caitlin. "I thought he was casing the joint." Turning back to Michael, she added, "I didn't buy the story about waiting for a friend."

"I never lie," Michael told her, slowly turning back to Caitlin and sending her a knowing look. "Even though I've been reminded on occasion that I'm no Boy Scout."

Caitlin remembered the accusation she'd made after that long night in her San Francisco hotel room two months ago and smiled. "And I believe that observation is still correct."

Michael lifted her hand to his lips. "Let's get out of here."

The spark in his eyes made Caitlin go weak all over. She turned to Chloe, feeling flustered and embarrassed for the first time. "Ah, Chloe, Michael has asked me . . . Michael and I . . ."

"Get out of here," Chloe ordered, handing her her purse and coat. "The undercurrents in here are going to drown me." She gave Caitlin an enthusiastic embrace, whispering in her ear, "And if I don't get a full report this time, you're fired."

Caitlin squeezed Chloe tightly, then let Michael lead her from the shop. It wasn't until he'd pulled his sturdy four-wheel-drive vehicle onto the freeway on-ramp toward San Francisco that she realized, except for her purse, that she had nothing with her.

"Hey, wait!" she said, sitting upright and turning to him in the front seat. "I haven't brought anything. I don't have anything to wear."

"Don't worry," he assured her, leaning over and planting a quick, hard kiss on her mouth. "You won't need anything. I don't plan on letting you out of bed all weekend."

Of course, the distance was way too far, and the miles seemed to go on endlessly, but the commute to the bay area made the agony of anticipation that much sweeter. They didn't talk, only a word here and there. It was enough just to be together again. They would touch—hand to cheek, thigh to thigh—both waiting for that glorious moment when there would be no longer any need to hold back.

Finally, after what surely had been a lifetime spent waiting, Michael pulled his car into the parking lot of Cliff House Inn. Then . . . bed, blanket, sheets.

Clothes were disposed of with more speed than seemed possible. There wasn't time for leisurely renewals or bit-by-bit familiarizing. It had been two long months, endless nights filled with agonizing doubts and bitter dreams. Wounds needed healing, and needs had to be met.

"Caitlin." Her name tore from the depths of his soul— a plea, a prayer—as he made their bodies one. He gazed down into her clouded eyes and felt control begin to slip. "You're mine Caitlin. Do you hear me? Mine."

Caitlin gazed up at him, her world spinning frantically, tilting off balance. "Yours," she murmured. And she was.

Long after they lay on the bed—after needs had been appeased, passions had been sated and sanity had been

restored for the time being. In the distance the fog had begun to weave its way through the San Francisco skyline
across the bay. They talked—about Balcolar and what had
happened after his arrest. About the smugglers and Jorge's
tape. Michael told her about the grant and his discovery at
the dig. She told him about Chloe's reaction, about Agents
Newcomb and Lassiter and about the new pots she'd made
in ceramics.

Michael held her, slowly stroking her long, honey-
colored hair. It had been better between them than he'd
even remembered—the lovemaking and the sharing. With
her in his arms it didn't seem so difficult to tell what he was
feeling.

"In case I didn't mention it before, I missed you," he
said, lazily curling a long golden strand around his finger.
"I think we need to talk."

"Talk?" Caitlin braced herself. He was going to let her
down easy, set down the ground rules, not let her get her
hopes up. She knew what kind of man he was, what kind
of life he led. She'd known this would come sooner or
later; she'd just hoped it wouldn't be so soon.

Michael felt the tension spread through her body. The
coward in him wanted to run—to hit the road and get the
hell out of there. But he was through with running. He'd
allowed one bad experience with Alaura to affect his life
for too long now. This time he would stay and face the
music.

"I, uh, I realize we haven't known each other that long."
He blew out a little laugh. "Although, God knows, it's
been intense." The small smile left his face slowly. "What
happened between us . . ." He felt her body go rigid. "I
don't want to lose it."

Caitlin realized she'd been holding her breath, and she let it out now in a long, silent breath. Pulling back slightly, she looked up at him. "I . . . I don't understand."

"I know we have different life-styles—different lives! And things have happened pretty fast with us. I know you're used to certain things that will be difficult for me to give you—a home and stability. But I think if two people really want to be together, they're willing to compromise." He looked down into her sparkling eyes. "I'll compromise. I'll wait. I'll try to give you all the time you need."

"Michael," Caitlin whispered, emotion so tight in her chest that she was barely able to speak, "what are you trying to say?"

"That I love you, Caitlin." He gathered her into his arms. "Marry me."

Caitlin felt her heart stop in her bosom. "Marry you?"

"Please?"

One lone tear dropped from her lash and fell carelessly down her cheek. If this was a dream, please don't let her ever wake up. "All right."

Michael blinked. "All right?"

"Yes."

"Yes?"

"Yes, I'll marry you."

"Just like that?"

"Just like that."

He settled back against the headboard and looked down at her. Slowly he shook his head, bewildered. "In a million years I don't think I'll ever figure you out."

"Because I agreed to marry you?"

"No, because I've spent weeks trying to come up with all kinds of ways to convince you. I don't think you realize what you're getting yourself into. I haven't even told you about my new job yet."

She sat up, pulling the sheet around her. "You got a new job?"

"Yeah. I took a position at UC Berkeley. I'll be teaching a class there for half the year."

"That sounds great."

"But I'll have to do field research for them the rest of the year."

"Wonderful."

"That means living at a dig for six months out of the year."

"Great!"

"That means having to travel and live in a tent."

"I know."

"And ice-cold baths and no running water."

"Perfect."

"And sleeping in a sleeping bag and having very little privacy." He leaned forward and challenged her with a look. "How does that sound now?"

She leaned over and kissed his hard-set mouth. "Give me fifteen minutes to pack and I'll be ready to go."

He regarded her for a moment, shaking his head slowly. "I'll never understand you."

"What's to understand? I love you."

He placed a hand beneath her chin and kissed her long and deep. "You really don't mind about the traveling?"

"I really don't mind."

"And you're really going to marry me?"

"You still want me to?"

He tugged the sheet from her and pulled her beneath him. "I'll show you what I want."

They had a future now, and it gave their lovemaking a dimension that was both new and fulfilling. Caitlin surrendered to what she knew in her heart was right. She'd wasted enough time with staid, sensible behavior. She'd had it with drawn-out decisions and cautious control. From now on she would listen only to her heart, and her heart was filled with love.

"I want to do something more than make love," Michael whispered as he entered her slowly and completely.

"Something more?" Caitlin whispered.

"I want to make a baby. Our baby."

Caitlin closed her eyes to the surge of love that swelled inside her. "Oh, Michael, are you sure?"

Michael smiled down at her. He'd never been so sure in his life.

*   *   *   *   *

COME BACK TO

There's something about the American West, something about the men who live there. Accompany author Rachel Lee as she returns to Conard County, Wyoming, for CHEROKEE THUNDER (IM #463), the next title in her compelling series. American Hero Micah Parrish is the kind of man every woman dreams about—and that includes heroine Faith Williams. She doesn't only love Micah, she *needs* him, needs him to save her life—and that of her unborn child. Look for their story, coming in December, only from Silhouette Intimate Moments.

OFFICIAL RULES • MILLION DOLLAR MATCH 3 SWEEPSTAKES
NO PURCHASE OR OBLIGATION NECESSARY TO ENTER

To enter, follow the directions published. **ALTERNATE MEANS OF ENTRY:** Hand print your name and address on a 3″ ×5″ card and mail to either: Silhouette "Match 3," 3010 Walden Ave., P.O. Box 1867, Buffalo, NY 14269-1867, or Silhouette "Match 3," P.O. Box 609, Fort Erie, Ontario L2A 5X3, and we will assign your Sweepstakes numbers. (Limit: one entry per envelope.) For eligibility, entries must be received no later than March 31, 1994. No responsibility is assumed for lost, late or misdirected entries.

Upon receipt of entry, Sweepstakes numbers will be assigned. To determine winners, Sweepstakes numbers will be compared against a list of randomly preselected prizewinning numbers. In the event all prizes are not claimed via the return of prizewinning numbers, random drawings will be held from among all other entries received to award unclaimed prizes.

Prizewinners will be determined no later than May 30, 1994. Selection of winning numbers and random drawings are under the supervision of D.L. Blair, Inc., an independent judging organization, whose decisions are final. One prize to a family or organization. No substitution will be made for any prize, except as offered. Taxes and duties on all prizes are the sole responsibility of winners. Winners will be notified by mail. Chances of winning are determined by the number of entries distributed and received.

Sweepstakes open to persons 18 years of age or older, except employees and immediate family members of Torstar Corporation, D.L. Blair, Inc., their affiliates, subsidiaries and all other agencies, entities and persons connected with the use, marketing or conduct of this Sweepstakes. All applicable laws and regulations apply. Sweepstakes offer void wherever prohibited by law. Any litigation within the province of Quebec respecting the conduct and awarding of a prize in this Sweepstakes must be submitted to the Régies des Loteries et Courses du Quebec. In order to win a prize, residents of Canada will be required to correctly answer a time-limited arithmetical skill-testing question. Values of all prizes are in U.S. currency.

Winners of major prizes will be obligated to sign and return an affidavit of eligibility and release of liability within 30 days of notification. In the event of non-compliance within this time period, prize may be awarded to an alternate winner. Any prize or prize notification returned as undeliverable will result in the awarding of that prize to an alternate winner. By acceptance of their prize, winners consent to use of their names, photographs or other likenesses for purposes of advertising, trade and promotion on behalf of Torstar Corporation without further compensation, unless prohibited by law.

This Sweepstakes is presented by Torstar Corporation, its subsidiaries and affiliates in conjunction with book, merchandise and/or product offerings. Prizes are as follows: Grand Prize—$1,000,000 (payable at $33,333.33 a year for 30 years). First through Sixth Prizes may be presented in different creative executions, each with the following approximate values: First Prize—$35,000; Second Prize—$10,000; 2 Third Prizes—$5,000 each; 5 Fourth Prizes—$1,000 each; 10 Fifth Prizes—$250 each; 1,000 Sixth Prizes—$100 each. Prizewinners will have the opportunity of selecting any prize offered for that level. A travel-prize option, if offered and selected by winner, must be completed within 12 months of selection and is subject to hotel and flight accommodations availability. Torstar Corporation may present this Sweepstakes utilizing names other than Million Dollar Sweepstakes. For a current list of all prize options offered within prize levels and all names the Sweepstakes may utilize, send a self-addressed, stamped envelope (WA residents need not affix return postage) to: Million Dollar Sweepstakes Prize Options/Names, P.O. Box 4710, Blair,[fj NE 68009.

The Extra Bonus Prize will be awarded in a random drawing to be conducted no later than May 30, 1994 from among all entries received. To qualify, entries must be received by March 31, 1994 and comply with published directions. No purchase necessary. For complete rules, send a self-addressed, stamped envelope (WA residents need not affix return postage) to: Extra Bonus Prize Rules, P.O. Box 4600, Blair, NE 68009.

For a list of prizewinners (available after July 31, 1994) send a separate, stamped, self-addressed envelope to: Million Dollar Sweepstakes Winners, P.O. Box 4728, Blair, NE 68009.   SWP-1292

AMERICAN HERO

It seems readers can't get enough of these men—and we don't blame them! When Silhouette Intimate Moments' best authors go all-out to create irresistible men, it's no wonder women everywhere are falling in love. And look what—and who!—we have in store for you early in 1993.

January brings NO RETREAT (IM #469), by Marilyn Pappano. Here's a military man who brings a whole new meaning to macho!

In February, look for IN A STRANGER'S EYES (IM #475), by Doreen Roberts. Who is he—and why does she feel she knows him?

In March, it's FIREBRAND (IM #481), by Paula Detmer Riggs. The flames of passion have never burned this hot before!

And in April, look for COLD, COLD HEART (IM #487), by Ann Williams. It takes a mother in distress and a missing child to thaw this guy, but once he melts...!

AMERICAN HEROES. YOU WON'T WANT TO MISS A SINGLE ONE—ONLY FROM

IMHER03R

Experience the beauty of Yuletide romance with Silhouette Christmas Stories 1992—a collection of heartwarming stories by favorite Silhouette authors.

JONI'S MAGIC by Mary Lynn Baxter
HEARTS OF HOPE by Sondra Stanford
THE NIGHT SANTA CLAUS RETURNED by Marie Ferrarrella
BASKET OF LOVE by Jeanne Stephens

Also available this year are three popular early editions of Silhouette Christmas Stories—1986, 1987 and 1988. Look for these and you'll be well on your way to a complete collection of the best in holiday romance.

Plus, as an added bonus, you can receive a FREE keepsake Christmas ornament. Just collect four proofs of purchase from any November or December 1992 Harlequin or Silhouette series novels, or from any Harlequin or Silhouette Christmas collection, and receive a beautiful dated brass Christmas candle ornament.

Mail this certificate along with four (4) proof-of-purchase coupons, plus $1.50 postage and handling (check or money order—do not send cash), payable to Silhouette Books, to: **In the U.S.:** P.O. Box 9057, Buffalo, NY 14269-9057; **In Canada:** P.O. Box 622, Fort Erie, Ontario, L2A 5X3.

ONE PROOF OF PURCHASE	Name: _____
	_____
	Address: _____
	_____
	City: _____
	State/Province: _____
SX92POP	Zip/Postal Code: _____

093 KAG